Salmon Surprise

A MYSTERY

Introducing Miss Edna Winwood

by

W. MICHAEL HAY

ISBN: 145659589X
ISBN-13: 9781456595890
Library of Congress Control Number: 2011901830

London. November, 1935.

The cold of the November evening helped the young man decide to walk to Blackfriar's Bridge along one of his favorite, albeit circuitous, routes. He did not relish a long walk along the Thames on a November evening. He reckoned that he had plenty of time before his scheduled rendezvous, so he eschewed the Victoria Embankment in favor of Savoy Row which would lead him to Strand then to Surrey Streets and which would take him practically through the dining hall of King's College, London. He smiled to himself because he always enjoyed a late evening stroll through the King's College vicinity.

He wore a camel hair overcoat on his back and expensive boots on his feet. There was a silk scarf wrapped cavalierly around his neck and on his head there was perched a hat that was of the style popular with the young gentlemen of London that year. His attire was indeed expensive and the air with which he carried himself gave off the appearance that he was a young London gentleman, but there was something about him that gave the lie to the true person beneath the plumage. Perhaps it was the way his eyes shifted constantly, surveying the scene around him, as though he expected to be ambushed at any moment. There was the wariness of a cat hunting its prey about him that, upon close inspection, gave him a decidedly unpleasant look. He seemed to be a man looking to look like a person of means who was, in fact, a person of lesser means, yet, curiously, having the means enough to afford the expensive trappings of the moneyed class.

As he came upon King's College he slowed himself down a bit in his stroll. "No sense rushin' now, mate", he thought to himself, his eyes shifting and scanning for something. But what?

His hands fumbled a bit with his scarf. He knew better than to be late for his appointment at Blackfriar's. That particular engagement, though perhaps intriguing and hopefully lucrative, had its own thorns. "The guvner won't be none too pleased if I'm late," he reminded himself. Still, he could not resist taking the extra bit of time that he knew he had and use the opportunity to reconnoiter one of his favorite hunting grounds.

"'Allo! What's this?" he breathed silently to himself. A middle-aged man who had been approaching from the opposite direction had slowed down to a stop in an apparent attempt to light a cigarette.

"Well, now, rent's due and I'm sure he'll do," the young man surmised as he took in the would-be smoker before him. He drew nearer and pulled a gold-plated lighter from inside his coat. "Oi, mate! Need a light?"

A pair of brown eyes looked intently into the blue eyes of a younger man and the gaze lingered just a bit longer than it might. The offer was accepted and the cigarette was lighted as the gaze continued to hold.

"Oh, yes. He'll do, I'm sure."

In another part of the city another young man appeared to be waiting for someone. Huddled against the cold of the night air in a small doorway in the façade of a building, he puffed a cigarette and looked up and down the street, somewhat anxiously.

"Where is the little cow?" The scruffy looking young man, who was, even to a casual observer, not a gentleman, looked irritated and edgy. "She's always late. I don't care who she thinks she is. If she wants to play games I can show her some pretty ones, I can." He flicked the butt of his cigarette to the street and tried to calm himself as a bobby walked by and gave him the once over.

"I hope the bitch remembers that we're meeting here tonight," he thought as he eyed the policeman, trying not to look nervous. He knew that he had to be careful because of the fact that smoking and drinking what he smoked and drank with his friends always made him a little bit too chatty for his own good and he had been smoking and drinking a wee bit already. "If I get pinched by a copper and he finds what I've got in me pocket, it'll be the Old Baily for me. Then I'll wring her pretty little neck!" the scruffy young man muttered to himself as the bobby continued walking his beat, determining for himself that this ras-cal was not rascal enough to bother with. "Probably out on the town and waitin' for a lady friend, he is," thought the policeman. "Kids today. Not like when we were young," he mused as he walked.

"The bitch," once again the young man was getting agitated at the tardiness of his companion for the evening.

"I hope, if it is a lady friend that he's waitin' on, that she's dressed more proper than him," thought the policeman.

Part I

1.

"Hmmm. Not a bit of mist. Odd that, for this time of year." Indeed, there was not a finger of mist in the air as young Roland Minnington emerged into the cold November evening, pulling the great old doors of St. Bartholomew's Church closed behind him. The night air was crisp and clear, deliciously clean for a London evening. "There's going to be a hard frost, I'll wager," thought Roland distractedly as he pulled the collar of his great-coat more snugly about his neck. He turned and looked back at the façade of St. Bartholomew's. Vespers had ended a short time before and Roland's day there had come to its end. The church and the hospital connected to it had existed on that spot since the twelfth century, when an ambitious monk named Rahere had pleaded with his superiors in order to convince them to build a church and a hospital to care for the poor. The pious monk had prevailed and St. Bartholomew's had stood there ever since, a continuing reminder of man's need to care for the sick and the destitute. Roland Minnington had just finished a day's work within the hospital wards, serving as an orderly and assisting the nurses in their care for their patients in whatever way he was able. It had been a long day and he was tired after it, but he knew there would be more days like it to come. The rector at Trinity College

Seminary had determined that the experience among the poor and infirm would be invaluable for young Roland, considering his background of privilege.

Roland Minnington wished to be ordained a priest in the Church of England and was studying his theology in Dublin at Trinity College. His wealthy, and therefore, connected, father, Sir Clifford Minnington, Lord Dogmoor, had arranged with the Archbishop of Canterbury personally to obtain permission for his son to study in Ireland. Roland's father had been reluctant to accept his son's decision to enter the priesthood. He had hoped that his son would have entered the family steel business and carry on with it, keeping it in the family. However, he acquiesced on the condition that his son be exposed to as much of the world as possible, more so than a seminary might normally provide. Trinity, after all, was a school of unimpeachable reputation and would provide Roland with the best available education. In addition to that, it was out of England. You see, Sir Clifford Minnington, Lord Dogmoor, was an American and, though he loved his adopted country well enough, he was not in possession of that peculiar English trait that would have him believe that the sun rose and set on the British Empire alone. By getting his son out of England and sending him to school in Dublin, Sir Clifford felt relief in knowing that some of Roland's horizons were certain to be broadened. How little had he realized just how true that would be.

With a quick pull, Roland secured his hands within his fur lined gloves and smiled to himself as he took leave of St. Bartholomew's for the day. He did not enjoy the work, but accepted the fact that the rector's mind was made up. It would be fruitless to challenge his decision that the heir to Dogmoor needed the experience provided in the ancient hallways of the hospital. Roland allowed himself a rueful laugh as he thought how the rector, and even perhaps old Prior Rahere himself, would surely be very greatly surprised if they knew just how much he was enjoying his apprenticeship. How much he was enjoying it after hours, that is. Being back in London had given him the opportunity to explore other new and enlightening interests besides his exposure to the less fortunate. His Dublin education had certainly far exceeded his own expectations and had opened many new vistas for him. His heart quickened as he turned south down the Old Bailey, excited as he was to be exploring this new territory right in good old Londontown.

The clock in the church tower chimed eight and Roland hurried along, eager to make his rendezvous that evening at Blackfriar's Bridge.

2.

Try as she might to concentrate on her work, Dora Finch found she was distracted by the news that old Fr. Burns was coming to London with "something wonderful" for her friend, Maggie O'Shea. The two of them had been having tea in the kitchen of Maggie's mistress's manor house when the telegram announcing the intended visit had arrived. The boy who delivered the telegram had, naturally, known nothing about the sender or the message. Dora had, in fact, felt foolish after asking him if he knew why Fr. Burns would be planning a trip all the way from County Cork and what that "something wonderful" might have been. Neither Maggie nor Dora was accustomed to receiving telegrams and both had become just a little befuddled at this one's arrival.

As she washed the dinner dishes in the kitchen of the "Tea Cozy", the public house in which she was employed, her mind wandered back to County Cork and the little village of Fermoy, the home of the orphanage she had grown up in as a child. The memories unsettled her. The Sisters of Mercy, the Roman Catholic nuns who operated Saint Saviour Orphanage, couldn't have been kinder, as was the case with Fr. Burns himself. But whenever she thought of her childhood she could not escape the unpleasantness of knowing that she had been unwanted by her mother. In spite of the loving care of the nuns and their optimistic "God brought you to us for a reason" explanation of her predicament, Dora's childhood had remained one long dark night of tears and abandonment.

Even the friendships she formed there had not eased the pain entirely. Maggie, who had been her bunk mate and who had a much more practical view of their mutual histories than did Dora, had been her strongest support during those bleak years. They became best friends and shared hopes, dreams, disappointments and ambitions well into the night after the nuns had called for lights out. Maggie, in fact, was the one bright spot of her past. The two of them had moved to London together five years earlier, just after Dora had turned 21 and just a few months before Maggie would do so. Having each found employment they began new lives with each other to lean on, but even that had not eased the empty pain in Dora's heart. No, there was just no way around the unpleasant memories Fr. Burns' telegram had stirred up.

A soup crock slipped out of her soapy hands and brought her back to the present moment as it banged against the sink. Checking the dish to confirm that it hadn't chipped or broken, she scolded herself to be more careful.

She recalled the many nights that she had knelt beside her tiny bed and prayed that God would bring her mother to her and how often she would cry herself to sleep. Sr. Mary Francis had once reprimanded her, on her twelfth birthday, having caught Dora crying in the girl's lavatory. The nun had firmly and coldly told her to be content with what good care the Lord was providing for her at the orphanage. Sr. Mary St. John of the Cross had had a somewhat kinder way of trying to coax Dora out of her doldrums. She had advised her to look to the Blessed Mother as her real mother, for indeed that is what she was.

Dora had tried commending herself to the Mother of God, but ultimately even the Blessed Virgin could not fill the void in her innermost heart, left there when she considered what it meant to be an orphan.

By her thirteenth birthday Dora was no longer an orphan. Eowan and Oona Finch had adopted the young girl and taken her into their home. There was great excitement around St. Saviour when an adoption occurred. The nuns were at once elated and just a bit sad to see one of their charges go. Saying goodbye is difficult no matter what the circumstances.

The Finches gave Dora a home and a name. This latter was of particular good news to Dora, since all her life she had known only the surname the nuns had given her, St. Dymphna. The good sisters, you see, had the pious habit of giving to the orphaned children the name of the saint whose feast day it was when they arrived at Holy Saviour. Dora had known Danny St. Francis, Georgie St. Dennis, Enid St. Brendan, and her best friend, Maggie St. Ita. It had been one more bit of bad luck that Dora had arrived in her helpless infancy on the feast of St. Dymphna, the patroness of the mentally ill.

Unfortunately, her new name was the only good thing to come of the time she had spent with her adoptive parents. You see, at almost thirteen years of age, Dora had given up hope of ever being adopted, because it seemed that most perspective parents were looking for younger children to rear. When the Finches asked specifically for a girl Dora's age, she could scarcely believe it. It all became clear soon enough, however, the reasons for wanting a girl Dora's age. Mrs. Oona Finch wanted help around the house. Mr. Eowan Finch could not afford a maid to satisfy his wife's first desire. They had had no children of their own for reasons only guessed at by their neighbors, so as a childless couple, Mrs. Finch was left to do the housework herself. Adoption seemed to be just the ticket to acquire inexpensive help around the house. Dora soon found out that, instead of being a daughter in a family, she was more a scullery maid, fed and boarded by her new and miserly masters. By the time she was sixteen, she actually missed the orphanage and longed to return to the much more tender care of the nuns.

Dora drained the dishwater from the sink and turned her attention to drying the dishes she had just washed. "Well, if nothing else, Mum and Da Finch helped prepare me for life in the world", she thought ruefully. At twenty one years of age, Dora had left Ireland for England and found herself a job in the kitchen of the "Tea Cozy".

The ringing of a bell brought Dora out of her revelries once again. It was the bell summoning her from the kitchen to the dining room of the pub. Immediately, her heart quickened. Perhaps it was Erskine? But then she realized it was probably just a call to help finish clearing what was left on the tables. At this hour, eight o'clock in the evening, the pub was getting ready to close and it was very unlikely that Erskine would be coming in now. By nine o'clock the doors would be locked. Nobody stayed late at the "Tea Cozy".

That was something else that didn't help Dora's present state of distraction. Her young man had not been in for several days and she was beginning to wonder where he might be. Erskine Randiffle was a young and handsome man who had a quick mind and an easy way with people. All these factors combined had aided him in getting his foot in the door at Applegate and Copperwaithe, one of London's more preeminent accounting firms. His personal background, while not as dismal as Dora's, was not one that would have given him immediate access to London's business community. His parents had been poor yet honest laborers in London, as had their parents before them. They had scrimped and saved in order to have money for Erskine to get into university, but it was barely enough. Erskine had had to go to work himself to help pay for his schooling. The family was completely unconnected to any one of any account in London's social or business circles. So landing a position as clerk at Applegate and Copperwaithe was testimony to his own native talents and charisma.

That same combination of looks, charm, youth and determination had been what won Dora's heart as well. When she first noticed him in the "Tea Cozy" one evening she had been taken by his sparkling blue eyes and beautiful smile. Initially, Miss Finch did not even permit herself to think of the possibility of becoming involved with such a comely young man. Even his clothes were impressive. His suits, while not the most expensive, were all well tailored and neat. Why would he even notice a poor working class girl who spent most of her days and evenings in the vicinity of the kitchen sink of a public house?

But he had noticed her. One day he had come in earlier than usual and sat alone at a table set for two, obviously waiting for someone else to arrive. He struck up a casual conversation with Dora as she brought him a basket of scones and some tea. It was a simple conversation—hello, what's your name, how long have you been in London—but Dora had almost lost herself completely when he spoke to her, she had been that quickly smitten. Hardly daring even to look at him as she answered, she had felt herself blushing profusely, much to the delight of young Erskine who seemed genuinely flattered at the effect he was having on the pretty young girl with the slight Irish accent.

Dora Finch was pretty. In fact, she was more than pretty. Despite the plainness of her dress and the severe way in which she styled her hair as a pub waitress, there was something about her that positively radiated beauty. Her hair was chestnut brown and her eyes were great hazel pools that betrayed at once innocence, sincerity, and just a bit of the pain she carried from her childhood. Her slim figure and delicate skin gave an appearance of elegance that even her inelegant clothes could not diminish.

There was also something about her manner. The nuns had instructed all the young girls in their care as to the proper way to comport themselves in polite society, but Dora had seemed to have an innate sense of bearing proper to a young lady. She always spoke quietly, directly and without frivolity, even in casual conversation with her girlfriends, and her speaking voice, although it was accented, somehow sounded very genteel and refined, more liked that of a fine Irish lady from Dublin than an orphaned girl from County Cork. So her demeanor the day that Erskine first spoke with her, rattled as she was, was all the more endearing because it was so genuine.

The bell that had summoned Dora from the kitchen had, indeed, not been sounded because Erskine had arrived but because it was time to begin to close down the dining room for the night. Petal Chalmers, the hostess and primary waitress for the those who dined at the pub, rang the bell when she needed Dora's help in the dining room or, more recently, when Erskine arrived. Petal and Dora had become quite friendly as they worked side by side providing hospitality to London's middle class, the primary patrons of their pub. Their friendship had blossomed immediately the day that Dora first appeared at the door of the "Tea Cozy", applying for the position that was advertised in the window. There had been something about Dora that Petal had taken an immediate liking to, and first and foremost was the fact that Dora had been raised by nuns. Mary Annunciata, Petal's given name, was a Roman Catholic herself, her mother devout almost to obsession. She had been named for the Blessed Virgin Mary and got her nickname because she loved playing in the flower petals that were always scattered on the floor of her child-hood home under the myriad of Mary statues her mother had raised altars to. When the quiet and dignified, yet impecunious Dora had asked for the job, Petal couldn't help but feel a strange kinship for her. She had always felt herself to be particularly sen-sitive and believed there was almost something psychic in the connection she'd felt for young Miss Finch. She had hired her on the spot.

As the last few years had passed, and as Petal's affection for Dora grew, so had her concern. Her young scullery maid and part time waitress seemed too often to be sad for reasons which apparently stemmed from her childhood at the orphan-age. Dora was so pretty and so graceful, Petal was sure that she was wasting herself hiding behind an apron and stacks of dirty dishes. When handsome young Erskine Randiffle appeared on the scene, and Dora seemed to be so chipper when he was around, Petal thought that she would play matchmaker for the two youngsters. Against the advice of her own boyfriend, Joe, who worked behind the bar of the "Tea Cozy" and believed that one should mind one's own business, Petal had encouraged the quiet young lovely to spend time with the effervescent and hand-some young clerk. She thought that Erskine was just the man for her Irish friend.

3.

"It's 1935! You'd think the goddamned English would have mastered electricity by now!"

Sir Clifford Minnington fussed and fumed as he lit a candle in the dark of his study. Apparently a fuse had blown, again, and Sir Clifford's patience was wearing as thin as his hair, again. "One of these days I'm going to get an American electrician over here to rewire this goddamned barn!"

The accursed barn in question was Manor Minnington, the manor house on the ancestral lands of Dogmoor, an old English family of minor nobility in the British peerage. The Lord of Dogmoor had held a seat in the House of Lords since 1680, when Charles II elevated a dog breeder named Blickstoke to the ranks of nobility because his dogs had pleased the queen. Catherine of Braganza had been so enamored of the gentle and bright English Shepherds that she had insisted her husband bestow a title upon Blickstoke. At that particular time in his life, Charles was beset by so much political turmoil and so many health problems that he almost distractedly acquiesced to his queen's demands and made Blickstoke an English lord with a stroke of a quill and granted him the lands that would come to be known as Dogmoor, named entirely for the moors that comprised the land and the dogs that had made him so well favored by Her Majesty.

No mere peasant, Blickstoke was a shrewd and successful merchant who had bred dogs simply because of his love for the animals. When Queen Catherine had taken such delight in them, he had seen his fortunes changing for the better still. Despite the growing power of the Roundheads in Parliament, Alfred Blickstoke had deftly sided with the royals as he was elevated to the nobility above his brother merchants, whom he happily left behind as commoners. The times and politics were rough, however, and a certain group of Roundheads, in order to wreak their revenge, started an ugly rumor as to exactly why these dogs were so special to the royal family. A truly ghastly tale circulated around London of unnatural attachments to animals and to a mysterious French baron, apparently concocted to completely embarrass His Majesty and his connection to the French king.

After Charles died of stroke in 1685, and his brother, James II, ascended the throne, all hell truly broke loose. James wished to return the realm to the Roman Pontiff, a desire that infuriated the Roundheads and Cavaliers alike. In the turmoil that ensued during the reign of King James, Sir Alfred Blickstoke managed to keep a very low profile and allowed himself to be forgotten, falling into the safety of obscurity as the fury of the anti-Romans roared about him.

When he found that he was no longer in danger of being at all interesting to new and powerful factions in the government in London, Blickstoke settled into the life of the typical country gentleman of his day. The land that King Charles had granted him was in Surrey, which in the 17th century was considered to be quite a way outside of London. Insulated by distance and as well as disinterest, Sir Alfred was able to quietly go about his business and to build his estate to his liking. A manor house emerged on the most prominent parcel of solid ground on the property, right at the edge of a bog, which was flat enough to accommodate its grand size. Surrounded by dogs and bogs, Sir Alfred Blickstoke became the first Lord Dogmoor.

Sir Clifford Minnington, the current Lord Dogmoor, found the flashlight he kept in his study for just such a contingency in which he currently found himself. In the flickering candlelight of his darkened study, he made his way to the door and called for his man-servant.

"Snippy! Check that goddamned fuse box!"

Cleves Snipwhistle heard his master's shout from his usual station in the butler's pantry and was already reaching for the lantern he had lit when the electricity failed. Snippy, as he was called by Sir Clifford and everyone else in the household, had grown accustomed to his master's gruff colonial language and his impatience with the shortcomings of British electricity, as well as plumbing, heating and a number of other things that had been taken for granted back in Pittsburgh, Pennsylvania.

"Coming, sir."

Cleves Snipwhistle considered himself to be very British, the very essence of an English gentleman's gentleman. Yet, he himself longed for the luxury and convenience of life in America. When Mr. and Mrs. Minnington had first married they spent three years in Pittsburgh at Mr. Minnington's home there. Snippy had been a valet in Mrs. Minnington's family for 15 years already when young Opal Blickstoke-Jennings had landed her millionaire American husband. After a proper English wedding, replete with a tea reception in the garden, the new Mrs. Minnington had insisted that the newlyweds spend their honeymoon period in the United States. Snipwhistle had accompanied them to Pittsburgh at the insistence of Opal's father, who felt she needed proper supervision in the wilds of the New World.

Though quite foreign and often uncultured according to their British sensibilities, life in Pittsburgh had been comfortable. The Minningtons of Pennsylvania had done quite well for themselves in coal and steel and were very wealthy. The home they occupied in Pittsburgh was almost opulent, even by British standards, and had every modern convenience of the newly emerged 20th Century. When old Blickstoke-Jennings, Mrs. Minnington's father, died suddenly, three years after they had married, Lady Opal had insisted that the family move back to England and her ancestral home to look after her aging mother. Clifford had been reluctant to move but, as his wife pointed out to him, her father's death made him Lord Dogmoor by virtue of his marriage to her. This had had a certain appeal to Minnington, who loved looking down his nose at his peers in America anyway. His beautiful British wife had been a trophy he had proudly paraded around Pittsburgh society, but the thought of actually being an English lord was too much a plum for him to resist. After his considerable success in the business world and having amassed a fortune while building up the family business concerns, Sir Clifford Minnington thought it only meet and just that he should enjoy all the benefits of his most recent acquisition. Within a month of Opal's father's death, the new Lord Dogmoor was ensconced in Surrey.

Snippy, while homesick for Great Britain, especially during the long, hot Pittsburgh summers, nonetheless enjoyed his American sojourn. Everything had seemed so much bigger, brighter, and faster in the States. There was no need unmet and convenience was the rule, not the exception. He remembered his days in the Colonies fondly, especially so at moments like this, when the electricity in the manor house failed.

"Damn your hide, Snippy", bellowed Sir Clifford. "About time you got your British butt in here. Change the fuse down in the cellar."

"May I use your torch, Sir Clifford?" inquired Snipwhistle.

"Goddamn it! It's a flashlight, not a torch! I'm not sending you off to burn down Frankenstein Castle with the rest of the villagers!" Sir Clifford was an aficionado of the Universal Picture Studios in Hollywood. In fact, he owned shares in the studio and loved the movies they produced. "Take the damn thing and find that blown fuse!"

Snipwhistle, the ever faithful gentleman's gentleman, did as he was instructed.

4.

With a quick snap of his wrist, Jasper Dunwoody closed his pocket watch as he walked along the Old Bailey. He had heard the bells of St. Bartholomew's ring the hour moments ago and he had checked his watch's time against the ancient towers. "Eight fifteen on the nose. I'm going to be right on time," he thought to himself. The ancient cobblestones clicked under his heels and he hurried along in the chill of the evening.

Jasper Dunwoody was what one might call a "man about town". One might be tempted to say this about Jasper because he was unattached, at 30 years of age, and seemed to be always somewhere where something interesting was happening. Some people who knew him could not understand why he had never married. He was, after all, 30 and had a wonderful position with Sir Oswald Bunbarrel, an elderly minister of Parliament and himself a member of the British peerage. Sir Oswald employed Jasper as a personal secretary to help him keep his appointments in order and various other duties for which an elder statesman might need a personal secretary. Being very wealthy in his own right, Sir Oswald paid Jasper handsomely for his services.

Other than his age and his position, the truly most noteworthy thing about Jasper that had people wondering why some young lady had not been able to succeed in getting him to the altar was his incredible good looks. Jasper Dunwoody was perhaps the most strikingly handsome man in London. Extraordinarily well-put-together for a man of 30, he looked like he was a man in his 20s. He was tall, blond and blue-eyed with flawless skin and a perfect set of pearly white teeth that flashed beautifully when he smiled. Heads turned whenever he walked into a room, both of men and women alike. He had a way of charming the ladies at social gatherings that would have made Don Juan envious. But his flirtations never amounted to anything more than that. A laugh, a smile and perhaps a kiss on the hand was the extent of Jasper's exchanges with ladies, young and old.

He was efficient in his job. Sir Oswald Bunbarrel had had personal secretaries for many years, but none quite as good, or as good-looking, as Jasper. All of Sir Oswald's previous secretaries paled by comparison. There were those in town who wondered about Sir Oswald's long line of handsome young men who had attended him. They all had been good looking young professional men. Some had come from other noble families; most had been hired, as was Jasper, from chance interviews when Sir Oswald had needed to replace one secretary for another. None, however, had matched Jasper for looks, charm or suitability for the task, but especially for looks. For a man approaching 80, Sir Oswald's appreciation for all things beautiful seemed to be getting keener, especially with the acquisition of Mr. Dunwoody.

Jasper had appeared as if out of nowhere to interview for the position. He had gone to university at Eaton and, though not top in his class, had performed fairly well in school. His work history had been mostly clerking for a legal aid society for foreign nationals, but when he heard "through the grapevine" that Sir Oswald was seeking a new secretary, he jumped at the opportunity. He had decided to make the application because he had felt fairly confident of securing the position, considering he possessed the abilities and talents which he had heard Sir Oswald always looked for in his secretaries.

As it happened, he had secured the position and everything he had heard about Sir Oswald Bunbarrel turned out to be true. Jasper got the job and kept his employer satisfied and happy.

Tonight, however, his mind was not on his job. Sir Oswald was resting quietly at home after a long day in Parliament and Mr. Jasper Dunwoody, man-about-town, was a man about the town. He worked his way to the pub that he had been frequenting for several months and which had become the favored drinking and socializing spot for his circle of friends. His pace was quick and he was in a very good humor as he walked past the intersection that would have taken him towards St. Paul Church and continued on towards the Smithfield area of London. Even the handsome young man passing him on Old Bailey had only momentarily distracted him. He had seemed familiar, dark haired, young and handsome. Jasper was certain he had seen him somewhere before. Perhaps one of the students at King's College that Jasper was always and forever passing as he made his way to Fleet Street and on towards Smithfield for his evening outings. There were always handsome young men in that neighborhood. As they passed each other on the street, their eyes had met and the handsome stranger held his gaze just long enough to be considered the edge of indiscretion. Jasper smiled and gave jaunty nod of his head and continued his way to the "Boar's Head". He was meeting his friend, Erskine tonight and very quickly the nagging feeling of familiarity with the handsome young face in the night faded as anticipation of a pleasant evening of camaraderie loomed before him.

5.

As she waited for the lights to come back on and for her husband to stop his customary tirade, Opal Minnington sat quietly in her dressing room, looking out into the cool November evening. Mist was beginning to rise over the moors, but not very much. She thought that rather curious considering the time of year. But it had been an unusually warm autumn for England. She remembered the Novembers of her years in the United States. How lovely the trees would be around the neighborhood of large estates where she and her new husband had lived. How blessed hot it could still be there in September and October after a completely unbearable American summer. Yet, with electric fans strategically positioned about the large and commodious house, even the warmest weather did not seem to be too terribly intolerable, until you had to go out into it. And the electricity seldom failed in that house, except during the intense storms of the spring and early summer seasons. Once, a terrible American thing called a "tornado" had brushed through the Pittsburgh area and had caused the electricity to fail all over the city. She remembered how Mr. Minnington had fumed at the loss of power under those dramatic circumstances and how uncomfortable she had been then with his complaints. She looked back on those days now and wished for them again, considering his present state of rage over the wiring in Manor Minnington.

Still, it was good to be home in England. She had missed her ancestral lands and house, even though she had enjoyed America, to a point. When her father had died, she was devastated, of course, but also acknowledged that it was good news in as much as she could return to Great Britain and be at home again. Once she got her husband here, there would be no turning back to the States. Opal had known that the lure of British peerage would turn her husband's head and that he would not be able to resist the chance to be the lord of an English estate. When she had explained to him that, with her father's passing and she an only child, he would be the next Lord Dogmoor, she felt certain that he would not be able to pass up playing that role, even though he would have no standing in Parliament whatsoever. She had pegged her husband quite correctly. The irony that the new Lord Dogmoor hated dogs did not seem to impress itself on anyone. After settling into his new estate, it did not take him long to make up his mind to keep England as their primary home and return to the United States only enough to maintain residence and citizenship and, of course, to keep his finger in business matters there.

Business matters. "What a wonderful expression," thought Lady Minnington. It was certainly true that business matters mattered to her husband, not that she was complaining. After all, it had been through his family's business and his own dedicated effort and attention to business matters that he had earned himself the rank of millionaire several times over. Clifford Minnington had a hard nose for business and was the quintessential American tycoon. Even though there had been a modest amount of family money waiting for him, he had not allowed that to make him complacent. He had worked hard in his father's shadow until he had made his own share of the American Dream come to fruition. He had always boasted that he himself was a self-made man and not an idle heir to a vast fortune and had hoped his son Roland would follow in his footsteps. He was not, one might say, altogether thrilled to hear of his son's desire to don the cloth because, to Sir Clifford Minnington, Lord Dogmoor, business matters mattered most.

But, Lady Minnington had to confess to herself, they had mattered to her and her parents, as well.

The lights came on and the house was warmly alight again. Opal extinguished the candles she had lit when the electricity failed and stood in her dressing room in front of her make-up table. She was still an attractive woman, though in her 40s now, if she had to say so herself. Her figure was still slim, her skin still soft and creamy, and her hair was a beautiful dark brown with very little grey in it. Her age was beginning to show in only the smallest ways: her great green eyes surrounded by small wrinkles (laugh lines, her American husband called them—nothing funny about it to a woman, in her opinion), the beginning of a bit of a sag under her arms, which she vigorously exercised in an effort to maintain their youthful tone. At first glance, no one would suspect that Lady Opal Minnington of Dogmoor was a woman of her age with two grown children. She relished that thought as she admired herself in the mirror.

Opal began once again the task she had started before the lights went out, applying her evening make-up. She and her husband were going out to dinner that particular evening. Their plans were to go into London and eat at one of the new restaurants that had opened in the fashionable theatre district. When the lights went out and her husband went off, Lady Opal worried about what might happen if the same thing should happen on Saturday evening, when they were expecting to host a dinner party of their own. Sir Clifford, though he loved to affect English ways, was by no means an English gentleman when it came to being inconvenienced. His temper flared, his veil of decorum abandoned him, and he would become the belligerent beast to whom the household had become accustomed. But Opal simply would not have it at a dinner party.

"I hope to heaven he does get an American electrician over here soon!" she mused at herself in the mirror. "At least then England would be off the hook during the next failure."

6.

"Jaysus, I hope he's done with it." Maggie breathed a sigh of relief as the lights came on again. Even from the kitchen she could hear her employer's voice bellowing for Snippy. It would have been a perfectly lovely evening if the power hadn't failed. What with her employers out of the house for dinner, Maggie had envisioned an evening of leisurely polishing the silver in preparation for the big dinner party planned for the next weekend. The stress-free evening she had envisioned evaporated as the irate master of the house howled at the beleaguered butler. Perhaps once they were out of the house, she thought, it would be quiet for the remainder of the evening. At least she didn't have to try to prepare tonight's dinner and risk having to listen to a continued barrage from Sir Clifford.

Maggie O'Shea especially needed this particular evening to herself. She had been very much unsettled by the telegram from Fr. Burns earlier that day. Whatever could he be coming to Surrey for? Pondering it all day while trying to do her normal chores had given Maggie a headache. Unaccustomed to anything out of the ordinary, other than her master's temper tantrums which had become, frankly, ordinary, it had completely unnerved her.

She was happy that she hadn't had to hear the news alone. Dora had been there with her when the boy came with the telegram and had been just as perplexed as Maggie by the news. The normally cool and composed Dora even asked the boy if he knew why the venerable old priest was coming; an idiotic question in hindsight—how could he know. But the very fact the question was asked underscored just how rattled the two young women were.

Maggie and Dora had been through so much together from their childhood days at St. Saviour that they were now practically sisters. Perhaps they were even closer than sisters. Maggie could remember the day the two of them met. She had been six years old when her parents were killed in a farm accident in a little village in County Cork and she had been sent to the orphanage. Dora was also six at the time and had been at the orphanage for as long as she could remember. Dora St. Dymphna had been the girl assigned by the nuns to help little and bewildered Maggie St. Ita settle into life with the other orphaned children. She had always been so kind to her and Maggie loved her from the start but there was always something about Dora that made Maggie wonder. She could never articulate it as a child, but as they had grown up and were both now well into their adult years, Maggie realized that there was something about Dora that seemed deep and secret, so deep and so secret that Maggie suspected that even Dora herself did not know what it was that seemed to bother her, what it was that lay so far beneath the surface of that exquisitely delicate skin.

The two of them had sat in complete silence after reading the telegram and wondered what "something wonderful" might possibly mean. For both young women the orphanage had been quite tolerable, but still the experience of being orphaned was painful. "Ach, now. What in the name of St. Brigid could be so wonderful coming from the orphanage, unless it's the retirement of mean old Sr. Mary Francis?" Maggie had finally surmised. Her ruefully witty remark in regard to the old nun had eased the moment and the two shared a laugh. With that they continued their visit, trying unsuccessfully to put the mysterious missive out of their minds.

It was a true blessing for both of them that Dora was able to get out of the city and come calling in Surrey occasionally. She did not often get days off from the "Tea Cozy", but when she did, Dora made it a point to spend time with her old friend. Maggie seemed to think that part of what enticed Dora out to Manor Minnington was the long and tranquil ride it took to get there.

Lots of trees and the ever vaporous moors seemed to have an evocative effect on the quiet and pensive Miss Finch.

By 8:30 the manor house was quiet. The Minnington's had left for the evening and were motoring into London. Maggie settled herself into a chair at her work station in the pantry and began to methodically polish the silver as she mused over the events of the day.

7.

The end of her father's rant did not help Claudia Minnington concentrate any harder on her school work. She fiddled with the pencil in her fingers as she looked past the map hanging on the wall of her room and successfully avoided studying her geography lesson. She sighed as she thought of how Mrs. Tuddel would scold her in that high pitched, whiney voice of hers. "Claudia," she would say, "your father is *wasting* his money having you tutored for your university classes. You *ought* to apply yourself, young lady!"

Of course, Mrs. Tuddel was absolutely correct. Her father *was* wasting his money and Claudia would happily shout that from the roof tops if it would get her out of school and not result in restrictions on her allowance. Embracing wholeheartedly her British heritage and conveniently forgetting that she was also her father's daughter, she often referred to him as a "typical American git". She just could not fathom why he thought that she should spend so much time at university when the family was wealthy beyond reason.

"What does he think? That I'm going to go to work as a secretary, like old Winwood?" Claudia ruefully pondered, referring to her father's personal secretary, Edna Winwood. Miss Edna Winwood was the quintessential English professional woman of her day: prim, proper, exceedingly correct in manner and unbearably efficient. Claudia despised her at times. She had been her father's "gal Friday", as he so vulgarly put it, for the last several years and kept his files and business and personal correspondence in complete and total order. Nothing was out of place with Miss Winwood, nothing escaped her notice, and she always seemed to be one step ahead of Lord Dogmoor, anticipating nearly everything, as far as Claudia could tell.

She was good at her job and had been educated at the same woman's college in London in which Claudia was now enrolled. Bedford College, at least, was located in London and not in Surrey, as was Royal Holloway. It had been Claudia's fear that her father would make her go to school closer to home rather than in the city. Although she had protested continuing her education at all, she realized that her father was determined that she would one day be able to contribute to the family business, and once Sir Clifford's mind was made up, it was made up and it was made up especially since Roland was off to divinity school. "The pious git," she called him.

She had decided to try for the least offensive alternative and had suggested that since Miss Winwood had turned out so well from Bedford College that she would love to have a go at it there, too. It had practically choked her to say it out loud, but she knew that it was the most persuasive argument her father might listen to. Counting on her father's high opinion of his secretary, Claudia had carefully laid out the reasons why Bedford College would be to her better benefit. As it turned out, it was easier than she had thought it would be. Her father went for it right away, half because of the influence of the Winwood factor and half because he was happy to have an end to the protestations against higher education which had been raised by his only daughter.

Being out of Surrey, even for the short time she was in class, was important to Claudia. Sir Clifford's original concerns, fueled by her mother, were that a young woman should not travel back and forth to London so frequently. Claudia had pointed out to her parents that the roadways were sufficiently surfaced and travel by motorcar had reduced the distance between Dogmoor and the city. "It's not a big deal, mum. It's not like I have to travel by carriage and fend off highwaymen." Sir Clifford was assuaged, though her mother still had her doubts. In the end, Claudia had prevailed and was thus in her first year at Bedford.

She looked wanly at the map on the wall and focused on Persia. With her parents going out for the evening and the servants busy preparing for Saturday's dinner party, Claudia was easily able to excuse herself for a study trip to the library at school. She turned to the window to see if her ride had arrived. She listened at the door and heard nothing to indicate anyone stirring about. Her parents would be preoccupied with their own trip into town that night and more than likely not even notice that she was slipping out of the house at that hour. Even so, she decided to wait for her friends downstairs so she could make a quick exit. She had a vague idea where the library was on campus, she had been there before. The real use Claudia Minnington had for the library was that it gave her a perfectly legitimate reason to be in London, even though the reason she wanted to be in London was far from legitimate.

8.

Elinor Drumville sat on her dilapidated davenport and smiled at the invitation that she held in her hand. It had been delivered by post that afternoon and had kept her spirits lifted for the rest of the day. She poured herself a bit of brandy before settling further into her sofa with her feet as close to the coal fire as she could get them. Turning the envelope over in her hands, she took pleasure in perusing the return address once again. Manor Minnington.

Elinor had been invited to the next soiree at the Minnington's. Of course, she was almost always invited to the manor house when there was a big dinner party. She had been in that house so often in the last twenty years or so that she knew where every piece of furniture was placed in every single room. Her natural powers of observation, coupled with her natural predisposition to snoop, had provided her with a mental map of the Minnington home. She had even become very familiar with what was held inside some of the bathroom cupboards.

She shifted her shawl about her shoulders and sipped her brandy. It was not very good brandy, not like the brandy that she would enjoy at Manor Minnington on Saturday, but it was passable. Elinor could not afford the best brandy, or even the second best. In fact, Elinor could not afford the best or second best of anything. Plainly speaking, she was nearly broke. The couch upon which she sat had been new when she was a younger woman, some forty-odd years ago. She kept it clean and covered it to hide the frayed and faded upholstery, but it sagged under the weight of many years of use. Not that it got much wear and tear from visitors. Elinor seldom had anyone in her own home. She preferred spending her visiting time in the homes of her more well-heeled acquaintances.

Anyone outside her particular social circle might wonder why Miss Elinor Drumville, ostensibly an elderly busybody with nothing to show for her life, was always in attendance at some of the finest dinner parties in the west side of London. Frowzy in her antique evening gowns, Elinor could be found sitting in some of the finest parlors and dining rooms of the upper middle class of the south of England, looking very out of place but appearing to be perfectly at ease, smiling knowingly and giving slight nods of her head to other guests as though she were the dowager empress of Russia and keeping up with the general chit chat about whatever were the current events of the day. The other guests at these events always showed her a certain wary courtesy as they paid their respects to her.

"I suppose old Bunbarrel will be there," she thought distastefully. Elinor hated Sir Oswald Bunbarrel with a deep and abiding hate. Contemporaries, they were forever adversaries. Sir Oswald never failed in Elinor's presence to bring up how grateful he was that his ancestors had been prudent in their financial dealings and had been able to preserve the family fortune. Sir Oswald and Elinor both were members of the old British aristocracy, albeit the Bunbarrels had been higher up the social ladder than the Drumvilles. The Bunbarrels had been successful in keeping the family money together and had not frittered away the ancient estate and had even been able to increase their fortune over the years by wise investments in business. The result was that Sir Oswald was very well set for himself financially, as well as still having a seat in the House of Lords.

The Drumvilles had not been so fortunate. Like so many other members of the British upper class they had been unable to keep the family fortune and family lands in the family's possession. Things had gotten particularly bad in Elinor's grandparents' days and because of that her parents had very little left but the name. Young Elinor, while not a beauty exactly but attractive enough in her own right, might have been married off to a wealthy member of the merchant class, as so many others had done in order to infuse cash into the wheezing family bank accounts, but her parents were too proud to do that. Rather than sell their daughter into a loveless marriage, they had hoped that Elinor would find love among the peerage and marry well, and honorably, and on her own merit.

In fact, that is where Sir Oswald Bunbarrel came into the picture and made his first mistake that resulted in a lifetime of crossing swords with Elinor. Her parents had set their hopes on young Oswald as a suitable mate for their daughter. In those days Oswald was a handsome young man who had a bright future in politics before him. He also had money; in fact it was a considerable fortune. He had been friendly enough with the Drumvilles and their only daughter and Elinor had done her best to charm him into romancing her but Oswald had remained aloof. The Drumvilles extended invitations to the Bunbarrels for every conceivable occasion that might bring the two young people together, but their invitations were almost always declined, due in no small part to the fact that Sir Oswald's parents were not all too keen on the Drumvilles, given their somewhat desperate situation.

With no other prospects in sight, Elinor's youth faded over time and she had remained unmarried. Young and handsome Oswald never married, either, and had continued his life as a *bon vivant* in and around London, as well as retaining not only his seat in Parliament but his money as well. Over the years, he and Elinor had developed a cold and distant, barely civil, relationship with one another, merely tolerating each other at social gatherings. Sir Oswald never missed a chance to mention his wealth and Elinor would sit quietly enduring what she, and most others in attendance, knew was a personal dig at her impecunious state. Silently, she wished him dead.

Elinor reached for an andiron and poked at the grate to add vigor to the fire. Another sip of brandy and she neatly placed the invitation and on the table next to her. She reminisced about other dinner parties she had attended at the Minningtons'. Of all the well-to-do acquaintances off of whom she was fond of sponging, the Minningtons were her favorite. Despite old Bunbarrel's inevitable appearance, the social events at Manor Minnington were always the most enjoyable. The manor house was stunningly decorated, incorporating the best of the old along with some very fine new pieces of art and furniture acquired with the courtesy of Sir Clifford's American wealth. The food was always spectacular, prepared by, of all things, an Irish girl who had somehow learned to cook fine Italian cuisine. The Minningtons were always generous with their hospitality, serving the finest wine and liqueurs, as well as gourmet dinners. Yes, Sir Clifford always hosted splendid events.

Finishing her brandy, Elinor set her glass on the side table and smiled shrewdly to herself. She enjoyed the Minnington affairs for another reason, too. Her key to Manor Minnington, as well as to all the other social events of her circle, was the quiet blackmail she was able to press on her various hosts. Her snooping ways had paid off for her in a number of ways with a number of families. Her subtle extortions kept her on several guest lists, despite her lack of true status. And with what she knew of the Minningtons, she was fairly certain that she would continue to receive invitations to Dogmoor and her presence there, while not entirely welcome, would be secure.

9.

Edna Winwood stepped through the doors of her favorite little neighborhood public house just in time to order a cup of tea before the proprietors closed up for the evening. The "Tea Cozy" was handy to her Smithfield flat and also did not attract an unsavory crowd that plagued the pubs that remained open longer into the evening. At this hour, just a little before 8 o'clock in the evening, the place was already practically deserted, and that suited Miss Winwood just fine. She took off her hat and coat and sat at a booth near the kitchen, away from the windows, her favorite spot, as her desire was to be alone and in quiet.

Miss Edna Winwood, personal secretary to the current Lord Dogmoor, the wealthy American who had married into British aristocracy, was happy to be away from Manor Minnington. She was always happy to be away from Manor Minnington, if for no other reason than to spend time in her own apartment in London. Miss Edna was a person possessed of a very independent spirit and, although Sir Clifford provided her with personal quarters at the manor house, she loved the freedom of knowing that she had a place of her own to escape to when it was not necessary for her to be in Surrey.

Edna Winwood's independent streak had served her well throughout her life. It had gotten her into and through Bedford College with very high marks and the possibility, unique among the young ladies of her day, to find a professional position as a single woman in the English business landscape. Miss Edna was one of the front runners of women's suffrage in Great Britain, although she, naturally, did not see it that way. She had a mind of her own and was determined enough to conduct her affairs as she saw fit, and that's all there was to it. Having a place to call her own, simple flat though it was, was for Edna a symbol of the independence she worked so hard to attain. Having a sense of "my home is my castle" made Edna feel encouraged to deal in the male dominated world of business and less like the dainty, wispy ladies of English society of whom she was somewhat disdainful. Edna was proud of her accomplishments and appreciated being able to enjoy them at home, alone.

Another reason Miss Winwood liked being away from the Minningtons was that, lately especially, she sensed there was some tension in the air. It was not anything definite, such as an argument between Sir Clifford and Lady Opal, although, Lord knows, that happened frequently enough because of Sir Clifford's short temper. And it was not as though she had had to listen to Sir Clifford's tirade about English wiring when the lights went out since she had left the manor house before that sorry event occurred, although that would not have surprised her, either, since she had heard her employer's rants on many, many occasions. No, there was some other tension in the air and it was something she could not quite put her finger on. Something foreboding yet ethereal, such as the way the air becomes so calm and still just before a storm hits.

Edna Winwood did not like such uncertainties. She, like most of the women in her family, had an extremely practical view of life and saw things for exactly what they were and usually called them that way, too. Plainly speaking, she was plainly outspoken. In fact, she was without doubt one of the most plainly outspoken women in her profession. And, until she met Sir Clifford some dozen or so years ago, this quality had caused her a fair share of trouble with her British employers. It seems that many of the men who had availed themselves of Miss Winwood's services in the past had not been particularly pleased to be told, in plain language, when they were wrong. The wealthier members of British society, the class most likely to employ the Edna Winwoods of London, did not enjoy having women confront them so openly in their need to be corrected, either in business matters or whatever else happened to need to be corrected in Miss Edna's opinion. Most British men wanted secretaries to politely and dis-cretely work to make them look better not only to others, but to themselves as well. After all, they had their wives to point out their shortcomings. They paid enough for that, in one way or another, so why pay wages to a secretary to do it, too?

At least that's the way Edna Winwood viewed it—a problem of married men and their egos. She herself was an unmarried woman, an unplucked rose from the garden of love. She was not bitter about it, as so many suspected, those who had been stung by one of her blunt and unerringly truthful remarks. She had had her chance at marriage, many years before. A handsome Belgian gentleman had courted her for a brief time when, as a young student, she had summered on the continent. She had to admit she had been taken with him as he, obviously, had been with her. He, with his debonair manner and keen mind and darling moustaches, which he kept meticulously trimmed and waxed; she, with her sharp wit and uncanny ability to see through the superficial trivialities of life and get to the underlying reality of any given situation. It seemed that they had been gifted by Destiny to have met.

But, alas, nothing came of their relationship beyond their summer romance. Young Edna ended up forgoing the pleas-ures of marriage in order to concentrate on her schoolwork and her career. She had long planned to be a professional woman who could make her own way in the world and not be depend-ent on anyone, either family members or any man. Even though marriage was never actually discussed between them, the two young lovers had parted ways after the age old fashion that star crossed lovers have been fated for and continued on with life. Though she was never a beauty, she was a handsome woman, even today. But no other offers of romance had chanced her way, a circumstance that had not bothered or upset her in the slightest.

Hers was, overall, a very happy life. After she graduated from Bedford she obtained her first job with a well-to-do merchant and began what would become for her a career full of ups and downs in matters of employer/employee relations. Her first boss, as had all of the subsequent ones, had admired her efficient use of time and her intelligence and diligence in her work. All correspondence and paperwork, even the most detailed of legal briefs, had been flawlessly processed. Miss Winwood was not given to making mistakes.

No, it was not her capable work skills that eventually wore down her employers' patience. It was her relentlessly blunt way of pointing out errors that always seemed to get her in trouble. It wasn't as though she were being overtly rude, arrogant, nasty, or intrusive into personal matters. It was simply that she was blunt and to the point. For instance, when her first employer, a Mr. James Trebblebus, after working with her for a year and a half, had made an obvious mistake on a sales report, Edna caught it and presented the corrected report to him saying, "You'd better learn how to add figures better than a first year preparatory schoolboy or the Crown will be auditing you for tax evasion". Men in her day saw that as compromising their status in relation to her. She needed to learn to be more tactful, as a proper British lady should be, or so they thought. Miss Edna's temperament was not well suited for such useless niceties attributed to the very British ladies whom she disdained.

In retrospect, much of what had plagued Miss Winwood's relations with her employers was, indeed, her fault. But she just could not seem to learn how to play the game they wanted her to play. After leaving Trebblebus' employ, she had tried to curb the tartness of her tongue, but always, sooner or later, she would let go with a remark that would cause a rift between her and her boss and not long after she would be seeking employment elsewhere. It was fortunate for her that she was more than qualified for any job she sought because, as far as skills were concerned, hers were indeed impressive. Each time she left an employer she also received a letter of recommendation, praising her excellent proficiency and efficiency, "to whom it may concern". (This held true even after she told Arthur Ticklesham that the chimney sweep that worked her building had a better sense of the King's language than had he. He wrote her letter of recommendation the very next morning.) She would inevitably find another position, last a couple of years or more, finally unnerve her employer with her "ill-mannered" way of speaking, receive a new letter of recommendation, and be looking for work once more. She had met many of London's wealthiest businessmen over the years in this way.

Still and all, she had made a very comfortable living for herself. Her employment history, erratic as it was, was no more erratic than other personal secretaries who, although they may have kept their place and minded their tongues better, were less capable and more prone to mistakes. As it was, Miss Edna Winwood was able to keep enough money coming in to maintain her flat in Smithfield and enjoy a few of life's simpler pleasures, which were the only pleasures she was interested in indulging anyway.

Competent, capable and self-confident as she was, she was not, however, herself this evening. There was a very uneasy feeling hanging over her, a feeling that something was about to happen. It seemed that there was some inner sense that was tickling her subconscious mind. It so distracted her that, as she sat in the "Tea Cozy", she had hardly even noticed the hostess serving her. She played at a scone that had been brought along with her pot of tea and she began musing to herself about the Minningtons.

Yes, that had been a lucky break, being introduced to Sir Clifford during the tenure of her last employ. Frederick Waffington, a lawyer with the Solicitor General's office had acquainted the two with each other one day when Sir Clifford came in to tend to some affair or another concerning his estate. At first, Edna had not been terribly impressed with the American. His request of the Solicitor General was to change the name of Dogmoor to something else, anything else. When asked why, Sir Clifford had simply and bluntly stated that he hated dogs. Edna had had to leave the office at that precise moment for she knew herself well enough to know that one of her characteristic remarks was in the making. It was one thing to say something to one's employer, but quite another to say something to one's employer's client. So Miss Winwood had discreetly excused herself to the ladies powder room and laughed until she cried into some toilet paper. By the time she had composed herself, Sir Clifford was out the door, still the lord of Dogmoor.

As unpromising as that first meeting had been, Miss Edna found that she had more in common with the American gentry-by-marriage than she ever would have anticipated. It had been by purest coincidence that, after leaving her position with Waffington (after suggesting to him that if he spent as much time concentrating on his work and less on the secretarial pool he might have a better sense of his own business), she had seen in the "Times" an advertisement placed by one Sir Clifford Minnington for a personal secretary. Never one not to take opportunity by its knocking fist, Edna had responded to the ad and, two weeks later, found herself as personal secretary to the American who hated dogs.

As fate would have it, Miss Edna Winwood and Sir Clifford Minnington were perfectly suited to work together. As she grew accustomed to her new surroundings and her new boss, Edna found that she rather admired Sir Clifford, not for his unpolished colonial manner but for his direct approach to business matters and, well, life in general. And Sir Clifford found in Edna Winwood a secretary who was, as he put it, "a straight shooter". Lord Minnington actually liked Miss Winwood's direct and, shall we say, to the point way of expressing herself. And he especially liked that she was as efficient as he had been led to believe she was, although he did not quite fully understand her. Compatible as they were, it did take them some little while to become accustomed to one other. When one day he complimented her by telling her she must have been educated in the States, she looked over her glasses at him and asked, "Why, what did I misspell?" After realizing what her remark was intended to convey, Sir Clifford laughed heartily and said, "Edna, my girl, you and I are gonna get along just fine!"

A clanging noise brought Miss Winwood back from her revelries, the noise of a dish dropping in a sink. Presently, the young lady who often waited table emerged from the kitchen to assist the hostess with closing down the dining room. She had breezed right past Edna without noticing her sitting there. She, too, seemed distracted. Edna recognized her as the friend that visited with the cook on occasion at the manor house. She watched as the lovely young woman wiped down tables, beginning on the opposite side of the pub. There was something about her that twitched an inner sense in Miss Winwood's brain, something that seemed to be part of the eerie feeling she'd been having all day.

The young lady, whose name Edna could not remember, looked up from her work and the two of them caught each other's eye for a moment. There was a brief moment of recognition and then, with a shy smile, the young woman went back to cleaning the tables. Miss Edna Winwood finished her tea, left her money on the table, and gathered her belongings to make the short walk to her flat in the cold November night.

10.

The stone gateposts of St. Elwydd's Church were imposing struc-
tures, guarding the entrance to the church named for the Welsh
patron saint of animal husbandry and midwifery. They stood
across the street and just down from the "Tea Cozy". A young
man hid himself in their shadows and kept watch for who might
be coming out of the pub. He had seen Edna Winwood enter just
a while before and had pulled himself further into the protection
of the great gateposts. Erskine Randiffle certainly did not want to
be observed by the personal secretary to Sir Clifford Minnington;
although he was not sure why it was that he felt that way, other
than the fact that Sir Clifford was influential in London's business
class and his secretary was known to never miss a thing.

However, it was a much younger woman who was on Erskine's mind. He watched across the street at the door of the "Tea
Cozy" for signs of the end of Dora's day and wondered if he had
time to speak to her or not. If he weren't careful he'd be late for
his evening appointment with Jasper and Jasper, although he
never remained truly angry for very long, did not like to be kept
waiting for people to show up for appointments. Even though
their encounters were social and not business related, Jasper
would become petulant and Erskine would spend a good part
of the rest of the evening cajoling him out of it, as he had done
on other occasions before.

Dora and Jasper. Erskine had both of these two individuals
on his mind constantly. His whole day was spent working on his
figures at his desk and often he found himself wandering off and
daydreaming about one or the other of them. Fortunately, his

work never suffered and his employer was none the wiser about his imagination's perambulations, but it bothered Erskine nonetheless. He did not like to tempt fate. After all, his clerking at one of London's finest firms, Applegate and Copperwaithe, was an enormous bit of luck for him and he did not want to get caught looking dreamily off into space and risk losing his plum position.

But tempting fate was something that he felt he was doing a lot of these days, ever since he had met Dora and Jasper. At first his meetings with Dora in the pub were merely casual flirtations and nothing serious. But he soon found himself genuinely attracted to her. She was pretty, yes. But there seemed to be more to her than mere beauty. She had a certain secret tragic sense about her, an air of sadness just under the surface of her calm and gentle manner. Soon he had found himself spending more time at the "Tea Cozy", just to have a chance to chat with her and wonder about the comely young lady in the plain clothes of a public house waitress.

Then there was Jasper. Mr. Dunwoody had come into Erskine's life at roughly the same time as Dora, oddly enough, and had captivated his imagination just as much as Dora had. Jasper was outgoing, sometimes outrageous, and well connected, his being the personal secretary to a member of the House of Lords. Jasper was also the most handsome man that Erskine had ever met. Over the months of their friendship, Erskine had found himself being more and more aware of that particular quality of Jasper's.

Sometimes, when he caught himself daydreaming, he would have Jasper on his mind. Often his daydreams about Jasper were about swimming in the summer down by the sea, or perhaps imagining Jasper as a member of a rowing team. Erskine did not immediately understand the nature of these images which he just could not seem to keep out of his mind. At first he attributed it to Jasper's outgoing personality and his natural athletic build. But as he spent more time with Jasper, Erskine felt that there was more to it than that. His attraction to the outgoing Mr. Dunwoody had as much to do with his splendid appearance as it did with his personality. And as this reality began to take shape in Erskine's conscious mind, he became a bit perturbed by its implication.

He was beginning to have the feeling that he was attracted to Jasper Dunwoody in the way that he should have thought would have been reserved for someone else. Someone like Dora.

Troubled though he was about what his attraction to Jasper might mean, Erskine could not help himself when it came to Jasper's company. Beautiful as Dora was, she could not compare to Jasper's jocular personality, his popularity around town, his position, of course, with Sir Oswald, and, Erskine shivered as he admitted it, his looks. Jasper Dunwoody was simply stunningly handsome. Tall, blond and blue eyed, with an athletic build, Jasper turned heads all over London. Erskine had seen women blush when he merely smiled at them. Even men often did double takes, as if to make sure that they had seen someone who was that incredibly good-looking walking among them. This, coupled with the way Jasper doted on him, led Erskine into a powerful, yet alarming, attraction to him.

Dora and Jasper. One was lovely and feminine, the other masculine and handsome. Both had qualities Erskine admired. Both held an undeniable attraction for him. Erskine felt somehow caught in the middle of the two of them, as though they were some sort of tug of war with him at the center of the rope. Of course, neither one knew of the other. Erskine's playful dalliances in the "Tea Cozy" were carefully kept from Jasper. And Dora, as far as he knew, had never laid eyes on Jasper. Their one common denominator was Erskine himself and Erskine was intent on keeping it that way. At least until he could get a handle on the emotional turmoil these two people were beginning to cause him.

The door to the "Tea Cozy" opened and out walked Miss Winwood. Erskine sank deeper into the protection of St. Elwydd's. He was intent on at least getting a glimpse of Dora before heading off to the "Boar's Head". While standing in the cold night air, he had decided to forego any conversation with Dora for that evening, that he had better, and actually would rather, be in Jasper's company. Still, he at least wanted to see her. He waited until she, too, finished her chores and came out the door. He watched her from the shadows and then, after trying in vain to satisfy the longing he had had for her, he left the gateposts of the church behind and set off for his evening with Jasper and the men at the pub.

His intention to have not been noticed had been in vain. Edna Winwood's ever-observant eye had caught the movement in the darkened gateway as she left the pub. She had immediately recognized the young man as a frequent customer in the "Tea Cozy", one who had been seen flirting with the young waitress. Edna had recognized him at once because of his stylish manner of dress and because Erskine Randiffle, though no Jasper Dunwoody, was a very handsome young man himself.

Edna smiled to herself as she made her way home. Although she had every appearance of the stern, cold, down-to-business type, Miss Winwood did have a soft spot in her heart for young love.

11.

Another figure waited in the shadows on the street down from the "Tea Cozy", a little further down the street from St. Elwydd's. A young man watched Erskine, carefully concealing himself in the shadows of the dark November evening. He wore a stylish and expensive overcoat with kid gloves on his hands and covered his head rakishly with a hat that could have been worn by George Raft in one of those American gangster movies. He was watching to see what Erskine was up to, if he would go into the "Tea Cozy" or wait to talk to that waitress when she came out. He took note of the fact that Mr. Randiffle hid himself when Edna Winwood came out. He thought that might be a helpful bit of knowledge for him to pass on.

As he continued to observe the unsuspecting Erskine, he made note of the time. "About time to make up your mind, Erskine old bean," he thought to himself. The night was cold and, stylish as his overcoat was, it was still unpleasant to be out in the night air. "At least there's no mist," he mused.

Suddenly, the door to the "Tea Cozy" opened and out walked the waitress, Dora Finch. Randiffle hid himself from her as well and she, quite innocent of the fact that two sets of eyes were observing her, turned in the other direction and headed to her own flat. When she was out of sight, Erskine made his own way to his evening's destination.

The strange young man in the stylish coat and kid gloves and rakish hat waited for a few more minutes in the dark shadows of the street before making his own way in the general direction of the "Boar's Head" pub.

Part II

12.

As she walked to her flat, Miss Winwood noticed how much better the cold air seemed to carry noises than when it was warm. The sounds of the motorcars and autobuses seemed amplified on the cobblestone streets. Footsteps, her own determined step especially, resounded and sometimes even echoed off the walls of the buildings around her. Lights from the various pubs and businesses and upper windows of residences pierced the night with a clarity that summer's humidity did not permit. Miss Winwood never ceased to wonder at how changes in nature could produce change in the human ability to perceive. On an evening such as this cool, crisp, dry November evening her senses, heightened as they were, seemed almost catlike as she took in the scenes of London around her.

As she mused to herself and continued her walk, Edna soon approached an intersection which she would have to cross in order to continue on her way home. As she neared the curb her ears pricked up with the sounds of laughter and the frivolous chatter of young voices. This in and of itself was not unusual on the streets of London, but one of those voices sounded terribly familiar. Turning in the direction of the voices, Edna saw, coming down the cross street to hers, a group of young people who were obviously out having a splendid time.

If Miss Winwood were the nervous type she might have been concerned for her safety, for this was a ragtag group, for the most part. Disheveled clothes and tattered footwear gave the casual observer the impression that these young people had emerged from the slums of the city and were out marauding. Their language was as crude as their clothing, adding to the vulgar class impression that they presented. However, none of that concerned Miss Winwood. What did concern her was the fact that one of these ragtag, foulmouthed youths was none other than Claudia Minnington.

"Claudia?"

"Miss Winwood?"

The group of young people stopped momentarily and gave the prim, older woman a cautious glance. Miss Edna stood perfectly erect and faced them, addressing herself to young Miss Minnington.

"Claudia, I thought you told your parents that you were going to be doing research at the college library this evening. I am sure you are aware that you are no where near Bedford?"

"Who's this, Claud? The Queen Mum?" snickered one of the young men in the group, as he wiped his nose with the back of his hand.

"Shut up you git!" hissed Claudia. "It's my father's secretary!"

Ignoring the young man and what was meant to be an insulting remark, Edna addressed herself to Claudia once again, "Claudia, what are you doing in this part of London at this hour?"

The group of young people seemed to become very uneasy rather suddenly at the prospect of having Claudia's father's secretary catch them with their knickers down, as the saying goes. They nervously fell back a step and waited to see how Claudia, whom they knew to be a quick thinker, would talk herself out of this one.

"Why, Miss Winwood, we had started pulling out books and taking notes on our geography research assignment when we all realized that we had not eaten. We decided to come to our favorite spot for fish and chips and had a couple of beers and time got away from us. I fancy the beer helped that. You won't be a fussbudget and tell my father, will you?" Claudia smiled as sweetly as she could force herself to.

Miss Winwood, noting the smile that would have looked more natural on a cat after eating a canary, shook her head slightly as she observed the dubious group of students. She had serious questions as to whether any of them had seen the inside of a library, ever, let alone this evening. There was something about them that was quite peculiar, and not the peculiar eccentricity of the academician.

Addressing herself once again to her master's daughter, Miss Edna spoke. "I won't say anything to your father, but in return I expect to see some very good grades this semester. A fair exchange, don't you think? And for pity sake, Claudia, do something about your hair. You look as if you just rowed a dingy across the Channel."

Having finished what she thought was necessary to say, under the circumstances, Edna Winwood turned on her heel and crossed the street, continuing her way home. The gang of youths turned in the opposite direction and were soon laughing and teasing Claudia, their sense of apprehension dissipating into the night air. Claudia alone turned and gave a brief and uneasy look at Miss Winwood's back as she furthered herself along. Miss Winwood could cause her a lot of trouble if she chose to. Someone in the group handed Claudia a flask from which she took a drink. Soon her own apprehension was gone and she rejoined in the general rowdiness of her group. They were, after all, on their way to their favorite little hideaway. Claudia knew that shortly there would be little room left in her mind for Miss Edna Winwood.

Edna Winwood continued her walk and reflected on the exchange she had just had with Claudia and her friends. There was something quite odd about the whole thing that Edna could not put her finger on. "A very different group of young people," she allowed. She was not immediately concerned that she had promised to conceal her knowledge of the evening's events from Sir Clifford. She did not feel it was really her place to baby sit her employer's daughter, who, after all, had reached her majority. No, that was not what was bothering Miss Edna. It was the strangeness of the group. And it was not simply the fact that they were all strangers to her that bothered her. It was something more than that. Their awkward silence and the fact that they had cowered like a pack of scared dogs when they realized who Miss Winwood was as she confronted Claudia made her wonder about them. Perhaps even more so than that was the odor that had hung about them. They had obviously been smoking, but Miss Winwood could not imagine what kind of tobacco produced that type of smell. She had been around men all her life who smoked pipes, cigars and cigarettes made from tobaccos gathered from around the world, yet she had never smelled such an acrid, yet sweet odor as that which had clung to the clothes of Claudia and her friends. The cold, clear November air had perfectly conducted that odor to her nostrils and Miss Winwood doubted that she would ever forget it.

13.

Most evenings at the "Boar's Head" public house were generally quiet. Only the neighborhood regulars, those with nagging wives and too much of a fondness for ale, were usually there. Snuffy Dolton worked behind the bar, tending to his few customers that evening.

"Snuffy" was a nickname, of course, because Mr. Dolton liked to pinch snuff and vastly preferred "Snuffy" to his given name of Silbey. It was infinitely better than another nickname he had had in his youth, simply the shortened version of Dolton. The call of "Hey, Dolt!" had made him cringe throughout most of his youth. Once he started using snuff somebody at the pub had ordered a beer saying "Hey, Snuffy, how about another round?" The name stuck and Silbey Dolton was only too happy for his new nomenclature.

Snuffy looked around the pub at the few men sitting there and then glanced at the clock on the wall. It was getting on to be 8:30 and he was anticipating more customers. Lately, there seemed to be a new group of men who were basing their evenings at the "Boar's Head". These were not the neighborhood regulars to whom he had become accustomed. No, these were young, professional men who did not seem to mind being up late during the work week. These gentlemen, and that's what they seemed to be, most of them anyway, were always very well dressed and perfectly behaved. They liked their drink, to be sure, but did not get sloppy drunk. They usually congregated around a few of the tables in the back of the pub and kept to themselves, never mixing or mingling with his other customers.

They were pleasant enough, but there was something about them that Snuffy could not quite figure out. For one thing, why would men of their class be in his pub, especially during the work week? What did their wives or girlfriends think of them spending so much time together there? How was it that they always looked as if they had just gotten out of a bath and been dressed by a valet? Nattily dressed and perfectly groomed, they seemed to have stepped out of an advertisement found in one of those popular new magazines.

Still, they *were* pleasant enough and they spent their money freely. They had not once caused any trouble since they started coming into his place almost a year ago now. He remembered the night that he had first seen the one who appeared to be the leader of the group. Jasper, he thought the name was. One night last Christmas, a tall and very good looking man with blond hair and blue eyes came into the pub and flashed a perfectly white set of teeth at Snuffy and asked how late he served. As he poured him a whiskey Snuffy told him "Open till midnight, or thereabouts, sir." With that the handsome young man looked around and smiled once again, finished his drink and said he'd be back. And back he came, almost every night thereafter and always with some other handsome young man, or men, in tow.

Over the ensuing months Snuffy came to learn that the leader, this Jasper, had something to do with government, because he kept hearing the word "Parliament" bandied about in his conversations. Being a proprietor with proper proprieties, Snuffy tried not to overhear their conversations, or at least tried to appear not to be obvious about it. Over time they had proved themselves to be polite, relatively quiet, and uninhibited in their spending, so Snuffy Dolton really did not care who did what as their occupation and was happy for the influx of business.

The bell over the door jingled and in he came. Tall and handsome as ever, Jasper Dunwoody took off his overcoat and went up to Snuffy and ordered a porter. As the barkeep drew it, Jasper took his coat to the coat rack, smoothed out his suit coat, tugged at his French cuffed shirtsleeves and returned to the bar to get his beer.

"A good night out for porter, help take the cold off," Snuffy offered as he finished drawing the dark beer into the pint sized glass.

"Yes, no wonder the Irish drink so much of it, damp as it is all the time over there," Jasper agreed amiably.

"Expecting many of your friends in tonight with you, Sir?" asked the barkeep, conversationally.

"Oh, the usual suspects, I suspect", smiled Jasper and he took his beer and headed for the back table where he usually held forth for an evening's conviviality. The bell at the door rang again and more faces which had become familiar entered the pub. Soon after, most of Jasper's usual suspects had arrived.

Jasper Dunwoody was the center of attention, as he almost always was, laughing and joking and telling stories about his employer and Parliament. The other men seemed to hang on his every word and laughed merrily at his quips. Not that they did not have quips of their own. The whole group seemed to be very witty and quick with a remark or barb. Every man in his group was very well dressed and groomed, rather young compared to the other clientele, and each of them decidedly handsome. None, however, as handsome as Jasper himself. He seemed to be the source of male beauty in which the others basked, soaking up his reflection and making his beauty their own. Jasper was, at the very least, the focal point of the group.

He seemed to be a bit preoccupied this evening, however. As he laughed and conversed with his companions in the back of the pub, he also kept looking up at the clock, as if he were anticipating the arrival of someone who was later than expected. Only the closest observer, however, would have noticed the slight crease in the corners of his eyes as he realized what time it was getting to be, he maintained his happy-go-lucky manner so readily. After each quick check of the time he would return his full attention to the men around him and made merry all the more.

It was past nine o'clock when the bell at the door jingled yet again and in walked young Erskine Randiffle. Snuffy recognized this one as one of Jasper's more constant companions of late. Erskine hung up his topcoat and hat and ordered a pint of

Guinness for himself before joining the group. Snuffy noticed his reddened nose and ears and wondered if he had been long outside in the cold.

Jasper noticed as well, but smiled broadly as Erskine joined the group. He threw his arm around his shoulder and drew Erskine into the story he was telling about the niece of Sir Ozzie's who was visiting London and had practically thrown herself at him by asking her uncle to arrange an evening's engagement for them. For reasons unknown to Snuffy, that sent the entire troupe into uproarious laughter, as though that were the most ridiculous thing any of them had ever heard. Jasper ordered another round of drinks and Snuffy busied himself making them ready.

Before he was finished pouring, the bell above the door jingled yet again and in walked the one member of the group that made Snuffy terribly uncomfortable. This one was also well dressed, sporting a very stylish overcoat, a hat rakishly settled upon his head and he even wore gloves that appeared to be made of kidskin. On the surface this young man looked as if he would fit in with the rest of the crowd that had settled on the "Boar's Head" as their favorite pub, but there was something distinctly different about him. Whenever he saw him, Snuffy could not help but remember an old saying of his mother's. "You can put a silk dress on a sow but you still end up with a pig." And that was what was different about this newly arrived customer. He had all the outward appearances of the other gentlemen, but did not have the class or breeding to be convincing. At least, that's how Snuffy saw it, as surely would have his mother.

It was not Trevor's custom to greet Snuffy upon entering the public house, which annoyed Snuffy immensely and strengthened his opinion that this was a man with no breeding. It was Trevor's custom to throw off his overcoat in a most flamboyant fashion and join the group. He usually did not remain long. He might have a drink, he might not. He would converse with everyone in general and no one in particular. He most often came in alone, but once in a while had a companion with him whom Snuffy had never seen before and would never see again. Very, very infrequently would he leave with any of the other men who clustered around Jasper. In fact, most of them seemed to be somewhat uncomfortable around him, too, and only seemed to grow more comfortable in his company the more they drank. He gave every indication that he belonged with this group, and yet at the same time was so obviously apart from it, apparently only tolerated by its members. When he had first started making an appearance at the "Boar's Head" Snuffy had been intensely curious about this paradox, but over time simply attributed it to the better breeding of the customers whom he preferred. "They know a pig in a dress when they see one."

The gaiety diminished a bit upon Trevor's arrival, as it always did, but soon picked up again, as it always did. Tonight Trevor seemed to have something on his mind and signaled Jasper with his eyes. Jasper separated himself from the group and conferred with Trevor in a booth nearer the front of the pub.

"He was there again, standing in the cold watching for her," Trevor said to Jasper. "I nearly froze my own arse off waiting for the bitch to come out at the end of her duties."

Jasper said nothing for a moment. He looked as though he were contemplating that bit of news. Finally he said "Thanks" and slipped Trevor five quid and returned to the group. Trevor put his coat, gloves and hat back on and went out of the pub into the night.

Snuffy observed that the frivolity continued as usual and that Jasper was buying plenty of rounds that evening, especially for the young man named Erskine.

14.

Wednesday morning dawned a dreary, rainy day in London. The mist was so thick that it obscured the tops of even the shortest buildings. It also made the November morning seem colder than it actually was.

Edna Winwood was in a taxi and making her way to Manor Minnington. Sir Clifford provided for this convenience for his personal secretary. Not given to gushes of any kind, Miss Winwood was nonetheless terribly grateful for this generous perk from her employer. She felt it extravagant on his part, but he was, after all, an American. She accepted it as the benefit of her job that it was.

On this particular morning she was given pause to think about the night before and perhaps to reconsider her decision not to mention to Sir Clifford that she had seen his daughter in London last evening. On one hand she felt she was being disloyal to him if she did not tell him what she knew. On the other hand, she was employed for business matters, not family matters, and, on top of it all, Claudia was old enough to make her own decisions. On the other hand—Miss Edna was sorry she only had two hands—Claudia seemed to be making some poor choices, from what Edna could tell from last night.

In the end, she decided to keep her promise to Claudia and mention nothing of their chance encounter to Sir Clifford. She had sensed enough tension in the manor house lately and, although she did not know why she sensed something was wrong, she certainly did not want to add to it. Having arrived at her decision, she settled back into the seat of the taxi and watched out of the window as London slipped away behind them and they made their way to Surrey.

The moors were barely visible at all as the taxi neared Manor Minnington and the fog was thickest around the bogs. Edna had long since become accustomed to the scenery in this part of England and hardly even noticed it anymore as she concentrated on the day's work ahead of her. Sir Clifford, she knew, was planning a business trip into London himself in the next day or so and would no doubt want her to sort paper work and itineraries for him, arrange his appointments with important people in the city and so on. Edna looked forward to days like this because it was easy for her to concentrate on her work when she had lots of it to do and thus keep herself from being distracted by whatever else might be going on at Dogmoor.

Her day started at 10 o'clock sharp with his lordship and since Edna usually arrived early, it was her custom to have a cup of tea in the pantry before seeing him. Today would be no different and, as Miss Winwood removed her coat and gave it a shake before Snippy took it for her, she was only too happy to avail herself of a hot cup of tea on such a nasty morning.

Maggie, the cook, was there to greet her, as usual, and poured her a hot cup of tea and offered her some fresh baked scones. Maggie was, in Miss Winwood's opinion, one of the brightest spots in Manor Minnington and she could not help but smile in response to the cheerfulness of the lilting Irish brogue as Maggie said her good mornings and served Edna her tea and scones. Today Maggie seemed especially animated and Miss Edna wondered why.

"Well, Maggie, you seem to be awfully chipper for such a dreary day. You act as if you've won the Sweepstakes," said Edna.

"Ack now. Sure'n it would not have been any better news for me, I'm certain, although winning the Sweepstakes would be darlin'," replied Maggie. "But I've only yesterday received news from Ireland that Father Burns is coming here to pay me a visit, all the way from County Cork!"

"You don't say. And who is Father Burns?" asked Edna as she stirred some milk into her tea.

"Father Burns is the parish priest in Fermoy that was connected to the orphanage I was raised in, ma'am. I've known him since I was a wee young thing."

"Why would he be coming all the way to England to visit? Is he on holiday?"

"No ma'am, not a holiday, I'm thinkin' but he says that he has some good news for me and is coming here to tell it to me his very self!" Maggie's voice was practically a whisper as she said this, as if to say it out too loudly would bring bad luck upon her.

"Well, now," replied Miss Edna, "that is good news, then, isn't it?"

"To be sure, I don't know. When I left the orphanage I left that part of me life behind forevermore. I never again wanted to remember those days. Dora and I both had been determined never to dwell on the sad past of St. Saviour's and the Sisters of Mercy. And now, with Father Burns coming, why ever since I received the telegram yesterday I haven't had a moment's peace. I'm excited, to be sure, but neither Dora nor myself could decide if it was good news to be excited about or bad."

Miss Winwood arched her eyebrows. "What's Dora got to do with it?" she asked.

"Well, ma'am, Dora and I were orphans together at St. Saviour's and we had a time of it there with those nuns. Most of them were nice, but a couple were holy terrors if ever there was one. We were both adopted as young girls in our teens. My family, the O'Sheas, were lovely folk. But Dora did not fare as well with the Finches." And here Maggie again whispered, "There was some great unpleasantness in that household, I'm thinkin'."

Miss Edna mused to herself what type of unpleasantness that might have been, but uppermost on her mind was that Dora had been orphaned in Ireland.

"You know, it never seemed to me that Dora was Irish, despite being named Finch. She just does not seem Irish. Please don't take that the wrong way, my dear," proffered Miss Winwood.

"No offense taken, ma'am, for often it has been that I've thought the very same thing meself about Dora. Her features could pass for Irish, maybe in the north, but it's her manner, her way. She definitely is not like the other Irish girls I have known. I have always supposed it was because of the Finches and what they done to her. But it seems to me she was that way, even as a wee one."

"So you've known each other since you were children?" Edna was intrigued.

"Yes, ma'am," replied Maggie. "We were bunkmates in the orphanage right off and have been friends ever since. When we became of age we both decided that we'd move out of Ireland and try to find better circumstances for ourselves here in Britain. I must say, I feel particularly lucky to have found this position with the Minningtons. Imagine, an Irish cook in a British manor house!" With that, Maggie threw her hands up laughing and turned to the sink to finish cleaning some artichokes.

"Dora works at the "Tea Cozy", doesn't she? As a waitress?" asked Miss Winwood.

"Indeed, yes she does, ma'am" replied Maggie from her artichokes. "It was the only employment she could find that she felt qualified to do. The Finches had used her as a maidservant, that's for certain sure, and so she sought work, and found it, in a public house. In a way, it made her feel a bit comfortable being in a public house, since we have so many over home," she said as she trimmed the stems.

"Yes, of course," said Edna thoughtfully before biting into a scone. This was interesting news. She had no idea that the girls had been in an orphanage together and that that was the genesis of their friendship. She had, of course, never given it much thought at all until now, but it still seemed surprising to her. And she wondered why that was. Why *should* she be so intrigued? Something about this conversation added to the tickling of her inner sense in the back of her mind, a sense that she was realizing she already had been feeling about this girl Dora.

"Tell me, Maggie," continued Miss Edna, "did you and Dora arrive at the orphanage at the same time?"

"Ack no, ma'am", said Maggie, now turning her attention to some cabbages. "Dora was already a long time resident when I got there. She had been abandoned as a baby, poor thing, and had lived her whole life in the orphanage, never knowing her mother or father or what family life was like, until the Finches got a hold of her, devil take them!"

"Abandoned as an infant, eh?" Miss Edna was more speaking to herself now. Still, she could not understand why this intrigued her so. Just then, however, the clock struck ten, and it was time to go meet Sir Clifford for the day's tasks. She thanked Maggie for the tea and company and, picking up her valise, went through the pantry door and made her way to Sir Clifford's office.

"She's a nice one, she is," thought Maggie as she watched Miss Winwood retreat from the pantry. "For an Englishwoman."

15.

By 10:30 that Wednesday morning the sun was shining once again on the British Empire, at least enough to burn away the morning mist from around its capital city. The day was looking less dreary as Petal Chalmers excused herself from the "Tea Cozy" and took her customary walk to the Tower of London. She told Dublin Joe, her barkeep and boyfriend, that it was her morning's constitutional to help her stay trim, which she was not. It was more that she enjoyed watching the ravens fly about the Tower and found it a relaxing break before the lunch and tea crowds descended upon the pub.

Surprisingly, it did not take her long to get to the Tower. It was a bit of a walk and although she was a plump one, Petal kept a brisk pace. She enjoyed looking at the shop windows she passed along the way, the people in their business clothes, and the flower girls in their shawls. A fact to which she would readily attest was that she enjoyed living and working in London.

Dublin Joe was just as pleased to have her out of the pub at that time of morning anyway. Without much to do to keep her occupied, since all the soups were already on the boil and everything else cut and readied for the lunch customers, Petal could be irritating to the barkeep. Dublin Joe, as he was called, was Joe Shannon, an Englishman of Irish descent who did not mind that people mistook him for an actual Irish man by his name and nickname. Truth was, people had come to assume that the capital city in Ireland was the source of "Dublin". That suited Joe just fine. In actuality, it was not "Dublin" but "Doublin'" that had been given to him as a nickname by some wag who was making sport of the fact that Joe was gaining weight as he helped himself to ale and stout when he thought Petal wasn't looking. "Joe Shannon, you're doubling up as we look at you!" he had shouted amid laughter some years earlier. "Doublin'" Joe Shannon eventually became "Dublin" Joe to everyone, due in no small matter to Mr. Shannon's ability to keep his mouth shut and not make a fuss about it all when the joke first was made.

He hummed a tuneless melody as he wiped down the bar in order to be ready for the upcoming lunchtime crowd, pausing only to pour himself a bit of the stout.

Meanwhile, Petal was at the Tower enjoying the ravens and the sights around her. She was in terribly good spirits for some reason that day. She did not know why, but she just felt that something was going to happen that day. Perhaps, she mused, it was going to be some happy news for Dora that was bringing on this feeling of optimism and good fortune. Maybe that young man of hers will finally ask her out to dinner.

She paused just long enough to daydream about these things and, taking one last look at the ravens, she turned to make her return trip to the "Tea Cozy". It was then that she happened to notice the two gentlemen on the other side of the street, nearer the Tower and it was then that she noticed that one of the gentlemen looked very familiar.

"Why, that's the young man who pays so much attention to Dora!" thought Petal as she decided to linger just a bit longer in the vicinity of the Tower. "And who is that other one? I've never seen a man so handsome as that!"

Jasper and Erskine were engaged in conversation across the street, unknowingly observed by Petal Chalmers. Erskine seemed perplexed, as if trying to make a decision and Jasper seemed eager to help him make it.

"Look, mate," said Jasper, "think about it, won't you? That's all I ask."

"I don't know Jasper," said Erskine in reply. "Suppose his lordship should find out and not appreciate the fact that I'm spending the night in his flat?"

"Sir Ozzie will never find out. I told you, he's gone to Scotland and won't be back until late on Saturday when he'll have to get ready to go to the Minnington affair. And besides, it is not as though we are going to be in his personal quarters. I have my own set of rooms in his flat. It is perfectly all right with him if I have guests over," Jasper used his most persuasive tone.

"It sounds like it would be great fun and, and I really want to do it, spend the night there, that is, but....." hesitated Erskine.

"Take today and tomorrow to mull it over, Erskine. You know how much I like you and enjoy your company. It'll be jolly fun for us to have a night in at the old man's place. Just at least think about it and get back to me tomorrow, alright?" With that Jasper gave Erskine a hug, a tight hug, and sent him on his way. The hug was a sudden and apparently impulsive gesture and Erskine was surprised by it, but also very much pleased. He left Jasper standing in the shadow of the Tower of London, wondering whether or not he would take him up on his invitation to spend the night in Sir Oswald Bunbarrel's opulent London flat.

Petal, though she could not hear their conversation, nevertheless paid close attention to what she had seen and wondered what the two of them had been discussing and why young Erskine had looked so perplexed. She hoped that it may have had something to do with Dora and that the handsome man he was with was encouraging him to make a move. These were her thoughts as she once again started to make her way back to the "Tea Cozy" but once again she was stopped in her tracks.

No sooner had young Erskine rounded the corner when out of nowhere appeared a young man in a stylish overcoat and a hat, worn rakishly upon his head. Petal recognized him from having seen him happen into the "Tea Cozy" on occasion. She was not sure of his name, but she was certain of his reputation. It was a bad one. His was the worst reputation of any individual Petal or her girlfriends knew. Once again, she could not tear herself away from her spot across the street and tried to look inconspicuous as the two men talked.

She needn't have bothered to try to blend into the scenery because the two men were completely oblivious to her. Jasper and Trevor, as soon as Erskine was out of sight confided briefly with each other. This time, it seemed from Petal's vantage point, that it was the very handsome young man who had the perplexed look upon his face. He said something to the unsavory man in the stylish overcoat, who simply nodded. The handsome Jasper reached into his pocket and pulled out what appeared to be some money which he pressed into Trevor's hand, who pocketed it and casually made his way along in the same direction as Erskine. The very handsome and striking young man then left, walking in the general direction of Parliament.

"What in God's name could they have been doing? And why was Dora's young man there? Could he possibly be part of anything with that seedy fop? I wonder, does he even know?" Petal was breathless with anticipation as she hurried back to the "Tea Cozy" to confer with Dublin Joe about what she had just seen and wished she had heard.

16.

Sir Clifford Minnington was his usual punctual self and had just been seating himself at his desk when Edna had arrived to review the morning's work. He looked up at his secretary as she entered and, although he appreciated the fact that she was always punctual, he was not likely to comment upon it since, after all, that is what he paid her to be.

"Do you have the file on the Fossbury account?" he asked in his usual gruff tone.

Unperturbed, Miss Winwood replied, "Yes, it's right there on your desk in front of you. I left it out for you yesterday as you asked me to then."

"Alright, then, let's have a look at it."

And so it went with the two of them. In many ways, they were a perfect working pair, neither one seeming at all to mind the other's curtness. The first part of the morning progressed in this way, as it always did, with Sir Clifford grumbling about one thing or another and Miss Winwood advising him when she had an opinion and pointing out to him why he was wrong when he made a mistake.

On this particular Wednesday, as morning gave way to mid-day, Sir Clifford decided that he needed some time to reflect quietly on a presentation he was to make to the Lord Mayor of London about establishing some offices in the city of London. After he had Miss Winwood pull out the necessary paper work, he felt he would like some coffee.

"Snippy, coffee!"

A crash was heard from the direction of the butler's pantry and Miss Edna thought it best that she go and fetch Sir Clifford's coffee and check to see what happened to Snipwhistle when Lord Dogmoor had bellowed for him. Excusing herself from the office, she went in search of the butler and some coffee.

Poor Snipwhistle! He had thought himself accustomed to his master's abrupt and brutal summoning, but this one for some reason took him by surprise. He had been so startled by the sound of his master shouting his name that he dropped the silver tea service he had just retrieved in order to polish it for the upcoming dinner party. "Perhaps I am getting too old for this job," he thought as he hurried to pick up the tea service and attend to Sir Clifford.

Miss Edna found the baffled butler stooped to the floor, picking up silverware. "Snippy, let me help you with that," the sound of Miss Winwood's voice was unusually comforting that morning. She had come into the butler's pantry to find the butler surrounded by several pieces of silver strewn about the parquet floor. Thanking her for her assistance, Snippy gathered a coffee service together for Sir Clifford and made his way toward his office.

For her part, Edna decided to take a bit of a break. When she was finished cleaning up after Snippy's accident, she returned to the cook's pantry for another cup of tea and perhaps another of Maggie's delicious scones. The cook was out, it seems, doing errands for the dinner party that was to be held Saturday evening but Edna was surprised to find Lady Opal in the pantry, looking over a list of things that needed to be attended to in preparation for the dinner.

"Excuse me, Lady Opal, I did not realize you were in here," said Miss Winwood and started quietly to excuse herself.

"Quite alright, Winwood, stay. You are no bother to me at all." Lady Opal had the habit of addressing a female servant by her last name, something which her American husband never did. Miss Winwood had come to appreciate the American manner over the British. At least it was better than how Maggie was usually addressed by Lady Opal. Simply as "Cook", Lady Opal did not even bother with a name, just her job.

Edna busied herself making her own tea, explaining to Lady Opal that Sir Clifford had desired some time by himself to look over his upcoming presentation to the Lord Mayor of London the next day.

"Oh yes, that," sighed Lady Opal. "My husband wants to open offices in London for his Pittsburgh steel company. He is of the opinion that, with the trouble brewing in Germany and that silly chancellor of theirs, there might be some advantage to his company if he were to maintain offices here. He certainly has a good head for business matters, if not social ones," continued Lady Opal distractedly.

Yes, thought Miss Edna, he certainly does, lucky for you. Miss Winwood, though not personally acquainted with anyone in the peerage, still had heard enough about the Jennings-Blickstokes through the rumor mill to have an inkling as to what the prevailing gossip had been in regard to their daughter's marriage. Though she would never describe what she witnessed within Manor Minnington to anyone outside its walls, she had, nonetheless, a certain sense of the depth of relationship between Lord and Lady Dogmoor. While she would not say theirs was a completely loveless marriage, there did appear to be less about love and more about mammon about them.

In an effort to clear her mind of such inappropriate thoughts, Edna decided to dare to make conversation with Lady Opal. It was unusual that she found herself in her ladyship's company like this, so she thought she'd approach her with neutral subjects.

"How are plans for the dinner party coming along? Have you decided on what you are going to serve?"

"Well, Winwood, the plans are pretty much made by this point. The opening courses are naturally already decided. What I'm worrying about is what to serve as the entrée. It depends on what Cook can find fresh at market. It must be perfectly fresh for our guests, and she knows it," said Lady Opal in an imperious manner.

What Miss Edna was thinking was one thing but what she said was "Oh, I am sure Maggie will do wonders with whatever you decide. She really is a marvelous cook, for an Irish girl. Remember that risotto she whipped up for that last dinner party you had. It was so creamy, perfectly delicious."

"Yes, she does a good job, especially since, as you pointed out, she is Irish. I don't know how I let my husband talk me into hiring her but, and don't you dare ever tell him I admitted this, but I'm glad he did. Papist that she is, she can nevertheless prepare delicious meals."

Miss Edna disliked the way Lady Opal spoke about the Irish with such disdain. But the remark about Maggie being a "papist" gave her a topic with which to continue this dubious conversation and so she said, "Oh, and did you know that Maggie is getting some good news from Ireland?"

"No, what good news could possibly come from Ireland?" wondered Lady Opal, still perusing her list.

"Well, Maggie does not know yet what the good news is, but she told me that a telegram had been delivered yesterday from a Father Burns in County Cork who was planning to come by for a visit and deliver some very good news to her. She seemed to be quite excited about it."

Miss Edna stirred milk into her tea and looked up at Lady Opal, anticipating a neutral response to anything having to do with "Cook" or Ireland. What she saw surprised her. Standing as if she were frozen in time, Lady Opal said nothing at all. Finally, she responded. "Father Burns, did you say? From County Cork?"

"Why, yes ma'am. That is the priest's name, I'm quite certain." Miss Edna watched with an increasing sense of alarm at the sudden change in her ladyship. "Are you quite alright, Lady Opal?"

Lady Opal did not appear to be quite alright at all. In fact, she looked downright wan. Miss Winwood feared she was about to swoon and set her own tea down to help the mistress of the house into a chair.

"I'm fine, Winwood. I'm fine. Thank you. It must be the excitement of this party we're throwing. We haven't had such a large one in quite some time and I think planning it is getting the better of me. I am quite alright now, thank you. Might I have some tea?"

The last was more an order than a request, but the dutiful Edna Winwood poured her employer's wife a cup and handed it to her along with the milk which she ignored and sipped the hot tea, pausing with the teacup at her chin. For only a moment Miss Winwood was able to detect a far away look in Lady Opal's eye, a look that seemed to search for a memory. But it only lasted a moment and then Lady Opal was back to her old self.

"Thank you for the tea, Winwood. You'd better get back to my husband. I am sure you could be of more use to Lord Dogmoor in his office than you could be to me in the pantry." And with that, Edna Winwood was dismissed from her ladyship's presence.

"My heavens!" she thought as she left the pantry. "What do you suppose *that* was all about?" Her lips were pursed and her brow was knit as she wondered about the startling display she had just witnessed. The same inner sense that had given her such a foreboding feeling earlier was at play again in her mind. She was somewhat tempted to return to Lady Opal to see what she might learn. However, realizing that she had already been dismissed by her and that, in fact, would be more help in an office than in a pantry, she returned to Sir Clifford's office.

17.

When she was alone again in the pantry, Lady Opal got up from her chair and took the tea cup over to the sink and poured it out. She stood for a moment, looking out of the window into the herb garden that Cook so carefully tended. "Fresh herbs always make the difference, Missus," she was always saying to her mistress, stressing the "h" in "herbs" in that annoying Irish fashion. But yes, she was an excellent cook.

Pushing herself away from the sink and the view, Lady Opal gathered her lists that she had been going over before being interrupted by her husband's secretary. Under ordinary circumstances, she would have been furious at Winwood for daring to interrupt her while she was busy, breaking her concentration. But she found that she was not under ordinary circumstances at the moment.

She climbed the back staircase and went to her room. She laid her lists down on her desk and took a seat at the window overlooking the moors on the north side of the house. What beautiful, rolling hills they were. The grass was still very green and now the sun was shining brightly on this late autumn day. Soon it would be winter. Would it snow, she wondered to herself.

Lady Opal fingered the collar of her blouse distractedly, a habit she had when she was lost in thought and she was deep in thought now. Or rather, deep in memory, trying to avoid thought. It was as though she were lost inside herself somewhere. Again her eyes took on a far away look, only this time no one was around to observe it.

"Father Burns," she whispered the name and shivered. It was a name she had almost forgotten and had hoped she would not hear again. "Hell and blast," she thought, suddenly recalling an expression her father used to use. "He must be in his 80s by now. Don't those damn Roman priests ever die?"

Her mind wandered to her own past and the part Father Burns played in it. Calmly she sat at her window, no longer seeing the green of the moors, but the green hills and fields of Ireland. The Ireland of her youth. The one and only time she had ever been to that godforsaken country.

As her mind's eye conjured images of the places and people she had known while in Ireland, she suddenly thought of her cook, Maggie, an Irish girl whose last name she could never seem to remember. And then, for some inexplicable reason, she thought of her cook's good friend who always seemed to be about the place. What was her name? Dora something? Lady Opal could not be certain she had ever heard Dora's full name and, even if she had, it would not have mattered to her. Dora was a simple girl from town who somehow knew her cook. Why would a person of Lady Opal's standing be at all concerned with the likes of her?

And yet, there was something about that girl that had always struck Lady Opal as intriguing, even discomfiting. There was nothing Lady Opal had ever been able to articulate about her, since she had never even spoken to the girl personally. Lady Opal had never let herself dwell on it, this feeling of discomfort brought about by a commoner. It simply could not have been anything important enough to concern her.

As Lady Opal sat looking out her window fidgeting with her collar, her thoughts continued to dwell on Ireland and Dora and the strange impressions she had in her regard. Suddenly, as though a veil had been lifted, she realized why Dora had made such an impression on her and why, indeed, it did in fact concern her.

18.

Breathless with excitement and the extra exercise she endured by hurrying as she did along the streets of London, Petal Chalmers returned to the "Tea Cozy" just after the lunch crowd had begun to file in. Dublin Joe was flustered to the point of exasperation because he thought he was going to have to do double duty as both bartender and waiter. It was unlike Petal to be late and when she finally returned to work he was relieved as much at seeing her safe return as he was at not having to serve at table. He was so relieved, in fact, that he decided to have half a pint, just to steady his nerves.

"You and those damn ravens!" he hissed at her as she took an order from the bar. "What, were they doing tricks today?"

"Hush now and wait till you hear what I saw today. It wasn't the birds that were up to tricks, I'm here to tell you," she replied and went about serving up lunch to her guests.

The crowd was pretty much the same crowd that was always in for lunch day by day, with one or two exceptions. There were some who happened in only occasionally and a few of them were scattered here and there among the "dailies", as Petal liked to call her regulars. No one seemed to notice her breathless excitement as she served them or even that she was in all that much of a hurry. She smiled and greeted everyone as she always did and left them alone to their own conversations, as she usually did. What she wanted more than anything was to relay to Joe what she had seen at the Tower.

When all her customers were settled and served, Petal took herself back to the bar, having made sure that Dora was safely ensconced in the kitchen catching up on the dishes from the morning's preparations.

"Joe," she whispered. "Come here to me, I have something I have to tell you."

"What's up with you now?" Joe said as he ambled over to her. Petal was an excitable type at times, but he had never seen her as excited as this before.

"It's about poor Dora," she replied.

"What about her? Is she alright? She was back in the kitchen just a bit ago wondering where the devil *you* were!?" Joe chided.

"It's not *about* Dora," Petal whispered, a little less discretely. "It's about her gentleman friend, that young Erskine who's been coming in here and chatting her up."

"Well, if it's not about Dora why did you say it was, then?" retorted Joe, not unknowingly egging his beloved Petal on. He did enjoy it when she got excited at times.

"Shut up and listen," Petal's voice grew a bit more audible, but most of the diners were busy with their lunches. "I think there may be something *peculiar* about that young man and I do not want Dora to be hurt!"

The way Petal said "peculiar" pricked Joe's ears and got his attention. "What do you mean by that?" he asked her.

Feeling that she finally had his full attention, Petal continued. "Well, I was down at the Tower as usual, watching the ravens, as usual, the way they fly about the parapets and all…"

"Yeah, yeah," Joe interrupted her. "Get on with the point."

"When suddenly I notices Dora's young man Erskine on the other side of the street."

"So, I don't suppose you are the only idjit in London who likes to watch birds," Joe observed.

"Shut up and listen," Petal repeated. "Anyway, there was the young man that has been spending time here with Dora, making her all flushed and excited and all, and there he is at the Tower of London having a chat with some *other* person," Petal said with a knowing nod of her head.

"Another woman do you say?" asked Joe.

"Not at all. It was another *man*!" replied Petal.

"So he was talking to another man, was he? Well, lass, if that's against the law you'd better duck, because your dining room is filled with men talking to one another," said Joe, tartly.

"Shut up and listen," Petal's voice once again rose in pitch, try as she might to be whispering. "This was no ordinary man that you wouldn't notice if you passed him on the street. This was the most handsomest man I had ever laid my eyes on. He was tall, blond and fit as a fiddle, all decked out in fine clothes. I think he might have something to do with the government, because when it was all over, he left in the direction of Parliament."

"When *what* was all over?" Joe was getting exasperated. "You haven't said anything yet worth talking about, let alone worrying over as you are!"

"Will you please hush and listen?" Petal was becoming more exasperated by all of Joe's interruptions. "The two of them were talking, all chummy and friendly like, and when they were finished, the very handsome blond man gave a hug to Erskine that made me blush from across the street!"

"Ah, go on. What's that matter? Maybe they're related?" Joe said when he suddenly realized where Petal was going with her story. He was reluctant to be drawn into it.

"They did not look like brothers to me. And besides, that's not the end of it. Young Erskine leaves to go and out of nowhere shows up that young fop who's been in and out of here on occasion."

"Young fop? In here? Who are you talking about?" In spite of himself, Joe could not help but to be intrigued.

Petal continued. "That young dandy who always wears expensive clothes but doesn't seem to have a job. You know him, he's been in here already, usually always alone, but sometimes with another bloke."

Joe scratched his chins and thought he knew who Petal meant. He was a young, flamboyant fellow who made most of the other customers uncomfortable when he was in the dining room. He never ate much food but was no stranger to drink and at least, Joe had always thought, he had always been generous with his gratuities.

"You know what they say about what he does for a living, don't you?" Petal asked pointedly.

Now, Joe, in fact, did know what *they* said he did for a living. Some of the evening regulars at the bar had commented on the young man when he had been in the pub. Joe did not let on, however, that he had heard that gossip, because he just couldn't wait to hear Petal try to tell him. He did not think she had it in her to talk about such unsavory things.

Petal, in her own right, had held some pretty interesting conversations with some of the "working" women of London. Always there with a prayer and some sound advice that they should give it up and take up a good, steady profession such as waiting tables, Petal had tried on more than one occasion to persuade the wayward girls of London's streets into a better life for themselves. She did not have much success, but had developed a rather tenuous rapport with them, because she also felt sorry for them and gave them extras if they came into the pub, which occasionally they did. So Petal was more versed than Joe knew in the seamier side of life.

"He does for men what some women do for men, and they both do it for the money."

Well, he couldn't believe she came right out and said it so bluntly! Joe had underestimated his Petal and suddenly found himself blushing despite himself. He decided he had heard enough about her trip to the Tower. "Hush now, and leave it be. It's none of your business and you don't know for certain sure what was happening there across that street! I tell you true, lass, if I don't keep you away from that damned Tower I'll be hanged for trying! Now tend your tables. Some of the dailies look like they are about ready." Joe returned to wiping down the bar and, to calm himself, put just a bit of a topper on his half pint.

Petal returned to her customers, her regular dailies who helped keep them in business. None of them had been even remotely aware of the conversation she had just had with Dublin Joe. She busied herself clearing plates and rang for Dora to come help. It was going to be a profitable lunch hour, or so it seemed from the interest expressed in what was being served for dessert that day.

There was one occasional customer who sat alone in a booth near to the bar. She was an older lady who came in frequently but not often enough to be considered a "daily". She also was picky and rude, as older women can tend to be. She sat so quietly enjoying her tea and a bowl of soup that Petal and Joe had forgotten she was there during their conversation. Even if they had noticed, Petal was sure that her whispering would not have been able to be heard by an old lady such as her.

But Petal had not been whispering, really, and Elinor Drumville, old though she may be, was not hard of hearing at all. In fact, she had managed to overhear every single detail of the story the hostess had just told to the barkeep. More than that, her mind was as sharp as her hearing and she knew of only one truly "handsomest" blond man in London who might work at Parliament. Jasper Dunwoody was one such fellow and Jasper Dunwoody was Sir Oswald Bunbarrel's personal secretary. What truly captivated Miss Drumville, however, was that Jasper Dunwoody had been observed consorting with a known person of ill repute, a male prostitute no less!

Elinor could hardly contain her glee as she finished her tea. Why, today she even felt like leaving a tip. If only she could afford to do so. She was sure her hostess would understand.

The elderly lady in the booth arose from her place rather hurriedly and made her way out of the public house. Petal noticed her departure but knew not to rush to the table for any extra money on it. "The old cow hasn't left a tip since Noah let her off the ark," she mused, and turned her attention back to her rosary beads which she had piously decided to offer up for poor, poor Dora.

19.

"'Allo, what's that?"

The bell above the door at the "Boar's Head" jingled, indicating that someone had just come into the pub. Snuffy Dolton was surprised by that, since hardly anyone ever came into his public house at this time in the afternoon. A very few came in for a quick snort during the midday break, but the "Boar's Head" did not see any regular activity until the evening hours. Snuffy continued to wipe down his glassware and looked up to see who had entered.

A tall, good looking young man came into the pub. This gentleman had the general appearance of the other young men who had become his evening regulars but there was something different in his manner and bearing. For all his youth and good looks, he appeared quite out of place at the "Boar's Head". He walked right past Snuffy as he looked around, obviously checking to see if someone else were in the public house. Snuffy suddenly felt as though he were invisible.

"Arrogant prig", he thought as he continued to watch the handsome young stranger make his way into the back portion of the pub where the tables were. Snuffy had never seen this one before. He was handsome and young and had a bearing that spoke instantly and loudly of "Money". That would have to be the one major difference Snuffy noticed about him, other than an apparent lack of manners, that set him apart from the other handsome young men who had started frequenting his pub. They all dressed well and groomed themselves to look like the well-heeled class. This young gentleman had it in his blood and it showed in the way he carried himself. He was obviously, no matter what he might have been wearing, of the upper class.

The tall, dark stranger re-emerged from the back portion of the pub, not finding what or whom he had been seeking and took a place at a booth near the door, absently ordering a glass of port as he did so, without so much as a glance in the barkeep's direction.

"This one thinks no small bear of himself, that is for certain sure", thought Snuffy as he poured out the wine. He could not remember when he had ever seen a more uppity human being in his establishment, if ever! Trying to stay inconspicuous, Snuffy served the port without a word to the customer at his booth and resumed his spot behind the bar, wiping down his glassware. Something told old Snuffy that something interesting was about to happen in the "Boar's Head". Both a bit anxious and a little excited for the break in the day's tedium, he waited and watched the handsome young stranger.

Roland Minnington took out his pocket watch and checked the time against the pub's wall clock. "The little trollop should have been here by now!" he thought angrily. His eyes narrowed a bit as he thought of the ways he would make his tardy appointment pay for keeping him waiting. He checked himself, however, knowing that he had to handle this situation delicately. Once he had the necessary agreements and arrangements made, then he would wreak his revenge for this breach in protocol. "Yes, I need to handle this with kid gloves," thought Roland, and he smiled to himself. "Kid gloves, just like the ones the silly little dandy wears."

After the elapse of ten or fifteen minutes, Snuffy went over to the booth to check on the glass of port and to inquire if "the gentleman would like anything else?" The young man ordered another glass of port and resumed his wait. He seemed to be perfectly calm, but Snuffy sensed a growing tension in the air. "If this one is waiting for an appointment to show up," he thought to himself, "I'll wager he's not used to being kept dangling. Pity the poor bit when he or she arrives."

At precisely that moment, as Snuffy was refilling the wine glass, the bell above the door of the "Boar's Head" jingled and in walked an all too familiar figure. The slight young man in the stylish overcoat was just removing his hat and gloves as Snuffy looked up to see who had entered. Stifling a groan of unpleasant recognition, Snuffy waited at the booth to see if this were the young gentleman's appointment and, if so, would the new arrival care for anything to drink. Long having grown accustomed to being ignored by this particular barfly, Snuffy was actually surprised to be spoken to directly by him.

"G' afternoon, Snuff" said the young man and smiled a mouthful of uneven and yellow teeth at him. "I'll have what the gent is havin'."

Snuffy was momentarily stunned, as much as for having been actually spoken to as by the poor quality of the young man's dental hygiene. He snapped himself out of it and quickly poured another glass of port and served it. He then returned to his bar, wiping down the glasses, this time at the end nearer the door, and the booth.

Roland waited until the bartender had served the port and left the two of them alone in the booth before he spoke. He sat staring evenly and coolly at young Trevor, choosing his words carefully so as not to reveal his anger and disdain.

"Well, Trevor, I'm glad you are finally here," he could not help himself with that one, "have a bit of a nip of your port to take the chill off and let's get down to business. Have you thought about my proposition?"

"Yes, Guvner, I 'ave and it's very interestin'," replied Trevor, his cockney accent grating on Roland's more refined ear. "Very interestin', indeed. But there are some things I 'ave to work out 'ere in London first."

"What things, Trevor?" inquired Roland. He was eager to wrap up this little business arrangement that he had in mind with the young fop. "Have you considered the amount of money you'll make if you come back to Dublin with me?"

"Sure I 'ave, Guvner, and I'm all in. It's been a long time for me in this town and a change of scenery would do me the world of good. But....," and here Trevor hesitated just a bit, "are you certain about the amount of money to be made off of Irish men? I mean, in my line of work?"

"As sure of it as I am of my own name," Roland assured him. "After all, it was an Irish bloke who showed me the happier side of life, and I have never been without companionship when I wanted it." Roland smiled as he recalled his chance encounter along O'Connell Street, two years before, when he happened to be asked for a cigarette by a young gentleman named Hobart Stockpeeper. Roland had been newly enrolled in Trinity College and was new to Dublin and had been terribly lonely. As he lit the cigarette for Hobart, their eyes met. One thing had led to another and before that night was over Roland had discovered a whole new side of himself that, as it turned out, he enjoyed immensely. It was not only because the sex was exciting. It felt good to him, as though he had finally uncovered some deep truth about himself. It felt real. It was not long before he realized yet another benefit from this moment of self-discovery. He knew that his father would take a stroke if he ever found out about it. Roland's ultimate revenge on his father for being sent to Ireland was to have discovered his homosexuality there. But other things were on his mind with Trevor.

"People from all over Europe and the even the States come to Dublin to study and enjoy a holiday," he said.

"They do that in London, too, Guvner," replied Trevor.

"Yes, but Dublin is a lot smaller than London, more contained. It's like catching fish in a barrel there. All you have to do is pick a spot in Temple Bar in which to loiter about and wait. They practically come to you!" Roland was watching his companion to see how he was taking it in.

"And you'd be sending them my way, all ready for the evenin's entertainment and me not hafin' to worry about what they'd be expectin'?" queried Trevor.

"Yes, yes, I have explained all that to you before. We'd find you a suitable spot and I would send 'interested parties' to you from Trinity. It's a perfect set up since Temple Bar and Trinity are so very close. And you would not believe how many 'interested parties' there are in and about Trinity College! Single men, married men, young men and old. Students and businessmen and even clergy!"

"Clergy?" Trevor repeated that last one in surprise. "You mean to say you actually get a vicar to pay for it?"

"So far, I have not had anyone 'pay for it', this is just a plan. But yes, there are plenty of priests who will, I'm sure. All Anglicans, of course. The Romans have no money for it and besides, they have too much of a sense of guilt. Although watching them wrestle with it afterwards can be entertaining." Roland smiled a cruel smile.

"And the pay again, Guvner, how would that work?" Trevor continued his questions, but was obviously already sold on the prospect.

"The pay is handled cleanly on my end. I set up the arrangements from the college and send the customer to you. All you have to do is use your special talents on them to make them happy and satisfied. No money would change hands between you and the "client" so the police could never be able to get you for prostitution again as they have here so often. All they could pinch you for is a morals charge. And, fortunately, I have somebody in Dublin who can help us out there, should that unfortunate circumstance ever occur."

"And I get my take of the money at the end of the night?" Trevor was really getting down to brass tacks now.

"Yes. I would arrange to meet you someplace where we could inconspicuously split the take. Half and half, seems fair enough, don't you think?" proposed Roland.

Actually, for doing all the real work, Trevor thought a split down the middle was not particularly fair. Still, this arrangement appealed to him because it kept his hands clean of money and possible prostitution charges. They had been real buggers about that, the London police. And, of course, there was the fact that Trevor did enjoy his work.

"Sounds like a deal to me, Guvner", responded Trevor. "But for one thing that's keepin' me 'ere in London."

"What's that?" asked Roland, relieved and agitated at the same time. He needed Trevor to commit to this. It was a grand scheme. Roland had worked out every detail in his head as to how to run a male prostitution ring out of Trinity College. What he needed was an experienced male prostitute like Trevor to be the working end, so to speak, of his business plan.

"Well, Guvner, there is a bloke 'ere in London what I'm beholdin' to at the moment," Trevor began to explain. "He 'elped me out of a tight spot a while back and pays me a bit now and then for information. I 'ave only to clear up one matter for this gent and then I would be free and clear for to go to Dublin."

"Who is it and what is it that you are trying to do for this 'gent'?" demanded Roland.

Without giving a moment's thought to the fact that he was betraying a confidence, Trevor explained. "None other than your old friend, Jasper Dunwoody, Guv," he said insouciantly. "Right now 'e is in deep for a bloke named Randiffle. Seems old Jasper has finally fallen 'ard for somebody. But Randiffle, 'e's on the fence. Seems to not be able to decide between Jasper and some girl named Dora Finch, like 'e's wantin' to have a go at both sides of the party, if you take my meanin'. I been following 'im around town keeping tabs on 'im for Jasper. Young Randiffle spends a lot of time at the pub she works at and Jasper is keen on knowin' 'is wheres and whens."

Jasper Dunwoody was a name certainly known to Roland, not only because of his association with Sir Oswald but because he was widely regarded as the most handsome man in all of London. Every homosexual male in the city knew of, and dreamed of, Jasper Dunwoody. This may be an opportunity for Roland to get a little revenge on the only man to have rebuffed him.

For some reason, the name "Dora Finch" had rung a bell in Roland's mind as well. But he was not at all sure why the name of a common public house wench would be familiar to him.

Roland narrowed his eyes at the cocky Cockney and said, "Are you telling me that if Jasper Dunwoody 'gets his man' as the Canadians say, you will feel free to leave London?"

"Yes, Guvner, that's what I'm tellin' you," Trevor affirmed.

"And the only thing standing in the way of connubial bliss for Jasper and this Randiffle is some bit of stuff who works in a pub?"

"Right agin, Guvner. Jasper's plannin' on takin' Randiffle in this weekend and makin' a man out of him, if you catch my meanin'. Got plans to get old Erskine well acquainted with some of the facts o' life."

Roland, despite his natural disdain for common people, could not help but to find this fascinating. "Fine," he said. "I am sure I will be able to help take care of things and hurry this happy little couple along. Just tell me the name of the girl again and the public house she works at."

The two men finished their conversation and their port and stood up to leave. They paid not the slightest bit of attention to the barkeep, standing behind his bar nearby. Good thing, too, for they might have noticed that he was not wiping the pint glass he held in his betoweled hand and wondered why his mouth was agape, giving him the overall appearance of complete and utter shock.

Once outside, the two men parted without a word. As Roland made his way down the street, Trevor watched his back receding as he went. "He's a cagey one, that one," he thought to himself. "He didn't flinch when I told 'im the name o' the girl. I wonder if the arrogant bastard even knows." Trevor had made it his business to know as much about Dora as he could and that included knowledge of the waitress's association with the cook at Dogmoor. "I wonder if he has the stomach for it. He talks big, but can he do it?" Trevor mused. "I got to get meself out of London. If the coppers nick me one more time they may never let me loose. If old Roland can't get it done, I'm sure I can find a way to get Miss Finch out of the way. I know lot's of blokes who owe me a favor or two." Trevor's eyes narrowed as he contemplated the many men who would do just about anything for him to keep their names out of police reports and newspapers. He turned and walked in a direction opposite of the one taken by Roland Minnington.

20.

By Wednesday afternoon, Petal had calmed herself down a bit, but was still quite worried about Dora. Her day had been spent desperately seeking an answer that would benignly explain the events she had witnessed at the Tower. Finally, she decided that she had to find a tactful as possible way to tell Dora that her young man, Erskine, was not honourable and that she should set her sights on somebody with, at the very least, fewer shady associates. Dublin Joe had sternly, and wisely she had to admit, advised her to keep out of it, but she simply could not resist the temptation to clue Dora in on what she had seen.

It was quiet in the "Tea Cozy", as it always was at that time of day and Petal had little to distract her from her musings. Young Erskine was so handsome and full of life and promise. It was a complete and terrible shame that he might also be, how should one say, a "fancy boy", as Petal knew them. But why would he have been spending so much time with Dora here at the "Tea Cozy"? Perhaps, thought Petal, he had not gone over to that other side or maybe he only needed the love of a good woman to save him and make him normal.

All these thoughts and concerns were racing through Petal's mind when she heard the door of the pub open and a customer came in. It was a lady. A real lady, from the looks of her, thought Petal. The woman in the fine clothes and neatly styled hair looked nervously around the public house dining room and took a seat in a remote corner away from the windows, almost looking as if she wanted to be hidden. Petal went over to take her order and, having done so, promptly went off to make the lady some tea.

Lady Opal Minnington did, indeed, wish not to be seen as she sat in the booth in the least conspicuous part of the pub she could find. "I wonder, is she here?" she thought to herself. "This is so terribly foolish of me! Why am I here?"

Lady Opal asked herself that question already knowing, deep in her heart, the answer to it. She simply had to see Dora. She had to look at her, discretely and from a bit of a distance, she hoped, but see her she must. It was suddenly an obsession for Opal Minnington to see, and really look at, Miss Dora Finch, her cook's best friend and frequent visitor to her home.

The door to the kitchen opened and out came the hostess with the tea she had ordered and a basket of scones. Opal sat perfectly erect in her place, her posture not betraying the sinking feeling she had inside. She had almost hoped that it would be Dora who served her. But how, in heaven's name, would she explain her presence at this public house to Dora? She had acted on impulse and the reality of the consequences were beginning to come to fore. "Thank goodness there's no one here at this time of the afternoon," she thought as she stirred milk into her tea.

Just then, the door to the "Tea Cozy" opened and in walked another customer. Petal rolled her eyes. "What's *she* doing back? She barely comes in twice a week, let alone twice in one day!" she thought with some dismay. She watched as the elderly lady made a bee line for the lady in the booth.

"Lady Opal! What a pleasant surprise to see you here!" Elinor Drumville sang out.

Lady Opal reopened her eyes, which she had squeezed closed as soon as she had seen Elinor enter the public house. She just could not believe her bad luck! "What this old busybody is doing here at this precise moment is just God's punishment, I'm sure of it!" cried Lady Opal to herself. Out loud she said, "Elinor, how nice to see you, too" and tried her best to look like she was smiling. "Whatever are you doing here?"

"Oh I just happened to see you come in here from across the street. My nephew has a mare that is ready to foal and I had stopped into St. Elwydd's to say a prayer and light a candle. I think I dozed off a bit. That old church is so quiet, don't you know. As I was coming out past the gateposts, there you were! Coming right into one of my favorite public houses. They have the best scones in the city."

Petal Chalmers bit the inside of her cheek to keep herself from making an indiscreet remark. She hurried over with another cup and another basket of scones because, whether she really thought they were the best in the city or not, the old lady certainly ate them as if they were. This also occasioned Petal to learn the lady's name. Lady Opal.

"That just *has* to be Lady Opal Minnington from Dogmoor," thought Petal. She had heard Dora speak of her often enough, and the Dogmoor estates in Surrey were part of local history, but Petal had never seen any of the Minningtons, to her knowledge, before. She realized that this was the first time she was ever glad to have seen the old lady come into the pub. Petal hesitated to consider whether or not to inform Dora that her friend's mistress was in the dining room.

"All ready for Saturday night, Lady Opal?" asked Elinor, as innocently as she could. She herself was ready for Saturday night because she had plans to expose Sir Oswald in front of as much of London's society as she could. She had asked the question with no real interest in Lady Opal's answer because she knew that, of course, things were being made ready. They always were perfectly executed affairs. Elinor's most immediate interest was why she was in the "Tea Cozy".

"Cook has everything in order, Elinor," Lady Opal responded. "And Snippy has seen to the china and silver. Everything will be perfect. All that's needed is to choose the main dish."

Elinor knew well enough that the choice of the main dish was always the last detail to be attended to before Maggie actually prepared the meal. Lady Opal had a reputation for insisting on the freshest of fresh ingredients at her dinners.

"So glad to hear it, Lady Opal. You always host such splendid dinner parties and the food is always exquisite!" Elinor twittered. "But tell me, dear lady, what are you doing in London at this time of day?" And why are you in the "Tea Cozy"? Elinor kept that last question to herself.

"Oh, I was just getting bored sitting around the manor house today, for some reason. Sir Clifford is busy preparing a presentation he plans to make on something or another and the children are both out of the house. I thought I might do a bit of shopping." Lady Opal surprised herself at how facilely she had lied.

"Yes, the winter fashions are lovely this year, are they not?. I might do a little shopping myself today," Elinor lied just as facilely. "Perhaps we can shop together for a spell?"

Sensing that she was about to be touched for a loan, Lady Opal was about to make some excuse, any excuse, when suddenly the door to the pub's kitchen opened and Dora Finch emerged with a stack of clean teacups and saucers for Petal to use at dinner time. She was concentrating on her work and did not even notice the two women sitting in the dining room. She would have simply returned directly to the kitchen and her chores if Petal had not cleared her throat and chucked her head in their general direction. Dora stopped herself and stared, in momentary disbelief, at Lady Opal Minnington.

For her part, Lady Opal Minnington stared as well, but hers was not an expression of disbelief. Hers was a curious mixture of surprise, curiosity, and just a little bit of horror. It was an expression that was not lost on Elinor Drumville.

Wiping her hands on her apron to make sure they were dry, although she didn't know why because Lady Opal never extended her hand, Dora Finch made her way to their booth to say a polite hello to her best friend's mistress and her elderly companion.

"Good afternoon, Lady Opal. What a pleasant and unexpected surprise to see you here at the 'Tea Cozy'", Dora said. She smiled at Lady Opal, who still sat with a somewhat dumbfounded expression on her face and did not immediately return the greeting. Dora was beginning to wonder if perhaps she had something smudged on her face or if her hair were in disarray. Elinor rescued what was fast becoming an embarrassing situation.

"Lady Opal and I thought we might do a bit of shopping in the city today, dear and decided to come in for a spot of tea. It's a lovely sunny afternoon, but it still is November," she said sweetly to Dora, but her eyes were on Lady Opal, watching her expression. "It's a bit cool for us to be out and about too long without a nice hot cup of some of the best tea in the city. Isn't that right, Lady Opal?"

Hearing Elinor speak her name, in yet another lie, brought Lady Opal back to her senses. "Yes, my dear. We were going shopping and decided to have some tea. And, um, how are you, my dear?"

"I am fine, thank you for asking," replied Dora, who could not remember ever having been offered such a social nicety from Lady Opal before. Usually, all she got at the manor house when she was visiting Maggie was a brief "how do you do" as Lady Opal concerned herself with her cook.

Elinor was most intrigued at this turn of events and sensed there was much more to come. She did her best to keep the conversation afloat.

"You are a frequent visitor to Dogmoor, aren't you, my dear?" she asked Dora as innocently as she could, keeping one eye closely focused on Lady Opal.

"Why, yes, ma'am. How did you know?" replied Dora.

"Oh, my dear, I have heard Maggie speak of her friendship with you many times," Elinor continued her lies. In truth, it was while she was snooping around the manor house during one of Lady Opal's dinner parties that she had seen Dora and Maggie together in the kitchen. She had only guessed at the frequency of her visits to the manor house. Her reason to keep the young girl engaged in conversation was that her suspicious nature had been aroused due to Lady Opal's presence at the "Tea Cozy" and because of her bizarre expression of a moment ago.

"Yes, ma'am, Maggie and I have been friends since our childhood days back in Ireland," said Dora. "In fact," and here Dora politely turned to Lady Opal to make sure she felt included in the conversation, "a mutual friend, acquaintance really, is coming from Ireland for a visit. Maggie just got the news yesterday in a telegram from Father Burns in County Cork. It seems he has some bit of good news for Maggie."

At the mention of Father Burns' name Lady Opal blanched once again, a fact that was not lost on Elinor, who ventured further, "And who is Father Burns, my child?"

"He was the dear, sweet parish priest who tended to the orphanage Maggie and I grew up in. Although the years in the orphanage were not the most pleasant, Father Burns is a happy memory nonetheless."

"The two of you, you and Maggie that is, were orphans together in Ireland?" A very fuzzy picture was beginning to take shape in Elinor's mind. She glanced once again at Lady Opal, who had regained enough composure to sip her tea, but still said nothing.

"Yes, St. Saviour's in Fermoy, County Cork. The Sisters of Mercy took care of us. My earliest memories are from there and I happily remember the day Maggie arrived. The sisters bunked us together and we became fast friends. It had been so lonely there before she arrived. Oh, but do excuse me! I should not be rambling on about myself while the two of you are trying to visit. Please forgive me, Lady Opal," Dora had suddenly become aware of herself and the obvious discomfort she was inflicting on the silent gentlewoman. "And yourself, missus, I am afraid I do not know your name."

"Miss Drumville. Elinor Drumville. And you have been perfectly delightful, has she not, Lady Opal?" Elinor eyed her frequent hostess carefully and waited to see what she would say.

"Perfectly charming, my dear, perfectly charming." The tea had calmed Lady Opal's nerves somewhat and enabled her to regain herself. "But I really must be getting along. It's getting late and Sir Clifford will want to have his tea. We must do our shopping together at another time, Elinor."

"Of course, Lady Opal," cooed Elinor. "Anytime that is convenient for you will be a pleasure for me, I'm sure. I'll just sit here and finish my tea."

With that, Lady Opal gathered her purse and coat in preparation to excuse herself from the "Tea Cozy". Her hand was trembling as she reached for the money to pay for the tea.

"Lady Opal," said Elinor cheerfully, "I have enjoyed so many lovely dinners at your home, allow me to take care of the tea for you."

Lady Opal smiled weakly and turned to leave the public house, just as a crash of dishes was heard coming from behind the hostess stand where Petal Chalmers had just dropped a stack of saucers.

21.

Even as they were speaking his name at the "Tea Cozy", Father Burns had arrived at Manor Minnington. Being a free Irish man and a Roman Catholic, he prided himself on his effrontery and had knocked at the front door. The butler, a timid looking older man, had met him and escorted him through the house to the cook's pantry, where he found Maggie O'Shea tending to her daily chores.

"Father Burns!" Maggie shouted as she threw her arms around the beloved old man. "Sure'n it's good to see you here! How was your trip over?"

"Fine and dandy, to be sure, Maggie darlin'" said the priest in reply. "The water was calm and the train was restful. And it was on time! I wish the trains in Ireland could say the same."

"Father Burns, you always prided yourself on being prompt!" Maggie found herself fairly beaming in the old priest's presence and almost forgot her manners. She sat the venerable father down at her table in the pantry and fixed him a hot cup of tea and offered him some scones. "Sure'n you must have a bit of the hunger on you, after your journey," she said. "But tell me true, sir. What is it that brings you to England? What is this 'good news' I heard tell of in your telegram?"

"Well, Maggie my dear, your fortunes have changed for the better," replied Father Burns. He sipped his tea and made a slight grimace. Suddenly, Maggie had another memory of Father Burns.

"Could I offer you something to sweeten your tea, Father?" she asked and bent down to a low cupboard and fetched out a bottle of Jameson's.

"May the angels watch over you forevermore, dear girl," said Father Burns as he dumped his tea down the drain and held out his cup to be filled with a more bracing beverage.

"And now, Father, please. Tell me! How have my fortunes changed for the better?" begged Maggie.

"Well, my dear," Father Burns said as he sipped from his teacup, "it seems as though you had a distant relative in County Galway who recently passed on. He was your mother's father's brother's second cousin, by marriage." Maggie had a bit of difficulty following the lineage.

"So he would have been.....?" she began.

Father Burns continued to sip his "tea". "Ack, now. Let's just say he was a distant uncle. At any rate, my child he has gone to his reward. As he lay dying he told his parish priest that he had something on his soul that he had to make right. Thinking the man wanted to make a last Confession, the priest, a one Father O'Reilley, put on his stole and prepared for the Sacrament. The man, Michael O'Toole, your distant uncle, told Father O'Reilley that he would need more than absolution to mend his soul in this case." Father Burns took another sip from his cup.

Maggie sat and waited for more. She could scarcely believe what she had heard already. She did not know at all that she had any living relatives in Ireland. She looked intently at the elder clergyman.

"Well, now. Where was I? Oh yes. County Galway. Anyway, it seems old O'Toole had had a niece or some kinswoman who had died some 20 odd years before, leaving behind a daughter, her only child. O'Toole knew the child's father had disappeared years before, even before the child had been born. It had been an embarrassment in the family to have a mother with a child and no husband."

"My mother?" Maggie's voice quivered just a bit.

"Yes, my lamb, your dear mother." Father sipped again. "In his last moments on earth, Michael O'Toole wanted to make amends for allowing his own flesh and blood to be abandoned to the care of the Sisters of Mercy instead of doing the right thing by the child at the time, so he told Father O'Reilley the circumstances and last known whereabouts of his distant relative and Father O'Reilley traced it to me and St. Saviour's orphanage."

Maggie was wide eyed as she refilled the priest's cup. What in the name of the Mother of God did all this mean?

As if he read her thoughts, Father Burns continued. "What this means, young lady, is that your distant uncle has left you a sum of money in the exact amount of 750 Irish pounds!"

"Seven hundred and fifty Irish pounds?" Maggie repeated slowly. The amount, while not a fortune, was more than she would ever have imagined having at one time at any point in her life.

Father Burns gingerly set down his teacup and reached into the breast pocket of his black broadcloth coat. Withdrawing his wallet, he extracted from it a cheque issued from the Royal Bank of Ireland in the amount of 750 pounds. He handed it to Maggie and smiled broadly as he resumed his afternoon "tea".

Maggie held the cheque in hands that trembled ever so slightly and stared at it in disbelief. Things like this simply never happened to her and she never looked for them to. She was much too practical a girl for silly daydreams. But this! This was reality! She could not even think at that precise moment. The most she could do was stare at the cheque in her hands.

"You are now a well propertied woman, Maggie O'Shea. That money will make a fine dowry for your marriage to good Catholic boy someday soon, God willing," said Father Burns, who smiled again, this time as much from the Jameson's as from the occasion.

"Dowry, indeed!" Maggie suddenly found herself able to think. She certainly did not think she'd be using this windfall to land herself a man. Whatever for? Had not Father Burns just sat here and told her that her own father had abandoned her before she was born? No, whatever she might do with the money, it would definitely not be used for a dowry. She caught herself and returned her attention to her reverend friend.

"Father, will you stay and have a bite to eat before you go on your way?" she inquired of the priest.

"Thank you, no, girl," he replied, "but haven't I already made arrangements with my classmate, Father Gilfoyle of St. Ignatius in London, to have dinner with him before I return to Ireland tomorrow. It was pleasure enough for my old heart to see you again and bring you this good news."

With that, Father Burns picked up his hat and was almost out the door. Suddenly he stopped and turned around. "But sure now, where's my mind? Do you ever hear anymore from your friend, Dora Finch? I hear tell that she came to England, too, after her sad experience with her adoptive parents. Do you know anything about her whereabouts?"

"Why sure'n I do, Father," Maggie was happy to report. "She's right here in London and works as a waitress in a public house. We see each other all the time! In fact, she was here with me yesterday in this very pantry when your telegram arrived." Maggie smiled her broadest smile at the priest who had remembered her happiest memory, Dora Finch's friendship.

But Father Burns looked a bit strange. For a moment Maggie thought that perhaps the drink had gotten to him. His face had the faintest hint of a frown and he stared ahead with unseeing eyes that had become somewhat glazed. In a way, he looked as if he were lost in memories that were not all that pleasant. He blinked his eyes as if to clear his head of cobwebs and looked at Maggie. "Dora Finch is in London? And has been in *this* house?" he asked in a tone that almost suggested that he did not want to hear the answer.

"Why, yes, Father. Of course she has been here," replied Maggie, wondering about the sudden change in Father Burns' demeanor. "Sure'n and why wouldn't Dora come and visit me here, or anywhere else for that matter?"

"No reason at all, my child," Father Burns replied, as if to no one, and turned his hat in his hands, looking at it as if it weren't his own. "No reason at all!" Having suddenly regained himself, he looked back up at Maggie and smiled. "And now, my dear, I must be off to St. Ignatius." He turned once again for the door, this time the back door out of the kitchen that led to the herb garden. "I'll find me way around to the front of the house. No need to bother the old gentleman who let me in."

As he reached for the door handle he hesitated briefly and Maggie was worried that another spell was coming on him. Instead, he turned his head in her direction and said, "And, oh, by the way," almost as an afterthought. "My friend, Father O'Malley in the next village just informed me last week that he was planning to send me a shipment of fresh salmon that some of the boys of his parish had planned to catch and give as a donation to the church. I believe they were going out this very day, in fact, or perhaps it's tomorrow. I will telegraph him from London and ask him to send a healthy portion of it here to you, as a gift and sign of God's good will. Good-bye to you now, Maggie O'Shea!"

With that, as quickly as he had arrived, he was gone. Maggie looked once again at the 750 pounds she held in her hands and then out the door Father Burns had just exited. She wondered about the strangeness of the last few minutes of his stay and his apparent surprise that Dora Finch had visited her at the manor house.

"Well, if the salmon get here quick enough and fresh enough, I'll know what to serve on Saturday night." Maggie had returned to her more practical view of life.

22.

Maggie was not the only one in Manor Minnington who wondered about the behavior of the old priest. Claudia Minnington wondered about it, as well, because Claudia had made it her business to listen in on the conversation the cook was having with the papist priest. "Those damn Irish," she had thought. "Probably planning to steal the silver and melt it down for those silly beads they keep fingering." Claudia did not have much respect for the religious sensitivities of others, including her own family. Not that there was a terrible amount of religious sentiment in her family, save for her brother Roland, the would-be Anglican priest. She despised him most of all.

Still, when she had seen from her upstairs window the old priest arrive, bold as you please, at the front door of her home, she could not help but to sneak down to listen in on their conversation. She was able to do this easily enough. She had taken off her shoes and slipped into the butler's pantry in her stocking feet, fully aware that she'd be alone in there since the butler, after having shown the priest in, returned to her father's room to finish his valet.

She had become quite intrigued when she heard of Cook's little inheritance. "Somehow I'm going to have to talk her out of a piece of that," she had thought. "It would come in handy on one of my trips to the library." She almost giggled as she thought that! She knew, of course, that getting Maggie's money away from her would be like trying to peel the white off of rice, but she would figure out some way of doing it. Her allowance did not provide much in the way of extravagant spending and some of her newly acquired habits were beginning to get costly. She eyed the silver candlesticks sitting on the counter.

She had almost given up on hearing anything more worthwhile when the Finch girl's name came up and Cook told the priest that she had, indeed, been there to visit with her. The priest's reaction to that news had been as strange as her mother's had been to news of his own planned arrival at the manor house. (Claudia had been eavesdropping on that conversation, also. She had turned into quite the clandestine little sneak, she proudly thought.) First her mother's reaction at the thought of the priest and now the priest's at the thought of a waitress in her house. Claudia felt there must be a connection in there somewhere but, although she was a good sneak, she was not yet much of a sleuth. Besides, she was beginning to feel a nagging tension in her that signaled the need to take a trip into the city. Vowing to herself to get to the bottom of it later, she slipped the two silver candlesticks into a bag and went back to her room to make plans to go into London.

23.

Edna Winwood sat perched in her chair in Sir Clifford's study, perusing reports he intended to use in his presentation to the Mayor the next morning in London. Her desk was small and functional, a mere twig of oak compared to the massive desk used by Sir Clifford himself. Oddly enough, Edna knew more about what was in his desk than he did, for the most part, because she was the one who had to constantly locate files and various papers that he could never seem to keep handy for himself. Still, he looked very impressive as he sat behind it, smoking his Cuban cigars and applying himself to what he knew best—business.

"Miss Winwood," he addressed her always in this manner, not like his wife who only used her last name—Miss Winwood appreciated that American nicety—"go and fetch us something to drink, but not tea. I've had it with tea. Get Maggie to make us some coffee. And bring in some of her scones, too. I know Mrs. Minnington will be expecting to sit down to tea soon, but I want something now. Now, scoot."

Miss Edna arose from her chair and set about fulfilling her employer's request. At one time in her life, she mused to herself, she would have been completely miffed to have been spoken to in such a peremptory fashion. "Now scoot!" indeed! At another time she may have let loose with one of her characteristically salty remarks and gotten herself in trouble with the employer who spoke to her thus. But over time she had grown so accustomed to Sir Clifford's manner of speech that it did not even faze her in the slightest when he did so.

It did not even bother her to be asked to do the butler's job. She was aware that Snipwhistle was upstairs tending to Sir Clifford's wardrobe for tomorrow's meeting in London. Lord knows, she did not want to have him interrupted from that chore and risk his being dressed down by Sir Clifford in one of his rants. She wondered how much more of that sort of thing Snippy could withstand. So without the glimmer of a grudge, Miss Edna Winwood made her way to the kitchen to ask Maggie for some fresh coffee.

As she walked through the house towards the kitchen, Edna thought of what a good idea Sir Clifford was onto with his upcoming proposal to the Lord Mayor. Opening up a branch office of his steel empire in London seemed to her to be a very good proposition. The way things looked in Europe, war was sure to be immanent. She did not know what else *could* happen, with what she was hearing of that fanatic little German and the trouble he was causing over there. She found that she admired her American employer for his foresight.

Upon reaching the kitchen she looked about but Maggie was not there, so she crossed the room and looked into the cook's pantry. There she found Maggie, sitting in her chair, staring at a bit of paper in her hand. Maggie looked up when she heard the pantry door open.

"Miss Edna!" Maggie exclaimed. "Excuse me, ma'am, please. Is there something I can get for you?"

"Fret not, my child," Edna soothed. "Sir Clifford just wants some scones and a pot of hot coffee. His American taste buds can only take so much tea, you know."

"Sure'n I do know that, for certain sure," agreed Maggie. "It took me months to learn how to make coffee the way they do in America. I don't know how many pots got dumped down the drain because they weren't to the master's taste. I'll be after making a fresh pot for you. Sit down, if you please," she said as she nudged past Miss Edna through the kitchen door and set about busying herself with the needs of her employer.

Miss Edna pulled up a chair and sat herself while Maggie prepared to make the coffee. "What did I interrupt?" she asked. "You appeared to be quite absorbed in something when I looked through the pantry door."

Maggie took the cheque from her blouse, where she had placed it when she got up to go into the kitchen. She handed it without a word to Miss Winwood. Edna looked at it and gave a low whistle.

"Well, well. What have we here? So you did win the sweep-stakes?" she said and smiled at Maggie as she handed the cheque back to her.

Maggie laughed. "No, ma'am, to be sure, I did not win the Sweepstakes. It's even better than that. This is an inheritance, you might say, from a long, lost uncle in Galway. I did not even know the man existed. Father Burns, the one I told you about? He was here today and gave me that cheque and told me about my relative. I did not know what to make of it. It just doesn't seem real to me at all at all."

"That's splendid news! Congratulations! What are you going to do with all that money? That's quite a bit for a cook, you know," observed Miss Winwood sagely.

"Sure'n it is indeed," agreed Maggie. "To be honest and true, I do not have the faintest idea what I'm going to do with it, other than put it in the bank. I have never had so much as two quid to rub together before, so this is going to take me some time to consider it, to be sure."

"I'm sure you'll find a good use for it, dear," said Miss Edna warmly. She genuinely like Maggie O'Shea and was happy for this good news.

"Ack sure'n one thing is for certain. I won't be puttin' it into a dowry as Father Burns suggested. No ma'am!" At that both women laughed heartily.

"That's right!" Edna agreed. "Put it away for a rainy day. So, your Father Burns was here today," she continued. "What else did he bring you beside the cheque? Any other news from Ireland?" More than simply taking up time while the coffee perked, Miss Edna was truly enjoying the conversation with the unpretentious Irish girl.

"Not much else from Ireland, to be sure," Maggie replied. "Savin' the load of fresh salmon he promised to have sent post haste from County Cork. That was almost out of nowhere that was. Still, 'twill be useful on Saturday for the big dinner party, if ever it gets here in time."

"Well, that is a good bit of news," said Miss Edna. "We both know how fond of fresh fish Sir Clifford is. But why do you suppose he'd send you such thing? Is that some Irish way of celebrating good fortune? Sending each other fish?" Once again, the two women shared a laugh.

"No ma'am, sure'n 'tis not an Irish custom to send each other fish," smiled Maggie. "And to be true to you, I do not know why he's sending it. As I say, it was almost out of nowhere it came. Like an afterthought on his part. It was after I told him that Dora Finch was here in London and visited me often here at Dogmoor. It seemed to strike him rather queer, it did."

By then the coffee was finished and Maggie poured it into the service and offered to take it to Sir Clifford herself. Miss Winwood told her not to be silly, that she was quite capable of pouring a cup of coffee and that Maggie should relax and enjoy her moment in the sun. As she carried the tray back to Sir Clifford's office, something twitched in the back of Edna's mind about what Maggie had just said. *"It seemed to strike him rather queer, it did."* There was something about Dora Finch that suddenly seemed to be making several people a bit queer. She wondered what it might be.

Concentrating on the task at hand, Miss Winwood served Sir Clifford his coffee and scones and, by way of conversation, mentioned to him about the fresh Irish salmon headed their way, thanks to a clerical friend of Maggie O'Shea's. She could have anticipated his response almost verbatim. "Good of the old mackerel snapper to send us something decent, eh?" Miss Edna smiled indulgently at her employer's insulting remark and resumed her place at her desk.

24.

Dinner at Manor Minnington that Wednesday evening consisted of one of Sir Clifford's favorite dishes. Boiled ham and bacon with potatoes and cabbage. It was one of Maggie's specialties, of course, simple peasant Irish fare that it was. Sir Clifford enjoyed it because it reminded him of his mother and some of the simpler fare she had prepared for her family during his childhood, dishes very similar to this one. Sir Clifford loved to reminisce about the simple life he had led as a child—even though eventually they had servants of their own—because that allowed him to remind himself of how he had succeeded in the business world so well on his own, with no help from anyone. Yes, on evenings such as this, Sir Clifford enjoyed himself very much, lost in his own thoughts of self-congratulation.

But on this particular Wednesday evening, Sir Clifford seemed to be the only one enjoying himself. The other members of his family seemed to be lost in their own thoughts, if not even somewhat edgy. Usually there was at least some conversation around the table. Lady Opal insisted on drawing her reluctant daughter into one at every meal. Roland was always at the ready to boast about some accomplishment or another he had achieved at school. (Sir Clifford could not understand that annoying trait and wondered from which of his wife's relatives he'd inherited it.) Lady Opal herself was normally able to chatter on about absolutely anything in order to keep the proper dinner atmosphere alive, and it was especially noticeable that she was so quiet with a major affair just a few days away. Yet, there they sat, quiet as a cemetery, each lost in his or her own thoughts.

Lord Dogmoor was concerned. He did not like change in routine, especially his domestic routine. The whole family and staff in Manor Minnington knew just how and when the master of the house liked things. So, while he was never actually interested in the family chatter at dinner time, Sir Clifford missed it because it was always there. Usually he was able to enjoy his own thoughts while Mrs. Minnington kept the dialogue going with her children, only bringing her husband into the fray when she thought it appropriate and necessary to do so in order to make him seem like part of the proper family dining experience, as well. In an attempt to bring things back to normal he made the most unusual decision to promote conversation himself.

"Well, now, Claudia. How is school going?" he asked, causing everyone at the table to look up with a start. "I understand you are spending a lot of time at Bedford's library doing your work. School's not such a bad thing after all, now, is it?" trying out his best fatherly tone.

Claudia looked at her father more wary than alarmed at this change in *his* routine. Her father seldom spoke to her directly except to tell her "no" when she asked for more money when her allowance was spent. "No, father, school is not nearly as bad as I had thought it would be," she said. "I am so happy to have been enrolled at Bedford College," and she smiled her best "loving daughter" smile at him, the best she could muster anyway.

Roland looked at his sister and rolled his eyes. "Yes, sis, how is that geography project coming along? Ever figure out where the Thames is on a map yet?" Roland held his sister in contempt. Due to his own clandestine activities in the city, he knew exactly what Claudia had been up to these last months when she claimed to have been at the library. He had figured that out after smelling the marijuana smoke that had clung to her clothes when he had happened upon her and some of her friends one evening. And, as if he needed more proof for himself, he was able to exact a confession of sorts out of one of those very friends about a week later when Roland had chanced upon him again one evening. He found him to be high on something and had been able to charm his way into his flat and then into his bedroom. That had been a serendipitous night. Not only did he find out exactly what his sister was up to but he had found a virgin as well. He was always happy to correct that condition in a man.

Claudia sneered at Roland across the table. She knew he had the drop on her because she heard all about said serendipitous night from the friend in question. A few weeks later, during another night of abusing drugs and marijuana, the young man, high yet again, had confessed to Claudia the encounter with Roland and everything that had happened. The marijuana seemed to have had the effect of making this young man want to admit to everything. Claudia's first reaction had been fear (marijuana seemed to make her feel a bit paranoid) but, as she thought about it, she realized that she had just as much on her brother as he had on her. He was a poof! She had long suspected as much but now, thanks to her friend and companion and his constant state of drug induced stupor, she had proof. Since that night, an uneasy détente had existed between Claudia and her brother.

"Now Roland, leave your sister alone. It's not every man who gets the fine education you are getting in Dublin. Your sister's only a girl and is getting the best that she is going to be able to get. You should be proud of her. I have to say I am" and here Sir Clifford bestowed another of his best fatherly beams at his daughter. "I'm as proud of her as I am of you, although it took me a while to get used to the idea of you being a priest. At least you'll be able to get married and have a family, not like the mick that was here today to see Maggie." Now it was Claudia's turn to roll her eyes, but she stifled a snigger.

Lady Opal barely noticed the tension between her children that evening. She had hardly even heard what they had said. She, too, had been startled by her husband's decision to ask a question of Claudia but she had continued to absently pick at her cabbage, her least favorite meal, as the conversation had ensued. However, at the mention of the words "priest" and "mick" she suddenly looked up. She fairly jerked her head up and the movement caught her husband's attention. Her expression reminded Sir Clifford of deer hunting. For some reason, she had that same look a deer had in his sights just before pulling the trigger. But, taking the opportunity to draw her into conversation, Sir Clifford forged ahead.

"Yes dear, a Roman was in the house today," ventured Sir Clifford, jovially.

"Oh really? What did he want, do you suppose?" Lady Opal offered her question, trying to sound casual.

"Who knows," Sir Clifford continued. "Something to do with Maggie and Ireland. Some old relative kicked the bucket and Maggie is benefiting in some way. The old priest brought the news to her personally for some reason. But there's good news for us too, my dear," Sir Clifford smiled at his wife. "He's sending a load of fresh Irish salmon to her. If it arrives in good enough condition we can keep it in the ice house and use it for Saturday's dinner! What do you think of that?"

Lady Opal knew her husband loved salmon, and Irish salmon was some of the best in the world. It would be perfect for the dinner. But it was not she who responded to her husband. Roland chimed in with "I wonder what bit of blackmail Maggie was able to hold over the old papist in order to get that extravagance out of him?" He laughed at what he considered to be his own cleverness.

At the mention of the work "blackmail" Lady Opal's face completely drained of color. Both of her children and her husband noticed this. The men thought that perhaps she was getting sick and suggested she go to her room and lie down. Claudia simply watched her mother and began to wonder more about the day's events. The rest of dinner was enjoyed in a very discomfiting silence.

25.

Not everyone associated with the Minningtons was having such a dour time with their dinner. In her humble little flat in London, Elinor Drumville was enjoying hers very much, indeed. After the events of the day, she had decided to splurge on herself and indulged in one of her favorite culinary passions, one that was affordable to her on occasion any way, shepherd's pie. She had ordered it from the grocer across the street and had it for her supper.

As she savored the taste of the lamb, she reflected on her day, turning each of her great discoveries over and over again in her mind. She was having a hard time deciding which of them she found more wonderful.

After her chance encounter with Lady Opal, Elinor was sure she knew who Dora Finch was. Lady Opal's reaction to the young scullery maid had been too obvious not to notice, especially to eyes that had been long trained in noticing such things. Why would Lady Opal have even been cognizant of someone in such a low station in life? Why, indeed, was Lady Opal even in the "Tea Cozy" in the first place? In her long association with Opal Minnington, an association long enough to remember her as Opal Jennings-Blickstoke, Elinor had never known her to venture into a public house. She would have thought that beneath her.

Elinor's long held suspicions about Lady Opal, and the quiet hints she had dropped in her direction over the years, hints that had kept her firmly ensconced on the manor house guest list, seemed to be coming to light with the discovery of Dora Finch.

Dora appeared, to Elinor's practiced eye, to be right about in her middle 20s and was, after all, a truly beautiful girl. A foundling in Ireland? Elinor wondered.

Dora was at, or near enough, the center of the other beautiful little controversy that had presented itself to Elinor that day. "I really *must* spend more time in that public house!" she reflected giddily. Having finished her meal, she cleared away her supper plate and poured herself a brandy. She took her cane and made her way to the chair by the fireplace, tossing an extra lump of coal onto the grate in celebration of her day's accomplishments. She settled into her chair and put her feet close to the warmth of the fire.

"Jasper Dunwoody, a dandy! That is just too, too much good news," Elinor thought to herself. Elinor was almost certain she knew who the other young man was, the one that had been referred to as "Dora's young man" by the hostess. She had been in the "Tea Cozy" often enough to have seen a handsome young man flirting with the lovely young girl. And Elinor was positively certain that she knew who the other young man was, the young man who Petal had hinted was a homosexual prostitute. Her keen eyes and suspicious nature had already pegged that one. The one thing she had never witnessed, nor even guessed at, was that Jasper Dunwoody would have ever had anything at all to do with the likes of him. She had never seen the two of them together, Jasper and this fop. Elinor scolded herself for not knowing his name *and* for not ever putting him together with her archenemy's personal secretary before this.

"After all these years of innuendo, I finally have some *proof*!" Elinor's inner thoughts were most self-congratulatory. "Proof he's a poof," she thought merrily. She could hardly contain herself. Sir Oswald's long line of handsome young secretaries was about to come to an abrupt end, at least if Elinor's plans came to fruition. Sipping her brandy, she wondered exactly what to do with this information. How could she best use it to finally deliver a mortal blow to old Bunbarrel?

"Sir Geoffrey would probably love to know this!" Elinor, her grey and hoary eyebrows raised as she considered a point, had arrived at a conclusion. "I am sure he would be most interested in this information."

Sir Geoffrey Tidwell was also a Member of Parliament and had a seat in the House of Lords. His family was also of the old British peerage and had retained its money and influence over the years, as had the Bunbarrels. Elinor did not know Sir Geoffrey personally. He moved in quite different circles than did she, but she did know that he, also, was an old nemesis of Sir Oswald's and that suited her just fine. As she understood it, the two of them were always clashing heads in Parliament, Sir Geoffrey a social conservative and Sir Oswald being possessed of a more liberal bent.

Elinor stared into the glowing coals as she considered her next move. How would she best be able to chat with Sir Geoffrey? How would she best be able to deliver this news? Would he be able to bring the old goat down in the House of Lords with it? Certainly there must be some morals charge that could be leveled against old Bunbarrel and he would then be driven out in disgrace?

Smugly, Elinor settled herself further into her chair and sipped her brandy. She had decided for herself which of the day's events was most important for her purposes. All she needed now was an introduction to Sir Geoffrey Tidwell. "I am certain he'll be happy to know this," she thought. "I am sure he'll want to show his gratitude in an appropriate manner." Elinor smiled into her snifter as she envisioned a whole new social circle opening up for her.

26.

The evening crowd of regular's was gathering at the "Boar's Head" pub, readying itself for another night of revelry. The handsome and handsomely dressed young men ordered their drinks as freely as ever and their banter was as cheery as it had always been. Each time the bell above the door jingled, heads would turn and merry welcomes would be made for whoever the latest arrival was. Things were on this Wednesday evening as they had been on every evening for the past many months. The only difference, it seemed, was in Snuffy Dolton.

The sole proprietor of the "Boar's Head" public house had spent a most anxiety ridden afternoon. After the departure of the two men whose conversation he had managed to overhear, Snuffy did something that he had never done before. He had closed the pub.

It had taken him several minutes to regain his senses after hearing what he had heard. He had stood behind the bar in absolute and total shock. Never in his life had he heard such talk. He knew that "people like that" existed in the world, but he had never known any of them personally. And more than that, what the two men in his pub earlier in the day had been discussing seemed to be beyond anything Snuffy Dolton might ever have even been able to imagine, if he were prone to imagining such things! Such twisted skullduggery!

After the initial shock had worn off, Snuffy had something along the lines of a revelation. His public house, it was suddenly becoming clear to him, had become the favorite haunt of a group of "people like that". When he realized this, Snuffy had

had a bit of a panic and that's when he decided to lock the door to the pub for the afternoon, fix himself some tea, and do some serious thinking about what he should do next.

Initially, Snuffy was not at all happy about being the owner of an establishment that catered to homosexuals. He had had in his mind an image of what such an establishment might be like. Discrete entrances, dim lighting, dirty linens—these were the sort of thing "those people" were attracted to, not clean, bright, upstanding businesses like his own. He could not understand why they had started congregating at his place.

He also could not understand how it was that he had failed to notice it. Hadn't he always wondered who these gents were who were suddenly finding themselves at the "Boar's Head"? And hadn't he often wondered why there was never any talk about their lady friends or wives? Somehow, though, they had not seemed to fit the image he had in his head of the homosexual persuasion. He always thought homosexuals were obviously effeminate types who liked to dress like sissies. Or they might also be the disgusting and degenerate types that loitered around parks and loos. What they were not like, he had previously imagined, were the men who had been coming to his pub. These were fine young gentlemen who dressed well and behaved themselves, albeit they did drink a lot.

Yes, and that was something to consider, they did drink a lot. That thought had struck Snuffy many times over the last several months, especially since he was realizing such a nice cash flow. It occurred to him that very afternoon to take a good look at his ledger of accounts. As he paged through the book he discovered that business had taken a turn for the better precisely when this group had started coming into the "Boar's Head". As best he could, Snuffy tried to remember exactly when that was. All he had to do to help himself remember was to turn the pages of his ledger back to just about a year ago. The black ink had finally begun to show up more often than the red and it had happened just a year ago September. Last fall, as Snuffy had finally recalled, was when the first group of them had come into his place after watching a rowing tournament on the Thames. He remembered, now, thinking that they seemed awfully enthusiastic about the rowers, without having much to say about who won the match. By Christmas, it was Mr. Dunwoody and his friends who had become regulars at his pub.

Closing his ledger that afternoon, Snuffy arrived at what was for him a cataclysmic decision. He would do absolutely nothing about the fact that his beloved "Boar's Head" was now a homosexual habitué. The money was just too damned good. Besides, as he had reflected, these boys were very well behaved and mannerly. What difference could it make as long as things stayed that way?

As he unlocked the door to his pub again, an act that seemed a bit futile in face of the fact that it didn't really need to be locked in the first place—nobody ever came into the "Boar's Head" at that time of day—Snuffy did think of one fly in the ointment. The young fop who had been in his tavern earlier with the other gentleman. Snuffy had seen him come in and out of the "Boar's Head" on a number of occasions, had observed him lately chatting it up with the one called Jasper. So far there had been no trouble with him. But after hearing what he heard today, Snuffy decided to draw a line. The rest of them were welcome, but not that one. Snuffy had determined that he would speak to Jasper about it at the first possible opportunity.

As fate would have it, that opportunity knocked right away. More accurately, it jingled, as the bell above the door announced another arrival for the evening. Heads turned and this time the greeting from the crowd was directed toward the handsome Mr. Jasper Dunwoody himself.

Exchanging greetings around with the circle of his friends, Jasper turned his attention to Snuffy and ordered a whiskey.

"Snuffy, old man, you have this mahogany shining like onyx!" Jasper observed cheerily. (To work off his nervousness, Snuffy had been wiping down the bar. He did not enjoy confrontations and imagined that this would be one.) "Expecting a visit from His Majesty?"

"No sir, no royalty here at the "Boar's Head"", replied Snuffy, who drew a deep breath and continued. "Actually, sir, I was hopin' to have a word with you, if I may."

"Of course, old man, anything you need. What can I help you with?" asked the ever jovial Jasper.

With that, Snuffy launched into his rehearsed speech about certain people being welcome and how he did not care who did what with whom as long as they kept it to themselves and so on. Jasper listened with smiling eyes, for he found the barkeep's discomfort both amusing and endearing.

"But, sir, I run a respectable place here and there are certain friends of yours who are no longer welcome," Snuffy finished and let out a breath.

Jasper's eyebrows raised in surprise. He could not imagine who the barkeep would be talking about. Who among his friends had done anything to offend this dear old chap?

"What do you mean?" he asked. "Has someone said or done something they ought not?"

Snuffy drew another breath and related to Jasper what he had heard earlier in the day. Jasper listened intently, blushing slightly at the mention of the male prostitute.

"Fair enough, Snuffy," said Jasper at the end of the narration. "Trevor will never darken your doorway again. But please be assured, neither I nor any of my friends you see here tonight engage his services. Well, *those* services. I have asked him to do me a favor in keeping an eye on someone for me, as you heard today. I think that will be coming to an end very soon now, anyway. But you say you do not know who the other man was, the one Trevor was talking with about going to Ireland?"

"No, sir, I cannot say as I heard the gentleman's name," replied Snuffy. "He did seem to be quite the gentleman though, I mean real gentry. It was in his bearin' and all." What Snuffy meant was that he was an arrogant snot, but he did not want to say that.

Jasper thanked Snuffy and promised once again that he need not worry anymore about Trevor. And that, as long as the welcome mat was out, his friends would continue their evenings at his establishment because they had come to be quite fond of it. He then ordered another whiskey and rejoined his friends in the back of the pub, his mind, however, wondering with whom it was that Trevor had been discussing his affairs.

27.

Thursday morning dawned a cool but yet another dry day in the south of England. The sky was cloudless and amazingly blue as the sun slowly rose over Britannia. The moors around the manor house were clear and green; the only mist visible at all was that around the bogs, a perpetual presence at Dogmoor.

Edna Winwood arose early from her rooms that were provided for her at the manor house. Last night had been one of the rare occasions that Sir Clifford's secretary spent the night in Surrey rather than return to London to her own flat. Her employer's appointment on Thursday in London precipitated the need for Miss Edna to remain the night in order to be ready to assist Sir Clifford with any last minute details before seeing the Lord Mayor.

Edna had not slept well during that night. She seldom slept very well at the manor house simply because it was not her own flat and her own bed. Last night, however, had been even less comfortable for the venerable assistant to the lord of the manor. That certain twitching at the back of Miss Edna's mind lately was last evening even more noticeable to her. There was simply something wrong in that house and some inner sense she had was on a high degree of alert. There was nothing concrete that she could point to as evidence to justify this strange feeling and Miss Winwood certainly did not claim to be psychic. It was all the little things that would go unnoticed by most people but which were noticed by Miss Edna and, as they piled up, she felt sure they were pointing to something unpleasant yet to come.

There had been Claudia's strange behavior. Claudia was a bit off-beat in the first place, but lately she had been secretive and surly with other members of the house, especially her brother Roland, home from Trinity until after the Christmas holidays. Even her appearance had changed. She was taking on a sickly and pale look about her, no matter how much she tried to clean herself up for dinner. Her mother had noted it one evening but her father had dismissed it as "too much time in the library".

Speaking of the library, what had she been doing with that strange group of young people in London when she was supposed to be at the college library? It had been abundantly clear to Miss Winwood that she had not been studying at all and was, therefore, not on any kind of study break. Her companions all had the same overall appearance as she had acquired. They were all ashen and disheveled looking and had a rather wild look about them. Miss Edna had never seen young people who looked so, well, threatening.

Roland Minnington was another story. For a divinity student he seemed to be the least divine of people. He was arrogant and rude to nearly everyone. He was even adopting an insouciant tone with his father! Sir Clifford, surprisingly to Miss Winwood, seemed to be very indulgent with his one and only son. He never corrected his son for his tone, except where Lady Opal was concerned. Roland had once spoken rudely to his mother and caught royal hell from his father for it. Miss Edna noticed an oily and obsequious manner in Roland toward his mother since that incident. Roland, it seemed, was crafty enough to know when not to cross a line.

"*Crafty enough.*" Those words struck Miss Edna as perfectly suitable for the young man. He always seemed to be plotting. She could see it in his eyes. But what on God's earth could a divinity student be plotting? "Perhaps he'll be the one to finally overthrow the Pope," Miss Edna considered, only half jokingly, to herself.

Lady Opal had been acting oddly as well, especially these last couple of days. Miss Winwood knew it could not be the stress of the party. Lady Opal loved hosting dinner parties. Besides, the real stress of social events at Manor Minnington was shouldered by the servants. No, there was something else. In the last day or so she seemed at once distant and jumpy. Edna had witnessed her practically leap out of her skin as she, Miss Edna, had come out of the pantry and startled her, Lady Opal, earlier on Wednesday afternoon. Lady Opal had laughed a bit nervously and excused herself and went into London. It was just not like her at all.

Sir Clifford seemed to be the only member of the family who was remaining stable and by "stable" Miss Edna understood herself to mean "predictably normal, considering". He seemed unfazed by whatever was bothering the rest of his little clan. He was blissfully unaware of anything foreboding at all as his mind was on his business, especially this new business of hoping to open offices in London. He was like Gibraltar, as far as Miss Edna could see, with only *fewer* apes to concern him. (Sometimes, Miss Winwood could not keep her salty remarks away from herself.)

Try as she might, Miss Winwood could not make any sense out of the conglomeration of impressions that she had been experiencing. She finished her tea and scone, readied her attaché, and went in search of Sir Clifford.

28.

The house was very quiet when Lady Opal emerged from her bedroom suite. She was aware that her husband had already left for London with Winwood since he had announced his departure time last evening during dinner at least seven times, or so it seemed. Lady Opal, who was usually very patient with the eccentricities of her American husband, found herself a bit short fused with him lately, although she refrained from saying anything confrontational to him. She was simply on pins and needles around him and around everybody, really, and she did not like the feeling. Lady Opal, ever since she was the little girl of the manor house with her mother and father doting on her, always felt as though she was in control: of her parents, certainly, of her house, her husband and children, but most completely in control of her emotions. She had to have been. It was the only way she could have survived the last 25 years.

She was, indeed, very unhappy with the way she was feeling lately. Unaccustomed to jangled nerves, she felt quite unsure of herself. She had built a life around being sure of herself. Since the days she had allowed herself to be courted by the American millionaire, after her parents had practically moved the earth and sky in order to secure the introduction, Opal Jennings-Blickstoke Minnington had been the picture of imperturbable calm and self assurance. It was carefully planned. It was thoroughly rehearsed; at least it had been during those early months of courtship. Her cool and detached demeanor had been meant to convey to the American the posture of the proper English lady, and it had worked. Clifford had been smitten by the young Opal's beauty and her quiet style. She seemed an unattainable goddess to him, which is why he simply had to attain her. Clifford Minnington was a man who was used to getting what he wanted out of life. Always had been, always would be. Opal had been able to use that to her advantage as she had maneuvered the steel magnate into a wedding proposal.

Her parents had been so proud and happy for their daughter's success. The Jennings-Blickstokes, though their name would disappear into history, could rest assured that the family legacy would remain within the family. Every plan they had made, every snare they had laid, had paid off more wonderfully than any of them had ever even anticipated. Clifford Minnington was a wealthy businessman with a good head on his shoulders. He was not likely, once he assumed possession of Dogmoor, to allow his acquisition to slip away from him, neither Dogmoor nor its young heiress.

Lady Opal Minnington looked out of her bedroom door and listened. She heard no discernable noises in the house. "Perhaps they are all gone, please God," she virtually said it as a prayer. She needed to be alone right now. She had to get hold of herself. It was Thursday and she was anticipating guests the day after next. She needed to be able to regain that self restraint that had served her so well before and during her marriage. She could not come apart now. Not now.

Instead of calling down for her tea and breakfast tray, Lady Opal decided to go to the kitchen for it herself. She knew Cook would be hard at work already. A reliable little Irish girl, she thought. At least that was something stable in the house which Lady Opal could depend on. That thought almost made her smile. Almost.

"Good morning, missus," chirped Maggie cheerily, as she always tried to be in the face of her aloof mistress. "I did not hear you ring for your breakfast! I am so sorry!"

"Good morning, Maggie," replied Lady Opal. Upon hearing her name, Maggie went on immediate alert. The lady of the house had never once referred to her by name before. "I did not ring for my breakfast. I just came down for some tea and one of your scones," continued Lady Opal. "How are things coming for the dinner on Saturday?" Opal tried to make this sound as con-versational as possible.

"Ack, sure'n missus, it is coming along as fine as rain in Dingle. The greengrocer tells me he is able to get asparagus at this time of year! Has it shipped in from some place in North Africa. That will be delivered Saturday morning and I'll serve it *alla romana*, as you like it. That should impress your guests, having aspara-gus in November!" Despite the red flags in her head at being addressed by name, Maggie was pretty proud of herself with that bit of news.

"Yes, dear, that should be a culinary coup," agreed Lady Opal, who was, in fact, genuinely impressed. She wished she were more herself so that her excitement about making that type of impression at one of her dinners was not so muted as it was right now. "And the pigeons for the first course? Are they going to be fresh and delivered on time?" All the English guests loved pigeon, but Sir Clifford avoided it. "You've never seen pigeons like we have them in Pittsburgh," he would say, much to his wife's chagrin. She served them anyway, as much to vex him as to delight her guests.

Lady Opal's fingers found their way to her blouse's collar. "And have we decided for the main course? What's fresh in the market?" she asked.

Maggie poured the freshly brewed tea for her ladyship and looked up in delighted surprise. "Do you mean to tell me, missus, that you have not heard the good news? We are having fresh Irish salmon for dinner. It should be delivered by way of County Cork by no later than Friday afternoon, if the fishing was good, that is. And to be sure, missus, the fishing is always good in Cork." Maggie laughed and returned to her sink.

"Fresh Irish salmon! That will be another coup for a November meal. Your Irish fishermen are miracle workers. But tell me," Lady Opal continued to attempt a casual tone, "how is it that we are being blessed with such largesse from the Emerald Isle?"

"Oh, missus, it was an act of Heaven, to be sure. An old priest I have known since I was a wee girl in Fermoy came by with news of a small inheritance for myself. Oh, it's nothing much, missus, but will make a nice nest egg for my rainy days ahead of me. He had a drop of, um, tea and we had a nice little visit, catching up on the old days in the orphanage. He asked about our Dora, too. He seemed terribly surprised, for some odd reason, to know that Dora and I were still friends after all these years and that we still see each other often, right here in this very kitchen!" The shock of her inheritance had worn off and Maggie was happily remembering the events of the previous day which had brought her such good news.

"You and your friend, Dora you say? The two of you were at an orphanage together?" Lady Opal's fingers fairly tugged at the material of her collar.

"Yes, missus, we were at St. Saviour's together in County Cork. Ack, they were hard years to be sure. The Sisters of Mercy were sparse in showing it!" Maggie laughed at the old joke that had amused the orphans for so long.

"St. Saviour's Orphanage? Sisters of Mercy? I suppose that must be a very Roman Catholic institution. And the priest, he was a Roman as well?" Lady Opal's voice was beginning to acquire a tone that made more red flags pop up for Maggie. She knew her employers were devoutly Anglican. Well, as devout as Anglicans get. They were certainly prejudiced against the Roman Church, as any good little Irish girl or boy working in England would know. Maggie suddenly felt she should be careful of what she said.

"Yes, missus, Father Burns is a Catholic priest," she ventured.

Lady Opal Minnington seemed quite pale suddenly to Maggie and it looked as if her mistress was going to tear a hole in her blouse. "Lady Opal, ma'am, is it feeling ill you are?" asked Maggie, concerned. Lady Opal sat motionless on her stool for a moment, staring into space.

"No, dear, I am quite fine," she came back to herself. "I think it's the excitement of the promise of one of our best dinners ever. Carry on. I am going to go back to my room and I do not want to be disturbed." With that, Lady Opal exited the kitchen without another word.

"Yes, missus," Maggie nearly whispered as she left.

Lady Opal slowly walked through the house, vaguely aware that there were no sounds coming from anywhere in it, except an occasional sneeze from the butler's pantry. Snippy always had allergy problems at that time of year. She climbed the stairs and re-entered her bedroom. She closed the door behind her, thought about locking it, but did not bother to do so since she was alone. She went to her closet, pushed aside some dressing gowns hanging there, and stared at the combination dial on her personal safe.

She had had the safe installed shortly after her marriage to Clifford. Her husband was reluctant at first. He believed that anything valuable should be kept in the main safe in his office. Lady Opal had prevailed, explaining how inconvenient that would be for her jewels. "You know I take forever deciding on what to wear," she had cajoled him. In the end, she had persuaded him to accept her wish by pointing out that if there were dogs back at Dogmoor perhaps she would not feel so vulnerable about her valuables. The safe was installed the next week.

Expertly she spun the dial on the combination and soon the door was opened. Lady Opal had been in and out of that safe an uncountable number of times since it was installed. She did not even have to think about the combination when she wanted to retrieve some bauble or another. Today, however, it was not diamonds, rubies, or emeralds that interested her. She carefully lifted up a tray of jewels in the back of the safe and reached in for a packet of papers hidden beneath. These papers were her real reason for insisting on the safe. They themselves were not exactly treasure, but the information they contained could mean the difference between being the pampered wife of a wealthy man or a scullery maid herself.

Opal untied the antique ribbon that bound the packet together and spread several papers and old letters out on her bed before her. Hesitating briefly, she trembled as she reached for one of them. It was a birth certificate which had been issued in Ireland, Fermoy, County Cork.

The years melted away as Opal remembered. She held the birth certificate and soon her hand stopped trembling. Looking at it, she was also looking past it as her memory swept the last twenty five years away and she was a young girl again. The baby's name on the certificate simply read "Baby Girl B.J."

What had Cook been talking about? Those nuns were gentle enough. Lady Opal was remembering. Her experience among the

Sisters of Mercy could not have been described as a holiday, but it was not at all what she had expected of these Irish women in black with their clinking rosary beads. They were kind to Opal, if firm. For all of Opal's fears about spending so much time there, her first true experience of Romans at such close quarters, and under the circumstances, was not as horrible as she had anticipated. They treated her better than they treated the Irish girls who were there for the same reason as she. This was because, as one of the girls had explained to Opal, that the nuns expected more of the Irish than of the English. Although she supposed it was meant to be insulting, Opal had been grateful to have been born an Englishwoman. It had garnered her gentler treatment at St. Saviour's, at the very least.

Opal was not even aware of how numb she was as she put the birth certificate down and reached for what appeared to be a letter. The pages of the letter were worn and stained, some of the words rendered illegible by the tears of the young girl who had received it. "My dearest Opal," it began and, after 25 years, Opal's eyes teared up still.

Once again Opal was a young girl. Carl had been the most beautiful man she had ever seen. He was the gardener and made his life's work tending to the estates of those who could barely afford his services anymore. He had had several clients among the friends of Opal's parents. He was respectful and not exorbitant and certainly good at his work.

He was also tall and handsome. He had dark hair and eyes, almost coal black. His complexion was also dark, as though he were perhaps of Spanish descent. But he was not Spanish, at least in his family's memory. He was one hundred percent Great Britain's finest, as he had proudly boasted to Opal as they walked over the moors.

Opal had been smitten with him from the first day he started working for her family. At first she surreptitiously watched him from the windows of the manor house. She nearly swooned that first summer, when he took of his shirt in the back field to work in the hot sun, exposing his muscular body to the fresh English air. She found herself making up excuses to talk to him: bringing him water, or tea, or perhaps something to eat. Soon enough they were taking walks together on the grounds of the estate.

Opal's parents were understandably upset at this attraction their daughter had allowed herself to develop. They threatened Opal many times to stay away from Carl but she only made it a point to spend more time with him the more they insisted she not.

Then, one October night the two of them took a walk in the early evening moonlight. It had been a full moon and was low on the horizon. Opal could remember it still. There was no chill in the air and only a slight mist hugging the bog. They had walked and talked and walked some more. By and bye they found themselves very far out on the moors and the manor house looked like a lighted up doll's house in the distance. Carl had stopped and stood looking at the moon. He had taken Opal by both her hands and turned her so they faced each other. Then he told her he loved her. Then he kissed her.

Lady Opal sighed at the memory of that night. She was that young teenage girl again, rebelling against her parents' wishes but at the same time undeniably drawn to the strength and beauty of the man who had held her. She looked back over the years and imagined she could still feel the cool of the grass as the two of them lay down together in the moonlight.

Suddenly, Opal burst into tears. The memories had overcome her and she was unable to maintain her cool, calm, self control any longer. It was as if a dam had burst inside her, flooding her with long repressed memories, emotions, and feelings of guilt. She went into a crying jag as she sat among the papers laid out upon her bed.

She flung herself fully into the unhappy feelings. So much for so long had been pent up within her that she knew she had to get it out of her system. Besides she could not control herself anyway. This jag was going to be had. As she cried, she felt the long buried pain of lost love resurface and the years of her basically loveless marriage span out before her. She then began to laugh, hysterically, as she realized the enormity of this situation. She truly was out of control, but she did not care. She had been in control of herself for so long that she actually embraced the building hysterics. Besides, she was alone in the house, so who cared what she did?

That would have been Claudia, because Lady Opal was not alone in the house as she had supposed. Claudia cared because she had listening at the door of her mother's room. During her customary skulking about, she had heard the beginning of her mother's crying jag and remained listening at the door as the laughter began. Claudia, a stranger to genuine feelings for even her own family, was actually shaken by this sudden breakdown in her mother's cold, calm exterior. Quietly, she pushed open the unlocked door to her mother's bedroom and was shocked at what she saw.

Lady Opal was supine on her bed amidst a scattering of old papers and ribbons. She was alternately bawling and laughing, loudly and lustily, giving full cry to an emotional outburst, much like the common people the whole family despised. Claudia slowly approached the bed and touched her mother's hand.

Opal jumped with a start and for the first time noticed her daughter in her room. Claudia was not sure her mother even recognized her, so strange was the look on her face. Rather than scold her for entering without knocking first, her mother simply cried again and fell back upon the bed. "Mum, you are coming unglued!" Claudia cried. Knowing she had to do something to calm her mother down, she reached into her omnipresent bag which she wore over her shoulder and retrieved from it a little silver flask. She unscrewed the cap and held it up to her mother's lips for her to drink. At first, Lady Opal resisted and made a face at it's oddly odiferous contents. Claudia persisted, however, and soon her mother took a sip. She waited a moment more and coaxed her to take another. Soon the laudanum had taken its intended effect and Claudia's mother calmed down and fell into a deep sleep, completely exhausted by her emotional release.

Claudia sat back on the bed next to her mother and took just a bit of a sip herself. She was still in shock at what she had observed. Her mother had nearly become a madwoman right in front of her! Claudia brushed the stray hairs off her mother's forehead and felt, for a moment, a certain tenderness towards her.

It was then that she turned her attention to the papers on the bed, the apparent source of her mother's disquiet. Randomly, she picked up one of the papers and started reading.

29.

At roughly the same time that his sister was drugging his mother to calm her down, Roland Minnington was making his way towards the "Tea Cozy". He was not sure about what, exactly, he'd say, but he knew he would say something. What he was sure of was that he wanted to do it when there were as few customers in the pub as possible. This had all the earmarks of a "scene" and, while Roland was no shrinking violet when it came to confrontations, he felt that this particular task should be handled with less spectacle. He was not concerned so much with Miss Finch or her co-workers as much as he was with his father finding out, should there be anybody in the public house who might know him and see or over hear what was about to transpire. Therefore, just early enough to beat the midday rush, Roland Minnington had entered the door of the "Tea Cozy".

A smiling, slightly overweight hostess greeted him as he came into the pub and showed him a table. She asked if anyone else would be joining the gentleman? (No.) and would he like some tea? (Yes, thank you.) Off she went to get him some tea and the list of the day's fare.

Roland sat in the nearly empty public house looking around, imperiously, at the conditions under which the common people he loathed dined. The longer he sat there and the more he looked around, the bolder he became in his mission. For one thing, no one here could possibly be part of his father's circle. Secondly, the very nature of the place raised his sense of indignation so much so that he fancied he would rather enjoy what he planned to do today. This was going to be much more entertaining than he originally thought it might have been.

As he scornfully surveyed the dining room he became quite full of himself. Maybe he would cause a scene after all. It would be rather amusing to see how much pain he could inflict on this girl and still be telling nothing but the truth. A blunt, forward attack had quite an appeal for Roland and he decided to go that route. "A lot of hurt, a lot of pain," he thought, "would not only be entertaining to witness in this wench, but also the most effective in achieving the real purpose for which I am here." With that Roland sat smiling and waiting for his tea.

The hostess served him his tea without delay and showed him the menu for the day. Without even looking at it or his tea, Roland asked her if there were a young woman working in the pub by the name of Dora Finch.

"Why, yes sir," exclaimed Petal. "Dora works for me tending to things in the kitchen and helping out in the dining room as needs be."

"Would it be possible," Roland poured on the charm, "for me to speak with her? I have some news in which she might find some interest." He smiled innocently at the hostess.

Petal replied, "Of course, sir!" and could not make her way back into the kitchen fast enough to fetch Dora. She had been aware that good news was supposed to be coming to Dora's friend Maggie O'Shea and wondered if this distinguished visitor might have something to do with that. She hurried through the kitchen door and took Dora by the arm.

"Dora, pet, there's a gentleman out in the dining room asking to see you!" she breathlessly whispered. "A fine looking gentle-man, too, I might say!"

Dora's eyebrows rose in surprise and Petal saw the smile jump to her lips and the hope in her eyes. She realized at once who Dora thought the gentleman might be and wanted to pinch her-self for not realizing sooner who Dora would naturally suppose the caller to be.

"I'm sorry, dear," she apologized, "but it's not Erskine. This young man is obviously much higher class that that young whippet!"

Petal thought she would try to sweeten the idea of a new para-
mour for Dora, since she knew Erskine to be no good for her.

Dora's heart sank a bit. She had hoped it was Erskine since
she had not seen him in several days. Still, she was curious as to
who would want to see her, especially such a "fine gentleman"
as her employer and friend had described.

"Who is he and what does he want?" she asked Petal.

"Lord, I do not know, girl!" Petal exclaimed. "Get out there
and find out! If you need me, I shall be very near by at the hostess stand." With that she gave Dora a gentle shove in the direction of the door to the dining room and hoped that there would
be no other customers coming in for a few minutes so she could
see and hear what she might.

Wiping her hands on her apron and straightening the bon-
net she wore while she worked, Dora Finch stepped through the
doorway into the dining room and looked around. When she saw
the young man sitting alone at a table, she drew in her breath in
surprise. "Mr. Roland? This is a pleasant surprise," she said, somewhat disingenuously. Although she did not really know the young
Minnington, she knew enough. "How may I be of service to you?"
she asked.

Roland, of course, recognized her as soon as she had come
through the door. "That's why that name sounded so familiar!" he
hissed to himself. "Dora Finch. Naturally, it would be the cook's
friend." He had seen her with Maggie several times at the manor
house but had, of course, paid little attention to her. But here
she was, approaching his table, and obviously wondering why
he was there to see her.

"Damn it!" he thought. "Now what?" Roland realized that he
could not, after all, cause a scene, that this was going to have to
be handled much differently than he had hoped. Almost immediately, a new plan hatched in his fertile little mind and, in his
most mannerly manner, he stood up and greeted Dora Finch as
sweetly as piously as his divinity school training had enabled him.

Smiling at her warmly he said, "Dora Finch! How good to see
you. I was afraid that you might not be here today. Please," he

continued, indicating an empty chair with his hand, "do have a seat for a moment."

The young woman stood with a bewildered expression on her face, but smiled at the invitation as she declined it. "Oh, no sir, thank you. I could not sit in the dining room with a customer. Miss Chalmers would not appreciate that, I am certain," and she gave a slight nod in the direction of the hostess stand where the hostess was looking awfully busy arranging menu cards.

"But of course, I understand," replied Roland. "I should have known better. I hope you do not mind if I sit and resume this delicious tea?"

"Of course not, sir," said Dora. "Please be comfortable. May I bring you anything else right now?"

"Not a thing," answered Roland Minnington. "The fact of the matter is that I have come here not so much for tea as to have a bit of a chat with you."

Dora's surprise could not have been any more hidden. In a most ladylike fashion she smiled calmly at young Mr. Minnington and urged him "Pray, continue."

There was a moment's hesitation as Roland prepared himself for what he was there to say. He looked at Dora and saw in her something that inspired a glimmer of recognition. There was something terribly familiar about this girl, but he was not sure what that possibly could have been. One might suspect that this feeling would mitigate what Roland would say, but it merely fueled his perverse desire to continue his hurtful mission.

Finally taking a sip of the tea, Roland put on his most distressed expression and looked with sad and concerned eyes at Dora. "I am afraid that what I have to tell you is not at all pleasant," he said. "In fact, it is most unpleasant. Are you sure you won't have a seat here beside me?"

"Sit, you fool!" Petal thought to herself and considered going over and telling Dora to do so herself. But that would mean that they would know she was listening in, so she abandoned the idea and simply kept checking her menu cards.

Dora once again declined the invitation and, with a growing sense of anxiety, tried to maintain her smile as she waited to hear what this young gentleman had to say.

"Very well," sighed Roland and he launched into his patter with earnest. "As you may know, I am studying to be a priest. As a divinity student I have been trained in counseling and caring for the flock which will eventually be mine after I'm ordained. It is through this part of my training that I am afraid I have come upon some rather unpleasant news that affects you, my child."

Dora could feel her anxiety level rising. She was not sure whether or not he knew it, but Dora was a Roman Catholic. It alarmed her somewhat to be about to be told something that Roland had heard as a confidence. A Catholic priest would never divulge such information, no matter what it may have had to do with her or anybody else. It also irked her, oddly, that he would refer to her so condescendingly as *"my child"* when she was fairly certain that she was a few years older than he. Still, she maintained her calm and ladylike posture.

Roland continued. "It has come to my attention from someone who was speaking from his heart to me in order to assuage a guilty conscience that you are acquainted with a Mr. Erskine Randiffle. Is this correct, my dear?"

"Yessir," Dora replied warily. "I am acquainted with Mr. Randiffle." She volunteered no other information.

"Yes, well it seems that, according to this person, Mr. Randiffle is toying with the affections of more than one person in London," Roland sadly shook his head and sipped his tea.

Dora fought hard to maintain her outward dignity as her insides crumbled within her. So this is why Erskine has not been in lately. He has found another girl, probably one more suitable to his station in life. Dora could not help imagining these thoughts.

Crafty young Roland knew he had struck a chord even though the young lady before him tried valiantly to hide it. He delayed just a moment in order to relish the moment before he went on.

"It appears that the young man who has been keeping company with you has also been keeping company with someone else."

"Mr. Randiffle and I had no understanding. He was a customer here, that is all," Dora tried to sound as calm as she could manage. Even though he was beginning to find it vexing, Roland had to admit to himself that he admired her self-control.

"Really? Now that is not what I have heard, my child." (*"He did it again!"* This was beginning to bother Dora.) "I have been led to believe that Mr. Randiffle has taken a particular interest in you and that, though you may never have accompanied each other out for an evening, he has been seen spending considerable time here at this public house in your company."

Calmly, Dora straightened her apron and feigned disinterest. "It is true, Master. Roland, that Mr. Randiffle has been here several times and that we have conversed on occasion, but if he is interested in another young woman, then that is his affair and not mine."

"Yes, my dear, it certainly would be his affair," Roland could not help smiling as he prepared to drop his bomb. "But you see, it is not another woman that has caught his interest." He watched to see Dora's reaction.

For her part, Dora just stood there looking at him. She was very obviously confused and hadn't the slightest idea what Roland was getting at. "Simple cow," he thought merrily to himself. "This will be sporting after all."

"Erskine Randiffle," he unctuously continued, "is seeing another man, not a woman. Do you understand what that means?"

Dora Finch may have been a simple kitchen maid from Ireland, but she certainly understood what that meant. She did not believe it, however. "What do you mean, sir?" she asked.

"What I mean, my child, is that Mr. Erskine Randiffle is a homosexual and has been keeping company with a man named Jasper Dunwoody, another homosexual. They have been seen in the most intimate of gatherings of other homosexuals in a pub that caters to that kind of clientele," Roland was really getting into his role now, managing to say *"that kind of clientele"* with utter distaste. He continued, "In fact, they have been seen embracing each other and leaving together late at night on any number of occasions. I am afraid, my dear, that your boyfriend has found his own boyfriend." Roland could not help himself with that last remark. He did, however, manage to keep from sniggering.

Dora knew that the color was draining from her face. She knew this because she could feel how much her throat constricted when she heard Roland Minnington say what he had just said. Still, she maintained her composure.

"Thank you, Master Roland, for stopping by. I am certain that you are telling me this in an effort to save me from some emotional distress or another, but I assure you, Mr. Erskine Randiffle is only a customer here at the "Tea Cozy" and means nothing more to me than that, personally or otherwise," she lied.

He had to admire her fortitude. He could see very little evidence of the pain he had just inflicted upon Dora Finch, other than the paled look on her face. He was forced to admit to himself that she was a lot stronger than he would have given her credit for and wondered whether or not she would be any further trouble to him and his overall purpose. However, he smelled blood, as it were, and was fairly sure that his poisoned arrow had found its mark. He was certain that his mission had been accomplished. Slowly, he rose from his seat in order to take his leave.

"Of course, my child, whatever you say. I am glad for you, then, if there was nothing between you. It would have been horrible, otherwise, to have set your hopes and dreams on a handsome young man only to find out later that he…" here Roland allowed his voice to trail off, knowing that he need not say anymore.

He bowed gallantly to the young kitchen maid and turned to leave the public house. As he donned his hat upon his head against the chill, he smiled to himself a most self satisfied smile. He knew that he had just taken care of the business he had come for and that Trevor would be free to accompany him back to Dublin after the first of the year. His lingering concern over Dora Finch waned as he continued on his way. Things were looking good for Roland, in his own opinion.

30.

Closing the door as she finally left her mother's bedroom, Claudia gave thought to the irony that that was the most amount of time she had ever spent alone in her mother's company. The afternoon had veritably flown by. She then cynically noted to herself that the laudanum had made it bearable, as her mother had been asleep through most of it. Claudia was certain that she would not have found out nearly as much as she had if her mother had not been under the influence of the lovely little narcotic that she was so fond of herself. She quietly clicked the door into its latch and turned to go to her own room.

She stopped and drew in her breath sharply in utter surprise. She was completely startled to find someone at the top of the stairs watching her every move! She had not heard a sound in the house at all.

"Roland, you creeping git!" she hissed, barely above a whisper. Claudia loved any excuse to call her brother names, but this time she was genuinely rattled by his sudden appearance. "Why are you sneaking about the house like some idiot?"

"Why are you sneaking out of Mother's room, dear sister?" Roland asked suspiciously. He had returned from London, still full of self satisfaction at his accomplishment of just a while ago, and just in time to catch his sister unawares. Apparently, she had not heard his car coming up the manor house drive. He eyed Claudia warily, suspicious of whatever motive his sister might have had for sneaking around in their mother's room.

"When Mother returns home, I am sure she will find it most interesting to know that you have been rummaging about her suite," purred Roland nastily.

"Give it up, you fool," replied Claudia tartly. "It just so happens that Mum is in her room now, sleeping like an angel."

"Oh?" said Roland, even more suspicious now. "And what were you doing in there, then? Surely not watching dear old mummy sleeping? What are you up to, sister dear?"

Roland's sudden appearance and his questions began to rattle her nerves and Claudia was beginning to feel the need for a little of her elixir herself, but did not dare take any right in front of her brother. She could not trust that he would not run to their father and expose her drug habit, although she had a few things she could pass on to daddy about his habits, if the need arose. In addition to the fact that he had seduced one of her male friends, Claudia had observed her brother in odd areas of town in the company of strange men while she herself was out carousing around London. One of these strange men was a known fop and Claudia and her friends were certain from that Roland, pious and imperious Roland, was a homosexual. She had kept this to herself in case she needed it at the proper time. That proper time seemed to be on the horizon now.

Still, in truth, Claudia held her tongue at this particular moment because she had been held utterly spellbound by what she *had* been doing in her mother's suite. She had spent all afternoon reading the papers scattered over her mother's bed after her mother had passed into the deep sleep experienced from her first taste of laudanum. While her mother slept heavily under the influence of the drug, Claudia had absently picked up one of the old letters. She had read it with amusement, since it was an old love letter to someone Claudia had never heard of. As she kept reading she had come across the birth certificate and other papers from County Cork. At first confused by it all, Claudia slowly began to realize the full meaning of what she had been reading. Her mother had another child, her father more than likely did not know about it, and she and Roland had a sister somewhere. And Claudia was certain she knew who, since her mother had muttered a name before the drug completely rendered her unconscious. For the first time in her memory, Claudia decided to confide in her brother.

"Roland," she started, casting a wary eye at her brother, "we ought to talk."

Thinking he had the upper hand, Roland felt himself about to gloat. Two victories in one day! "Yes," he replied sternly, "we ought to."

"Come to my room," said his sister. "You are never going to believe this."

31.

Dora had stood and stared straight ahead of herself as Roland had exited the "Tea Cozy". She did not even turn to watch his back as he walked out the door. Her expression had not changed from its calm reserve. She had struggled mightily to make sure of that.

However, once Roland Minnington was out in the street and had disappeared from view, all Dora's resolve shattered and she turned and ran, crying, into the kitchen. She simply could not hold herself in any longer. Embarrassing as it was for the beautiful young woman who was always in control of her emotions, she had to let go this time. She ran to her little stool in the kitchen's corner and laid her head on her arms on the preparation table, sobbing like she never had before.

Petal Chalmers who, because of her diligence, had heard every single word, decided to let Dora have a few minutes alone before she went in to her. Instead, she went over to the bar to confer with Joe and tell him all that had transpired.

"Of course, don't I know that already!" said Joe, for he had been just as diligent as Petal, "But I still say it ain't any of your business and now that them Minnington's is involved, you had better stay out of it!" Joe whispered this last part under his breath, fearful as he was of the power wielded by the wealthy class. He did not want to see Petal or the "Tea Cozy" hurt by any of these goings on.

As Petal and Dublin Joe engaged in their whispered conference, Dora had continued to cry in the kitchen, her mind reeling in disbelief at what Roland had told her about Erskine. How could it be true? How could she have been so blind? Surely, she would have realized it by now if Erskine fancied men over women. He always seemed so genuinely glad to be around her when he was in the pub. He even seemed to be flirting with her at times. How could she have been mistaken about *that*?   No, she just could not accept that Erskine was a homosexual and chose to believe that Roland Minnington, for whatever reason, had just told her a monstrous lie.

Dora knew very well that Petal had overheard everything so it had been no surprise to her when Petal finally did come into the kitchen and, more than that, it was of absolutely no help to her mood when Petal confirmed the worst by telling Dora what she had herself observed at the Tower of London. To make matters still worse, if that could be at all possible, Petal told Dora all that she and Dublin Joe had discussed about the matter, filling in for Joe's part what Petal thought he should have said, had he had the good sense to completely agree with her. She then clucked and cooed into Dora's bent head and patted her lovingly on the shoulder, trying in vain to comfort her and remind her that she was young and there were plenty of "normal young men" in London. Finally, realizing that her efforts were having little or no effect, she had suggested to Dora that she take the day off and get herself calmed down. Petal was a very loving and generous person, but she also knew that Dora would have been a danger to the crockery in the condition she was in. So, over Dora's muted protestations, Petal insisted that she go home and get herself a good rest.

Dora left the "Tea Cozy" and wondered the streets of Smithfield for a while. She walked aimlessly, looking at nothing, staring straight ahead. She noticed neither the passersby nor the chill in the air. Her face bore a blank expression that belied the pain behind it. She was aware of only one thing. She did not want to go home and be by herself. Finally, despite the risk of running into Roland, or any of the Minningtons for that matter, she decided to go see Maggie.

The bus had let her off, as it always did, near enough to the manor house that the walk was easily manageable. By this time she was recovering her senses and she felt the beginning of winter as she began the lonely walk along the road that ran through the moors. She bent her body against the cold, as the weather had grown quite chilly; at least it seemed to be so to Dora. Perhaps it was just her mood that made the cold feel worse than it was. As she walked through the moors and past the bogs, and finally coming to the main drive of Manor Minnington, Dora reflected on the afternoon's events, rolling them around and around in her head. She needed a strong dose of Maggie's common sense to help her through this miserable mental maze in which she had found herself. Hoping against hope that she would not be observed by anyone in the house, Dora made her way around to the herb garden and then to the doorway to the kitchen and knocked.

"Dora, darlin', what are you doing here?" Maggie asked as she let her in. "Why are you not at work at the "Tea Cozy"? Sure'n you haven't been given the sack?" Maggie's concern for her friend was genuine. Dora simply never missed work. As far as Maggie knew, Dora had never had so much as a cold that would have kept her from fulfilling her duties at the "Tea Cozy". For one thing, Dora could not afford to miss the pay. For another, she was just that dedicated to her commitments. So Maggie's concern was justified and she looked at Dora with eyes that spoke of her care for her friend. It was just what Dora needed. With Maggie taking her by the hand and leading her to the cook's pantry, she once again began to cry.

Now Maggie was really alarmed. Never, in all their days of friendship since they had left St.Saviour's had Maggie seen Dora cry. She had seen her smile and laugh. She had seen her concerned, thoughtful, and even a bit frightened when they had first arrived in the big city of London. But one thing she had not seen Dora Finch do was cry. Dora had always kept her emotions in check. Maggie put some water on to boil, arranged a teapot and cups, and seated Dora next to the small work table. She brought out some freshly baked crumpets and seated herself across from Dora, waiting for the water to boil and for Dora to say what she had obviously come to her to say.

For her part, Dora struggled to regain her composure, easier by a bit now that she was with her best friend. The long walk in the cold November air had helped her as well. The tears she was shedding now were not only pain but relief, relief that she was someplace with someone she knew she could trust and count on. By the time her tea was poured, Dora's weeping had stopped. She dabbed her eyes and wiped her nose, took a sip of her tea, and began to tell Maggie what had happened earlier at the pub.

Maggie's eyes widened as she listened to her friend's story. She was immediately relieved to know that nothing was wrong with Dora or that she had not lost her position at the pub. But she was drawn into the tale of unrequited love and rumors of homosexuality that was being laid out for her by Dora. Maggie could not imagine how such things could be real. She had, for instance, never believed the neighborhood bullies back in Ireland. After she had been adopted by the O'Sheas, Maggie had made friends with a young lad down the street who was always getting beat up by the local hooligans. Their claim was that he was a "girlie boy" and they mocked him by calling him "Ockie", after Oscar Wilde, the well known Dublin homosexual. Maggie had never believed the ugly things they had said about her gentle and quiet friend and had always felt very sorry for him after one of his encounters with the neighborhood toughs. In many ways, Maggie, though she now lived in a big city, was still very naïve.

As Dora continued her tale of woe, Maggie could not decide with whom she was angrier. Roland Minnington for being such a pious busy-body, Petal Chalmers for throwing in her two pence just for the sake of being able to spread gossip, or Erskine Randiffle himself for not being more direct and finally making a move with Dora. All three of them would be liable for a good old fashioned Irish tongue lashing, if Maggie O'Shea had any say in it a'tall a'tall. As Dora's story came to its sad conclusion, Maggie poured them both some more tea and looked with tenderness on her poor, dejected friend.

"Now, don't you be believin' any of that nonsense," Maggie soothed. "Sure'n there's a right proper explanation for everything. Why, Erskine Randiffle is a fine handsome man. It'd be a high crime against nature for him to be wasting himself on some fop, instead of settling down and marrying a fine young woman such as yourself. Don't pay them any attention, Dora," Maggie advised.

Dora, though grateful for the encouraging words, did not feel at all encouraged. In the time since she left the "Tea Cozy" , the bus ride, the walk through the moors and now retelling the story to Maggie, Dora had begun to realize that, deep down inside, this really did not surprise her. Oh, of course, the suddenness and bluntness of Roland's accusations had taken her off guard and she had been further confounded by the fact that Petal had had her own concerns which she had shared so soon after Roland left the pub. Despite the enormous pain and confusion, Dora, however odd it may seem, had begun to realize that a sudden sense of uneasy peace was settling upon her. It was as if a nagging doubt within her had finally been brought to light and questions unanswered were now answered.

Reaching across the table to take Maggie's hand, she said "I don't know, Meg, it does seem to make sense of some things that have been going on lately. He's been so distant recently. I mean, I have been wondering if there had been something I said or did that offended Erskine. I have thought and thought but could not remember anything other than our usual casual chats. Then I thought that perhaps he had grown weary of me because our routine had become just that, routine." She paused. "This, at the very least, would explain why he never asked me out for any engagement, even though he seemed to be on the verge of that on several occasions in the past. I just don't know what to think."

"Well," responded Maggie, "it would seem to me that an up and coming clerk with a firm such as his would not be wantin' the world to know he's a poof!" Dora winced at the use of that word. "Seems to me that he'd be wantin' to find a wife and be normal, if nothing else to help keep his position." Maggie's renowned practicality surfaced. "I would imagine that it would be a secret he'd want kept secret, not announced all over London!"

Dora smiled and tightened her grasp on Maggie's hand. It was refreshing, in a way, to have her point of view, even if it did nothing to solve anything. Dora agreed that it was probably something that Erskine would not want trumpeted around town and she was not at all happy to be privy to the information, even if she took a more benign view of homosexuals than it appeared Maggie did. Still, it was nice to have somebody like Maggie to be able to share the important stuff of life with. She was, as Dora frequently reminded herself, the truly only happy memory she had of her childhood days in the orphanage.

The afternoon passed into late afternoon as the two friends sat sipping their tea that November day, and as the shadows began to lengthen as the day grew later still, a sudden noise startled them both. The loud rapping at the kitchen door caused them both to jump, nearly spilling their tea. That broke some of the tension and they both shared a laugh as Maggie went to the door to see who was there.

"Ack now! Dora, come here!" Maggie shouted back to her friend when she saw who was at the door. Now it was Dora's turn to be concerned as she hurried from the pantry and into the kitchen. What she found, standing in the doorway, were two burly delivery men, carrying a large wooden crate between them.

"Dora, darlin', I completely forgot," exclaimed Maggie. "'Tis the salmon from Fr. Burns just arrivin' now!" She held open wide the door and allowed the two men and their crate to come into the kitchen. The deliverymen entered the room and set the crate upon the floor.

"Open it up for me, will you lads?" asked Maggie, excitedly.

The men pried the top of the crate off and Maggie and Dora looked inside. The crate had apparently been waterproofed by thick layers of oilskin and then filled with fresh ice. In the ice were some of the most beautiful looking Irish salmon Dora had seen in a very, very long time.

"Fresh from County Cork, ma'am," proffered one of the delivery men, taking off his hat. "Fr. Burns put us in personal charge of gettin' these fish here to you as soon as was possible under heaven!"

And fresh they were! Maggie lifted one of the fish out of the crate with both hands and felt how firm the flesh was. The ice had kept them so. She knew that if she kept them cold and icy they would be perfectly fine for dinner on Saturday.

"Thank you, lads," chirped Maggie.

"Where do you want them, ma'am?" the apparent spokesman for the pair inquired.

Thanking God for the drop in the temperature, Maggie instructed the men to take the crate back outside and directed them to the icehouse. The cold November air would assist the ice in its mission but the icehouse would ensure that the fish would not spoil before the day after tomorrow. It was located just to the left of the herb garden and the salmon would be easily accessible enough.

Tipping their hats, the Irish fishermen delivered their catch to its destination under Maggie's watchful eye and, declining an offer for tea, decided to head out for a night at a pub. The two women could hear the engine of their truck start up as they made their way out of the Minnington grounds.

"Two Irish men turning down a cup of tea on a cold evening?" mused Dora. "What is the world coming to?"

Maggie laughed. "Come now, Dora, sure'n you haven't been away from Ireland for so long that it would surprise you to find an Irish man who preferred a pint to cup of tea?" Dora laughed along with her friend, the first time she felt back to normal all afternoon.

"But tell me, Maggie," Dora asked, "what is this about? Why did Fr. Burns send you this salmon? This is quite a feat, even for a parish priest in Ireland to be able to pull off!"

"Sure, now, haven't I forgot to tell you," said Maggie. With that she launched into the story of Fr. Burns' visit, the good news in the form of the small inheritance, and his sudden and peculiar disposition after.

"Yes," she said, concluding her story, "he grew rather queer when he asked about you and found out that you and I visit frequently here. After that he suddenly decided to send over some salmon as a gift to the house. I cannot even imagine why he'd be after going to all this trouble, but sure'n I'm glad he did. This will take a burden off me for Saturday's dinner."

"Maggie, that's wonderful news! About your inheritance, I mean," exclaimed Dora. "I am truly happy for you. I am glad one of us got some good news this week!" The way she said it caused both of them to pause for a second, and then they simultaneously burst into laughter. Maggie was certainly the medicine Dora needed right now. With one last check to make sure the lid of the crate was securely in place, the two friends left the icehouse and returned to the cook's pantry to finish their tea.

32.

The "Tea Cozy was fairly quiet late that Thursday afternoon as Miss Edna made herself comfortable in her booth and ordered a cup of tea. The hostess scurried off to prepare it for her and Miss Edna Winwood looked at the bill of fare, deciding whether or not she wanted something more than a scone to eat. It had been a very long day and she was feeling a bit hungry.

She had spent the entire day with Sir Clifford at the Office of the Lord Mayor of London. The two of them had arrived precisely on time for their appointment with his lordship, but were kept waiting for nearly an hour before they were ushered into his office. It seems there had been some sort of emergency involving the Prime Minister's office that delayed the Lord Mayor's arrival at his own office that morning.

Miss Edna had fully expected Sir Clifford to exhibit some of the behavior she had grown accustomed to from her American employer. Being kept waiting, or almost any other inconvenience, was something Sir Clifford Minnington did not tolerate at Manor Minnington. To be kept waiting for three quarters of an hour for an appointment with someone was sure to provoke his temper. Edna had steeled herself against it when they were told by his secretary that the mayor would be delayed.

To her immense surprise, Sir Clifford had accepted the news graciously, as graciously as he could anyway, and had taken a seat, opened his brief case, and started looking over his proposal, occasionally questioning Miss Edna on this point or that. Miss Winwood sat on pins and needles as the time grew longer, anticipating the explosion that had seemed inevitable to come.

It seemed to her that the wait for the tantrum was worse than the actual event. She wished he would explode and get it over with. But Sir Clifford did not explode, nor did he grumble. He kept himself busy with his last minute preparations, leaving his dutiful secretary completely amazed.

Finally she asked him, "Who are you and what have you done with Lord Dogmoor?"

Sir Clifford looked up at her, not catching her meaning at first. Once he realized what she was asking, he looked at her over his glasses and said, "Don't you think I know the difference between this office and my own home? Business is business, Miss Winwood, and sometimes we have to expect this sort of rubbish to happen. Now, be quiet while I finish these notes." With that he returned to his papers.

Her American employer was truly at his best when he was conducting business. Feeling somewhat relieved at last, Miss Winwood sat back and awaited the arrival of the Lord Mayor.

When they had finally been ushered into his office, Sir Clifford was in rare form. He made a very impressive presentation to his lordship and his secretary could not help but to be impressed herself. In spite of his temper and bellicose attitude towards things British, Edna had to admire him for his style when it came to business. From his handling of the Lord Mayor to his reading his mail, Sir Clifford displayed a level of concentration and savvy that she had not seen in her previous employers. Miss Winwood could not help but smile to herself, reflecting on the day's events as she sat at the "Tea Cozy" and waited for her tea to arrive.

When the tea was served Edna had decided to have a bowl of pea soup and requested it of the hostess, who was only too happy to oblige. Along with some brown bread, the soup made for a nice late afternoon pick-me-up after the long day Miss Edna had had in the city. The impressive manner of Sir Clifford, Lord Dogmoor had apparently not been lost on his lordship, the Mayor, because Sir Clifford had been invited back to make his presentation before the High Commission of Commerce. It seemed, to both Edna and Sir Clifford, that things were going their way. Sir Clifford, in fact, had been so elated after the meeting was over that he had given Miss Edna the rest of the day off and the next day, as well.

Edna Winwood buttered her brown bread and was just about to taste her pea soup when she heard the door of the "Tea Cozy" open and observed a handsome young man enter. She also observed the look on the hostess' face when she looked up and saw the newest arrival to her public house. The round, jovial face that nearly always had a smile pasted on it turned sour quite quickly. It was obvious that the hostess was not pleased. Miss Edna could not help but to be intrigued.

"Good afternoon," began the young man. "Is Dora here? May I speak with her?"

"No, she isn't", replied Petal Chalmers curtly. "She has taken the afternoon off. After what she experienced earlier today I should think she needs some time for herself and I should think that you would be embarrassed to come in here asking for her!" Petal was beside herself with anger and disgust.

"Why, what do you mean?" asked Erskine Randiffle.

"As if you don't know!" snapped Petal. "Stringing that poor girl on like that when all along you had *other interests* on your mind!"

Erskine blushed a crimson red when he heard her say that. In her voice he could read exactly what she meant by the remark. He had had no idea that his secret was apparently so well known. How did this pub hostess find out? He decided to pursue the issue.

"What are you talking about, *'other interests'*? And where is Dora? What did she find out today?" he demanded.

"I told you, Dora is off for the rest of the day. She won't be back. And as for you, I think you should leave, now." Petal sounded resolute.

"Why? What have I done," persisted Erskine.

"You broke her heart, you unnatural beast!" hissed the hostess. "I saw you myself with that strange man near the tower, and then when young master Minnington came into this very public house this morning and told her what you were up to, why, it nearly caused poor Dora to faint!"

At the sound of the name "Minnington" Edna focused her attention on the conversation a bit more acutely.

Precisely at that moment, Dublin Joe came from the kitchen and found his lady friend and Dora's erstwhile boyfriend obviously engaged in some unpleasantness. He sauntered over to the stand behind which Petal stood and inquired, "What's going on here? May I help you, sir?"

"Yes, please, tell me where I might find Dora," replied Erskine.

"I am sorry sir, but I cannot tell you what I do not know. Like as not she's gone to her friend Maggie O'Shea at Manor Minnington. All we know for certain is that she's gone for the day and we would appreciate it if you were, too."

Sensing defeat, Erskine turned to leave and was considering whether or not he should try to see Dora at Dogmoor. As he prepared to depart, he noticed for the first time the lady in the booth with a bowl of soup, her soup spoon suspended in the air in front of her, interrupted, as it were, on its way to her mouth. Erskine recognized her immediately as Sir Clifford Minnington's personal secretary. He had seen her in the "Tea Cozy" many times and had been informed of her importance in the local business community by Jasper. He gave a quick and uncomfortable nod of his head in her direction and hurriedly left the pub.

Petal had puffed herself up with great pride at the way she had handled the rouge, even as Joe reminded her that she was going to have to do Dora's work that night as well as her own so she had better get cracking with preparations for the dinner crowd. Petal shot him an exasperated look and turned to go into the kitchen. Remembering that she had a customer in the dining room, she turned to check on her.

"Is everything to your liking, ma'am?" asked Petal.

"Fine, the soup is lovely," replied Edna. "But, tell me," she could not help but to continue, "what was that about young master Minnington?"

Petal, who did not know the lady's connection with the Minnington's, did not hesitate to rush into a detailed account of what had transpired concerning that young rascal and Dora and young master Minnington. She started at the Tower of London and ended with the awful announcement that the nice

Mr. Minnington had so dutifully delivered to Dora Finch, just that very morning, and how Dora was now taking some time off, no doubt with her friend Maggie O'Shea who, as fate would have it, was the cook for the Minnington family at Dogmoor.

Having counted on Petal to be unable to resist retelling this unhappy gossip, Miss Winwood sat in silence as the tale unfolded, feeling somehow, in the back of her mind, that she had stumbled onto what was causing that strange feeling she had been experiencing of late.

Erskine hesitated on the sidewalk outside of the "Tea Cozy". He felt panic rising in his throat. Apparently, Roland Minnington had revealed something to Dora about him that he, himself, was only becoming more aware of. But why? Why would he do such a thing? What would Dora do with the information? If this became public knowledge he would surely lose his position at the firm. Erskine was certain that Dublin Joe was correct, that Dora would be headed for Manor Minnington to be with Maggie. Dora had mentioned to him on several occasions her friendship with the cook at Dogmoor. He remembered seeing Miss Winwood in the public house. His sense of panic was growing stronger. In an impulsive rush, he hailed a taxi cab and got in. He knew what he had to do and he wanted to do it in a hurry.

Part III

33.

As Miss Edna was listening to Petal's story in London, Maggie and Dora were still visiting in Surrey. Dinner at the manor house was going to be delayed that day because of Sir Clifford's business in London with the Lord Mayor. He had anticipated the meeting taking much more time than it had and, when he realized that he had plenty of time to get back to Dogmoor before dinner, he had given his secretary the rest of that day off and rewarded her with Friday off, too. He celebrated what appeared to be a very promising interest on the part of the Lord Mayor by going to his favorite gentleman's club for a scotch and water and to socialize and rub elbows with some of London's other business elite. Business looked good.

The delayed dinner hour was serendipitous for the two friends since it allowed them a longer and more relaxed time to visit. Maggie would not have to start dinner for at least another hour yet and as she poured Dora another cup of tea she wondered if her old friend was recovered from the terrible ordeal of that day. Maggie could not believe that Roland Minnington would be so cruel as to tell Dora that the young man she was interested in was a homosexual. Even for the pompous young heir this seemed excessive! "Beyond the Pale," mused Maggie to herself, recalling an old Dublin expression.

Of course, it had not helped matters at all that Petal Chalmers had chimed in with her own fantastic observations. Silly old busybody. Just because two men are talking together does not make them homosexual. Goodness, all the lads in Ireland would be considered that way by Petal's reckoning, considering how they get a bit too much of the drink in them and hang on each other on the way home from the pubs.

Maggie had tried all that long afternoon to offer these perspectives to Dora and had succeeded in calming her down some, if not completely allaying her fears about Erskine and his choice of friends. Dora seemed to be much more herself, albeit saddened by the events of the day. In the end, Maggie resigned herself to the fact that Dora had resigned *herself* to the fact that she did no longer have a prospect in Erskine Randiffle.

"Talk about 'unrequited love'," Maggie heard herself saying before she could stop herself from saying it.

Dora looked up, stared for a moment at Maggie, and then burst into laughter. It was the inadvertent break that Dora needed and both young women shared a bit of a laugh. The happy news of Maggie's windfall from Ireland had also helped the day to be made more bearable for Dora. They had discussed all the things that Maggie might do with the money, ultimately deciding that it was for the best to bank it and save it for some occasion she might need it in the future. Although, in dreaming about it, using the money to open a bed and breakfast in Ireland had held a certain appeal for them both. The most important thing about Maggie's inheritance, at the moment, was that it helped Dora to transcend her own problems and enabled her to put her them into a proper perspective. They were such close friends that good news for one balanced out bad news for the other.

The sun was beginning to set and darkness quickly fell upon the manor house in Surrey. It was time for Maggie to begin the preparations for that evening's dinner for the Minningtons. She had implored Dora to spend the night with her at the manor house so they could continue their visit. On rare occasions, Dora had availed herself of the hospitality offered to her by Dogmoor's cook and had spent the night with Maggie when she had a day off coming to her or for some other special reason. This evening, however, Dora felt more like being at home in her own flat. The visit she had shared with Maggie had done her a world of good and she was certainly glad that she had made the trip to Surrey for it. She felt now that she was over the worst of her upset and that a few hours alone at home would help her finish sorting out the whole sad situation and reconcile herself to the new realities that faced her. Besides that, she had to work tomorrow at the "Tea Cozy" and she did not like the idea of having to rush all the way to London from Dogmoor in order to be at work on time.

"Thank you, Maggie, but I really need to be going back to the city," she had replied when Maggie asked her for the fourth time. The last bus from the end of the lane that would take her back to London would arrive within the hour, so Dora hugged her best friend and thanked her again for her sympathetic ear and the tea, put on her coat and hat, and left by the back door of the kitchen, out into the cold dark November night. Maggie watched from the window as Dora made her way through the herb garden, past the icehouse, and out the back gate. She knew that her friend would recover and move on. She only wished that things had worked out better for her and her young man.

It was a dark night. Dora disliked the winter months because it got so dark so early in the evening. With the clouds looming above the moors, it seemed even darker still. Having grown accustomed to the lights of the city, the darkness of the country-side was almost oppressive. Dora's pace was slow and even so as to be sure not to trip and stumble in the darkened roadway. As she walked down the lane she allowed herself to cry just a bit again. She could not help how sad she felt about Erskine, but also began to think about how difficult it must be for him to have been leading what was tantamount to a double life. For all the heartache he caused her, she could still feel compassion for him. Dora's heart was as big as England itself.

As she strolled down the lane, taking her care and knowing she had plenty of time to get where she had to go in order to catch the bus, she continued her musings on Erskine, Maggie, and her life at the "Tea Cozy". She thought that she might find another position somewhere else. Big hearted though she may be, she still felt it might be too difficult to continue on at the pub, especially under the pitying eyes of Petal Chalmers.

So lost in her thoughts was she, that she did not hear the twig snapping behind her. When the blow fell on the side of her head, she literally did not know what hit her. She fell to the ground in an unconscious heap, the darkness darker than she'd ever known— or would ever know again.

34.

Sir Clifford arrived home at precisely the time he thought he would and went upstairs to his bedroom suite to make himself ready for dinner. He still felt as if he were floating on a cloud, utterly pleased with himself and the positive prospects of having an office in London. He was in such good humor that he took extra care with his grooming. His wife would appreciate the effort, he was quite certain, for such niceties as that seemed to be so terribly important to her—as important to her as the subtleties of the business world were to him.

"Yes, we make quite a pair, we two," he reflected to himself. As he washed his face and looked at himself in the mirror, Sir Clifford smiled at the image looking back. He was not what you would call an unattractive man, certainly he would not call himself that, but he was not terribly handsome. He was a large man, not fat, but tall and broad shouldered with a stocky build. His dark hair, thinner now than it was those 20 or so years ago when he had first met Opal Jennings-Blickstoke, was still combed back in the same style as he had worn it then. Large as he was, his features were well-proportioned. His eyes were dark and sharp, set not too far apart nor close together. His nose was aquiline and prominent on his face, but not overly so. His chin was neither strong nor weak but seemed to be gaining a companion chin below it. A completely objective evaluation would have to be that he was neither handsome nor ugly.

But he was rich. Very rich indeed. He had been since he was young and had made much headway in American business ventures, particularly steel. He was wealthier than anyone he knew when, on a trip to Europe celebrating his thirtieth birthday, he was introduced to the beautiful and somewhat younger Opal. He had had an immediate attraction to her and sensed that she was attracted to him somehow. Certainly her parents had made much ado about their meeting. It was, as Sir Clifford recalled, at a ball hosted by the American Embassy to which, as a prominent American businessman on holiday in London, Clifford Minnington had been invited. The Jennings-Blickstokes were introduced to him and they, in turn, introduced him to their shy but beautiful young daughter.

Sir Clifford tied his cravat and considered a stick pin for it. He remembered how lovely Opal had been that night. Only in her very early twenties at the time, she seemed the very picture of English womanhood. Her breeding and status as an aristocrat were clearly evident, polished as she was in her poised and quiet manner. They had danced with each other most of the night, she laughing at his attempts at humor, he feeling awkward and unsure of himself for the first time in his life.

Her parents had invited him to tea the very next day and Mr. Clifford Minnington of Pittsburgh, Pennsylvania had his first experience of how high society in England conducted itself. The Jennings-Blickstokes had a beautiful home and had entertained young Minnington in grand style. Clifford, for his part, had been terribly ill-at-ease because he was the only guest for tea that afternoon and felt out of place and unsure of his manners. Soon he felt more comfortable when he realized that he was going to be able to become more acquainted with the charming Opal. In time, his confidence returned. It was not terribly long after having made her acquaintance that Clifford, bold as you please, asked her to marry him. Confident in himself as he was, he nearly passed out when she said "Yes" immediately. After a rather quiet wedding, a surprise to Clifford since it was, after all, the aristocracy, the Minningtons moved to America where they resided for several years until, on the occasion of her father's death, Opal convinced him to return to England and take up residence in her ancestral home.

He had very much enjoyed his life as an imported aristocrat. He enjoyed learning the ins and outs of British society, even though he was never able to incorporate them into his natural behavior. His next blunder always seemed to be a moment away. His wife and mother-in-law were terribly indulgent with their American relative and he knew why. As important as social niceties were to his Opal and her mother, his money was more important. He had suspected all along that that was why her parents had pushed them together but he had been so smitten with Opal that he played along. Returning to Great Britain gave him the additional trophy of a title and he very much enjoyed playing the part of Lord Dogmoor. Just as long as there were no dogs involved. He hated dogs.

Here he was, twenty or so years later, with two children nearly grown and out of the house, primping for his bride. Over the years Clifford Minnington had accepted the fact that his bride had married him for his money and not out of love. His primping was more out of habit than the desire to impress, these last many years. Their marital relationship was what might be called "cordial". After Claudia was born Opal had insisted on her own suite and very seldom did Clifford enjoy the bliss of the marriage bed after that. Still, they were quite a pair. Business was booming here in London and he was poised to become richer still. Lord Dogmoor adjusted his dinner jacket, smiled at his reflection one more time, and headed downstairs for dinner.

The evening meal at Manner Minnington was always a semi-formal affair because Lady Opal enjoyed such formalities. She had had a hard time training her American husband in the ways of mannerly dining. He had not understood why, when it was just family, they should be putting on such airs. But Opal had been resolute, with both her husband and her children, and had succeeded in turning her brood into proper, if not enthusiastic, dinner companions.

Dinner time at the manor house was usually not the casual family time that Clifford had been used to in the States. The children were children, however, and had tested their mother's patience for several years. Roland had, as he grew older, adapted to the proprieties, almost a little too well. Claudia never conformed, truly. Unruly as a child, she had settled down a bit during her later teen years, but lately she seemed to sulk more than anything else. Her mother was constantly nagging her to sit up straight and to dress better for dinner. Engaging her in conversation was such a labor that her mother eventually gave up trying. Still, they were all expected to be there for dinner, as a proper British family, unless, of course, Roland was away at school.

As he sat himself down at table that evening, Sir Clifford sensed a change in the atmosphere. As Snippy poured the water, Sir Clifford glanced around the table at his family and noticed that his wife looked quite unlike herself. She was slumped a bit, just enough to look like she was terribly tired. Overall, that is exactly what she looked like. Tired or overworked or perhaps sick. Sir Clifford knew she wasn't overworked and could not imagine what she might have done to tire herself so much as to result in this. He concluded that she might very well be coming down with something, which would be rotten luck, just two days before one of her big parties!

In contrast to his wife, his children were positively exuberant. Roland seemed especially cheerful as he talked about school and looking forward to the Christmas holidays. But Claudia was the most surprising. While her manner of dress had not improved much, that very casual and slovenly look she and her peers had adopted, her manners had. She chatted excitedly, almost annoyingly so, with Roland. Her father noted that her eyes were wide open, like a child's on Christmas morning. Her gestures were quick and jerky, like someone who had had much too much coffee. The three of them were so different than usual that Sir Clifford had the impression he was looking at a photographic negative of his family, if such a thing were possible.

Addressing himself to his children, he said, "My goodness it certainly is nice to see the two of you talking to each other in a civil fashion for a change," and turning to his wife, "don't you think so, dear?"

Lady Opal started as if she had been suddenly awakened from a nap. Her napkin fell from her lap to the floor and she nearly tipped her water glass as she started to bend over to retrieve it. Snipwhistle looked on in complete surprise at his mistress who was about to perform a task for herself.

"Opal, are you quite alright? You don't look too good. You're not coming down with something, are you?" asked Sir Clifford.

"I'm fine, just fine, Clifford," she fairly snapped. "Really, it is as if one were not permitted the odd accident now and again in this house!"

Sir Clifford arched his eyebrows in surprise at this response. Clearly his wife was not feeling too terribly ill. She still had her temper. Snipwhistle, for his part, decided never to allow her to do something for herself again.

Claudia let out a nervous giggle and Roland picked up on it and did the same. "Mum is just fine, aren't you?" he said.

"Yes, dear Mummy is just excited about her dinner party, aren't you Mummy?" Claudia chimed in. Sir Clifford could not remember the last time his children had been so chivalrous towards their mother.

"Thank you, dears," the weary sound came from Lady Opal by way of response. With that she seemed to get herself under control and, though it appeared that she struggled to do so, she maintained herself from there on as well as she might.

As dinner was served to the family, Sir Clifford kept a wary eye on all three of them. He wondered just exactly what was going on inside the heads of these three loved ones of his.

35.

It was a dreary English November day when Friday morning arrived in London. The mist clung to buildings, obscuring the sky. The chill of the incipient winter months made itself known in the damp air and Londoners pulled their mufflers and topcoats more firmly about themselves as they made their way about the city, conducting their various business enterprises. It was a day that most people would consider unpleasant.

Miss Edna Winwood, however, was not most people. She stoked the coal fire in its grate and finished her morning toilet. Today, Friday, was a day off for her, a reward from Sir Clifford for the success in the Lord Mayor's office the previous day. She had surveyed the city scene out of the window of her flat. Rather than be upset that her day off would be one of inclement weather, she felt a certain comfort in the grey skies. Days like these for Miss Edna were days when she was able to concentrate. Something about the dullness of her surroundings on such days enabled her to think clearly and focus on her tasks.

Of course, today's tasks would all be personal. There were letters and other correspondences that she needed to catch up on. She wanted to pay a few bills and also looked forward to doing a bit of shopping. Other than her correspondence, these were not things that required a great deal of concentration. However, Miss Edna sensed that she would need her mental faculties today, even if her tasks were mundane.

The wary feeling she had been having had not left her. In fact, that annoying, cloying feeling in the back of her mind that something was amiss had grown increasingly stronger after her experience in the "Tea Cozy" the day before. She did not know why, but somehow she knew that something was going to happen, something, perhaps, quite dramatic. Her sense of these things was very intuitive and she had been aware of this gift, for lack of a better word, since she had been a young girl. A sort of premonition of a big event would take shape in her subconscious and keep nagging at her conscious mind until she unraveled whatever it was. The "twitch" is how she sometimes had referred to it, especially when it was as active as it was now.

One thing she had never been able to unravel was what, exactly, caused the "twitch". Miss Winwood was, above all else, a very practical person and did not believe that she had any sort of extra sensory perception, like the fortune tellers she had seen at carnivals and such. They claimed for themselves powers that Miss Edna simply did not believe in, so she was firmly convinced that her own inner sense was something much more explainable, she just was not too terribly certain as to how to explain it. She assumed that her natural powers of observation and her uncanny ability to form fast judgments, both of which served her well in business, especially with Sir Clifford, were the very powers and abilities that created these uneasy sensations of premonition. Her "twitch", though she may not have explained it exactly this way, was her subconscious mind carefully registering everything she saw and heard and cataloguing it for her, eventually bubbling up to her conscious thought.

Unaware of the psychology behind it all, Miss Winwood simply accepted that there was something afoot and waited and watched. On this Friday morning, she finished her letters and assembled her bills for payment, donned her coat and hat, picked up her umbrella, and headed out into the streets of London to conduct her own business affairs. She began at the post office.

By the time Edna Winwood had finished her errands, but before she went to market, it was late morning. The chill and damp of the day had settled themselves into her and she decided that she would avail herself of a hot cup of tea before finishing. The market would be an easy last stop, since she needed only a few items. She would be attending the dinner at Manor Minnington the next evening and would more than likely end up remaining in the suite that Sir Clifford allotted to her for overnight stays there. She would have need only for provisions for this evening and for Sunday afternoon. The dinners at the manor house were always so ample that she had little concern as to what she would be eating for the next couple of days.

Although there were places closer which she could have patronized, Miss Edna found herself headed directly for the "Tea Cozy". She felt deep inside herself that something there today would likely be worth observing and she wanted to make sure that she was there to observe it. Ducking her head into the chill breeze, she made off to the public house that had suddenly become a very favorite spot for her.

Upon entering the pub she immediately sensed tension in the air. The place was nearly empty since it was still too early for the lunch time crowd to have arrived but there was, nevertheless, an urgency that was palpable, and it seemed to emanate from the hostess, Miss Chalmers. As Edna entered the public house, Petal had looked up, a mixture of expectation and consternation on her round and simple face. When she saw that it was Miss Winwood, only consternation showed. She shot a look at Joe Shannon behind the bar and came to the door to greet Miss Edna.

"Good morning, missus. Would you care for a seat near to the window?" she asked.

"Why, yes, thank you," replied Edna, who could not help but to notice the look of concern and worry on the usually jovial face of the hostess. She took her seat and ordered some tea. Almost as an afterthought she added, "And bring me some of those delicious scones that are baked here."

Upon hearing her request, Petal Chalmers froze in her tracks as if someone from Scotland Yard had ordered her to halt. The suddenness of her stop and the subsequent hesitation in her stance gave Miss Winwood pause to wonder just what was wrong with the portly matron of the "Tea Cozy".

Turning around to her customer, Petal finally apologized and explained. "I'm terribly sorry, missus, but there will be no scones out of our kitchen this day. We are a bit short staffed, you might say."

"Oh?" queried Miss Edna. "Has someone fallen ill? Not that sweet young girl who helps you out, I hope?"

"Well, missus, it is that sweet young girl, to be sure. Dora is her name. But we do not know whether she is sick or not. We haven't heard from her since she left here yesterday, as you may recall that scene, missus."

"Yes, I certainly do recall that scene. It was terribly unfortunate and most embarrassing for her, I'm sure," soothed Miss Edna.

"Right so," continued Petal, grateful to have someone of this lady's stature taking an interest. "Dora was terribly upset when she left here yesterday after what young Master Minnington told her. That Randiffle is a devil! Poor Dora!" Petal dabbed her eyes with the corner of her apron.

"And now you have not heard from young Dora yet today?" urged Miss Edna.

"No, missus, not yet. She was due here three hours ago to bake the very scones you've requested and start the soups for today's fare. I even had Dublin Joe there ring up the boarding house where she has her flat and they told him they had not seen her all morning, nor remembered seeing her come in last night!" Petal had said that last part in very much a whisper. She was very much concerned for the well being of her scullery maid. Miss Edna had the sense that the hostess was afraid that Dora may be prostrate with grief and unable to arise from wherever she may have landed the day before.

"Ah!" she said, "perhaps she is at Manor Minnington. She and the cook are great friends and I have seen the two of them together quite often."

"You are familiar with the manor house?" asked Petal.

"Yes," replied Miss Edna. "I am in the employ of Sir Clifford and, as I said, I have seen Dora and Maggie together there quite often."

"Begging your pardon, missus, but I did not know you were connected to the Lord and his family. It is my understanding, too, and my hope that Dora might be at Dogmoor. That Maggie is a dear sweet girl and Joe and I both are hoping that Dora is with her. But she should have let us know if she weren't coming into

work today." The hostess seemed, to Miss Winwood, to be vacil-
lating between concern and annoyance at this point.

"I'm sure it will all be fine," Miss Winwood said, not at all certain as to why she said it, for she herself felt that strange twitch
getting stronger. "It's only natural that she would want time alone
after what she went through yesterday. I'll just have my tea with
a ginger biscuit, if you please." Edna had decided that she
wanted her tea and to end the conversation with the hostess.
She wanted to be alone to let her mind wrap around the events
of the last days to see if she could find an explanation for what
was roiling around inside her head.

It had not been two minutes since the hostess left to fetch
the tea when the door to the public house opened again and
in stepped Mr. Erskine Randiffle. Miss Edna's eyes widened in surprise and could not help feel just a bit of exhilaration stirring within
her as she sat in anticipation of what this occasion might bring.
Assuming as innocent and detached a posture as she could
muster, she waited and watched to see what was going to happen next.

Petal returned from the kitchen with a tray of tea and biscuits
for her customer and, once again, stopped dead in her tracks
when she saw Erskine in the pub. Her eyes glazed over cold as ice
as she strode determinedly past him. The anger and hate were
very evident in her expression. She could barely contain herself
as she served Miss Winwood, her hands shaking with fury.

Ignoring her obvious discontent, young Erskine came up to
the table and, before he thought to excuse himself to Miss Winwood, asked Petal if he might speak to Dora.

"Speak to her?" she hissed at him. "If only you could. She's
not here."

"Where is she?" he asked, suddenly finding himself and
begged Miss Edna's pardon for the interruption.

"I don't know where she is and I certainly would not be telling
you if I did! We are worried sick about her and it's all your fault!"
Miss Chalmers nearly shouted the last part.

Erskine looked at the pub's hostess with complete surprise
when he heard she was not there and winced when she blamed

him. He gave a doleful look in Miss Edna's direction and, hat in hand, quickly left the "Tea Cozy".

"I'm sorry, missus, for that display," apologized Petal to Miss Winwood. Then, overcome with emotion, the portly hostess excused herself and went to the kitchen to cry.

Miss Edna Winwood sipped her tea and wondered.

Part IV

36.

It was a beautiful Saturday morning. The mist and clouds of Friday had been banished by the bright November sunshine. The day was promising to be splendidly bright, if not a great deal warmer, than had been the previous day. Cold and clear as it was the sun already generated enough heat to melt the frost on the moors and send it wisping into the air, almost as if the grass were smoldering in the morning light. Birds flitted about the bare bushes and trees that dotted the landscape made desolate by the oncoming winter. The sky was so blue that it put Wedgwood to shame. One could almost think that it was the end of winter, rather than its beginning. Onto this bright, yet chilly, scene came Packie Murphy and his dog, Riley.

Packie was a groundskeeper for Dogmoor, or at least he had been before retiring several years before. Though he was Irish by blood he was English by birth and was proud to be one of a long line of Murphys that had served Dogmoor for the last three generations. His great grandfather had arrived from Ireland in 1800 as a young man and found employment at the Surrey estate in the days before all of the family money was gone. Since then there has been a Murphy on the grounds of Dogmoor tending to its needs. Packie, as fate would have it, would be the last of that line. He and his wife, Mamie, had not been blessed with children and Sir Clifford, the current lord of the estate, had been forced to look elsewhere for Packie's replacement.

Still, Packie considered himself to be part of Dogmoor and, frankly, could not have cared less that he irked Sir Clifford by walking his dog on the moors. For Packie, it was a matter of pride. He appreciated Sir Clifford's generosity in allowing him to roam the estate, but just could not understand a man who did not like dogs. No dog in Dogmoor was more than Packie's old mind could comprehend. His American lordship seemed not to understand at all the tradition of the place, its very reason for being what it was.

To rectify that situation, Packie made it his duty to walk his dog every chance he could over as much of Dogmoor as he could. Riley was a four year old Irish wolfhound and was a beautiful dog of brindled wheaten coloration that most certainly enjoyed the long romps over the Surrey moors. No matter what time of year and no matter what type of weather, Riley was always eager to accompany his master as he fulfilled his personal pledge to keep the "dog" in Dogmoor.

Today was an especially good day for romping around the estate. Since it was so clear and so nice Packie reckoned that everybody would be in a good mood, so he had decided to walk Riley up near the front of the manor house. Of course, he stayed well away from the house itself, but he allowed himself and Riley to explore the driveway up to the house and the moors and the adjacent bog. Packie's secret aim was to gradually break down Sir Clifford's defenses against dogs by showing him how eminently proper they looked on his property and there was no better dog to demonstrate that than Riley. Of course, Packie had been doing this for the twenty years or so since Sir Clifford came to Dogmoor and had been through several incarnations of Riley and his kind. Yet, his determination never flagged and his resolution did not wane. Today just might be the day.

As the two of them, man and dog, walked along the drive, a good quarter mile from the manor house, Riley would frequently slip away from his master's side to go exploring. This was not exactly Mr. Murphy's favorite part of the walk, because whenever Riley got into the bog he came out of it covered in muck.

That is why Packie did not usually come along this particular route. However, today was as fine a day as you could ask for in November in England, so he had decided to do so. And, as he knew he would, Riley made a mess of himself in the bog.

Something was a bit different this morning, however. Riley, who liked to suddenly take off running or go sniffing around and acquaint himself with Mother Nature's morning news, seemed to have found something most particular in which he was interested. Packie stopped and lit his pipe, allowing his best friend time to satisfy whatever curiosity had been peaked by whatever it was in the bog. In due time Packie thought it was time to move on and whistled for Riley to come on ahead and continue the walk.

Uncharacteristically, Riley refused to obey and continued to sniff and paw at a particular spot in the bog only several feet off of the road. In fact, the dog seemed almost frantic in his efforts to uncover some hidden secret in the muck. Packie supposed that it might be an old bone that had captured his pet's attention. Whatever the case, Packie was getting impatient to move on. He whistled again and called Riley by name. Still the dog pawed at the ground. Growing a bit peeved, Packie walked over to where the dog was fussing.

As he came upon the patch of ground that Riley had been worrying, the dog suddenly lay down with his head between his paws, facing in the direction of the hole he had begun to dig. Packie stopped in his tracks and paled. He recognized that posture in an Irish wolfhound. Riley had found something, or probably, somebody dead. "A sign as certain sure as a banshee," thought Packie, recalling the familiar Irish myth. Carefully, he approached the spot where Riley had been digging.

As he approached, Packie halted, observing something that looked like it did not quite belong there. Unearthed by his dog's digging, there looked to be a piece of broad cloth, the type from which a coat might be sewn. Packie came closer and bent over the spot to examine it more closely. He took hold of the cloth with his hand with the intention of unearthing it to examine it. As soon as he tugged on it, he snatched his hand away from it and stood bolt upright.

"Come along, Riley," he said. "We have to summon the constable."

37.

The tall man in the black fedora and black overcoat looked lanky even covered as he was in his hat and coat. Holding a notebook with a pencil poised above it, Atticus Fingarrison, His Majesty's Coroner, stood on the lane that led to Dogmoor and squinted in the late morning sun. This gave his singularly hawkish face an even more bird-like appearance. The pale complexioned, darkly dressed official continued making notes regarding the location, position and general condition of the body in the bog.

Having been summoned by Chief Inspector Thornton Sheridon to join the investigation at Manor Minnington, Atticus Fingarrison had ridden out to the countryside with Sheridon, the Chief Inspector, and with Detective Milroy Frambley, all of them from Scotland Yard. The local constabulary, having been aroused into action by Packie Murphy, had put in the call to the Yard immediately upon assessing the situation at the ancient estate. Scotland Yard always assumed jurisdiction in these cases. Constable Dickey Olsen had been only too happy to call in his superiors in a case involving the aristocracy, even if the chief aristocrat at Manor Minnington was only honorific, being as he was an American and had attained to the peerage by marriage.

With several officers assigned to finishing the task of removing the body from its shallow grave, Chief Inspector Sheridon set himself to the task of conferring with the Coroner. He did not relish the thought of having to conduct an inquest at the manor house any more than did the local police but he knew that his duty was to do just that. As he watched the body of the young woman being placed ever so carefully on a gurney from the coroner's office, he turned to Atticus to hear his initial impressions.

"Apparently she suffered some blunt force trauma to the head", said Fingarrison in reply to the inquiring look given him from the Chief Inspector.

"So somebody did her in by bashing her head?" asked Sheridon.

"Well, it certainly started out with that, but the trauma to her head did not kill her."

"What did then?"

"Asphyxia."

"You mean to tell me that somebody hit this girl on the head and then smothered her?" It sounded odd, for some reason, to Thornton Sheridon, to be smothered after being rendered unconscious.

"No. She died of asphyxia from the bog itself. She was buried alive," replied the Coroner.

"That's a ghastly suggestion, Doctor. How do you know that?" As experienced as he was in these matters, Chief Inspector Sheridon never could find himself getting used to the idea of murder.

Atticus Fingarrison explained. "The evidence of blunt force trauma is indicated by the bruising on the side of the victim's head. Rather an oblong contusion, but not severe enough to cause death."

"Oblong?"

"Yes. It appears that the victim was struck on the side of her head by something hard enough to cause bruising from her temple to the back of her head, just behind her left ear. The depth of the contusion is indicative of a hard enough strike to have caused her to lose consciousness, but not enough to be the cause of death itself. There seems to be no fracture to the skull, although a complete autopsy will have to be conducted to be sure."

"What makes you say, then, that it was death by asphyxia from having been buried alive?" continued the Chief Inspector.

The coroner motioned for the Chief Inspector to look closely at the head of the corpse. "Do you see this hemorrhaging around her eyes and mouth? This is always indicative of asphyxia. In addition to that, there is the fact that she appears to have inhaled some peat from the bog, as I found some in her nostrils and mouth. Again, an autopsy will tell us for certain."

"Dead gruesome, that", said Constable Dickey Olsen from nearby. The inappropriate use of the common expression did not impress itself upon him until Detective Frambley cleared his throat and shot a glance at the portly policeman. Constable Olsen replied, "Beggin' your pardon, gents".

"What's the matter with you?" hissed Frambley, amazed at the lack of sensitivity of his underling. "Good thing you'll be staying here with the body and not going up to the manor house to get his lordship down here."

The corpulent constable could not have agreed more with that sentiment. Although he was only slightly embarrassed at his slip of the tongue, he did not feel up to the task of summoning Sir Clifford Minnington to the scene of what was evidently a crime on his property. Sir Clifford had a reputation in the village for impatience and being possessed of a vituperative spirit. Plus, he was an American. Olsen so preferred avoiding this particular titled gentleman that he was almost happy that he was clumsy in his speech. Suddenly, his lack of panache gave him a certain comfort. The thought that comforted him most at this time of unpleasantness, however, was that his favorite lunch of toast and beans was going to be waiting for him at home.

"No use putting it off," sighed the Chief Inspector. "Come along, Frambley."

A very few minutes later and Chief Inspector Sheridon and the somewhat jittery Detective Frambley were standing at the main doors of Manor Minnington and inquiring of the butler if his lordship were at home. They had driven to the manor house in a police vehicle in the hopes of lending a certain weight to their authority as they prepared to present the bad news to Lord Dogmoor. The Chief Inspector had hoped that the presence of himself as well as a police vehicle, lights and all, would impress Sir Clifford enough to persuade him to control himself.

Snipwhistle dutifully, if a bit doubtfully, ushered the policemen into the foyer and went off in search of his master. He dreaded

the idea of having to be the bearer of unhappy news to his lordship, but took comfort in knowing that the gentlemen from the
Met would receive the lion's share of his wrath. Snippy knocked
on the door of Sir Clifford's den and announced the arrival of the
representative from Scotland Yard.

"Scotland Yard," bellowed his lordship. "What in blazes do
they want, Snippy?"

"It seems there has been some unpleasantness down in the
bog, your lordship, and they need you immediately." As a mere
servant, Snippy would not have been informed of the nature
of the visit by the police, but, servant though he was, Snipwhistle knew trouble when he saw it, especially since he had been
observing what he could from a third floor window all morning.

"The devil, you say," said Sir Clifford. "It's always something
with these local yokels." Apparently, Scotland Yard was not
impressive to our American gentleman. "I'll wager some idiot
was caught poaching rabbits and now they want me to render
judgment! Will these people ever come into the 20th century?" It
was apparent that Sir Clifford still had certain misunderstandings
about the people among whom he had been living for the last
couple of decades. Gathering himself up from behind his enormous oaken desk, Sir Clifford Minnington did his best to mimic
English nobility and strode toward the entrance foyer, his hands
in his dressing gown pockets.

"Murder!" The word had shocked Sir Clifford and he had
repeated it to himself over and over again as he changed into
his overcoat for the trip out of doors. "Murder!" He continued to
repeat it as he was escorted by the policemen to the scene at
the bog. He could not believe it! On his property! Sir Clifford, it
would be safe to say, was flummoxed.

Arriving at the scene of the crime and nodding to the coroner
to remove the blanket from the face of the deceased girl, the
Chief Inspector asked, "Do you know who it is, Sir Clifford?" There
was a hesitation as Sir Clifford looked down at the corpse. "Can
you identify this body for us? And do you know why she might
have turned up dead on your grounds?"

"Identify the body? Are you crazy?" sputtered the lord of
Dogmoor. "I do not have any idea who this is! She does look a

bit familiar, I suppose, but so many of the villagers and townspeople stop and want to shake my hand....she could be anybody!"

Detective Frambley jumped into the conversation, surprising himself. "Yes, of course Chief Inspector. Someone as important as his lordship here couldn't possibly be expected to remember everybody who knows him. Why, he's almost a celebrity in these parts."

"Exactly!" said Sir Clifford, looking at Frambley as though he were the first intelligent Englishman he had met since marrying Opal. "More people know me, I am afraid, than I myself know."

Resisting the urge to roll his eyes, Chief Inspector Sheridon turned to Constable Olsen. "Well, Dickey, you'll need to set about inquiring after missing persons and checking around the village and all of Surrey if need be to identify this young woman."

"Right on it, Chief Inspector," replied Constable Olsen officiously. He rather liked the idea that he would be asking important questions of the townsfolk regarding Manor Minnington, without having to deal directly with his lordship. All in all, it was a satisfying turn of events.

Just then the sound of a motor car caught everyone's attention. A taxi cab was making its way up the winding drive towards the manor house. As it came upon the assembled group of men, police cars, his lordship, and Riley the dog, the taxi came to a stop and out of it stepped Miss Edna Winwood. Surveying the scene, she made straight away to Sir Clifford's side.

"Something dreadful, Miss Winwood," said Sir Clifford in answer to her inquiring stare. "There's been a murder! Right here at Dogmoor!"

"Murder!" Miss Edna could scarcely believe she had heard his lordship correctly, but the body on the gurney assured her that she had.

"Who?"

"Nobody knows," replied Sir Clifford in one of his sweeping generalities that Miss Edna had come to know so well. She turned her attention to the policemen.

"I'm Chief Inspector Thornton Sheridon, ma'am, of Scotland Yard. I am the lead on this case, called in because of the delicacy of having found a dead body on the property of local nobility." (This statement caused Sir Clifford to puff up his chest, a bit pridefully.) "And who might you be, ma'am?"

"I am Edna Winwood, Sir Clifford's personal secretary. Are you sure it's murder, Chief Inspector?"

"No doubt about it, ma'am, but the coroner will have to conduct an autopsy to be certain of the exact cause of death. So far it looks as though the young lady was buried alive in the bog."

Miss Edna blanched at the thought that some poor soul had suffocated in the muck of the bog. However, resolute in her duty to her employer, she continued. "It could not have been an accident then?"

"No, ma'am," answered the coroner himself, this time. "There is evidence of blunt force trauma to the head as well as suffocation in the bog. In fact, ma'am, if you would not mind, could you look at the body to see if you recognize the victim?"

"Don't be preposterous!" injected Sir Clifford, irately. "How could Miss Winwood know any more than I who this poor, unfortunate is?" Sir Clifford had afforded Miss Edna the same veil of ignorance as he had since, after all, she was *his* personal assistant. The fact that Miss Edna had a life outside of Dogmoor had not at this, nor any other, time, occurred to him.

Giving a brief, yet steely, glare in the direction of Sir Clifford, Miss Edna Winwood agreed to view the body of the victim. Her eyes widened instantly in recognition.

"Oh my goodness," she gasped. "It's Dora Finch!"

"Dora Finch, ma'am?" this time it was Detective Frambley who had re-entered the fray. "Are you acquainted with the deceased, ma'am?"

"Yes, of course I am! How else would I have known her name?" Miss Edna's words were not as sharp as the look she shot at the embarrassed detective who cleared his throat and made a note with his pencil.

Chief Inspector Sheridon, himself a bit baffled by the stupidity of the detective's question, inquired further of Miss Winwood. "And how is it that you know the victim, ma'am?"

"She works at the 'Tea Cozy', a public house in London, and is also the closest friend of his lordship's cook, Maggie." His lordship knit his brow, which led the Inspector to believe that now Sir

Clifford may have realized why the girl might have looked familiar after all.

Miss Edna returned her attention to the body. "Poor thing!" she thought to herself as she looked at the pale face, lovely even in death, but marred by the strange bruising on the side of her head. Suddenly, Miss Edna's head jerked up with a quizzical look towards the policemen. "She's missing an earring! The one from the ear on the side of the bruise. Did you notice that?" she asked.

"Yes, ma'am, we did," answered Fingarrison. "We've searched the bog where the body was found, but have found no sign of it so far."

38.

That Saturday afternoon was among the most unpleasant that Miss Edna could ever remember having endured. Her employer was in the foulest mood she had ever seen, and she had seen some pretty foul moods in his lordship. The entire house seemed to feel the tension that emanated from Sir Clifford's office den. He could not take in the reality of the terrible action that had occurred at his home and his anguish was palpable.

Maggie O'Shea, poor thing, had had to go to her room and lie down. She was, understandably, in total shock. Snippy took her a hot cup of tea and some biscuits which he left on her night table, where it all still sat, cold and untouched.

Lady Opal, Miss Edna could not help noticing, was acting in the most peculiar manner of all. After hearing the news, she turned, without saying a word, and went directly to her suite of rooms upstairs. There she remained, occasionally asking of Snippy if he had seen Claudia lately.

Poor Snippy. Not only had he not seen Miss Claudia, but he himself had taken more of the brunt of Sir Clifford's anger and frustration than he had ever before. When bringing him his tea, Sir Clifford had shouted so loudly and angrily that the already shaken butler had dropped the tray and the tea service was destroyed entirely.

As for Claudia, and Roland for that matter, they had not been seen around the manor house all day. Of course, it was a Saturday and they could be out and about anywhere in Surrey or perhaps London. Neither one of them had been observed leaving, however. Besides, it would been extremely unusual for either of them, even the aspiring priest, to be up all that early on a Saturday morning in order to leave and escape detection.

Yes, over all it was one very strange and unusual day at Dogmoor and, with all the tension, stress and misery of the day, work had come to a standstill. Miss Edna stared out of the window of her employer's office whilst he muttered and, occasionally ranted, about why did this have to happen on *his* property and about murder being bad for business. At one point she proffered that "Murder is always convenient for someone," a point that was lost on his lordship. Despite listening to her employer's blather Miss Edna found, to her own befuddlement, that her mind stayed focused on one thing only.

"What could have become of that earring?"

39.

Miss Edna had remained in her employer's office with him throughout the afternoon until it was time for tea. She had excused herself in order to tend to the brewing of the tea, presuming that Maggie would be quite inconsolable still and unable to perform such a simple duty. She was a bit surprised at what she found as she emerged from his lordship's office.

At four o'clock that afternoon the house had began to become alive again. This was of utmost necessity since Lady Opal's nearly forgotten dinner guests would be arriving within the next three hours expecting to be wined and dined in the manner in which they had become accustomed at Manor Minnington. Edna Winwood observed that Lady Minnington had finally emerged from her room only after her daughter had been located and directed to her mother's bedroom straight away by Snipwhistle. Miss Edna could not remember ever having been as impressed at any time previous with the closeness that the mother seemed to have for the daughter, or the daughter for the mother. In fact, before today, they seemed rather to dislike each other. It was a day for all kinds of surprises, as far as Miss Edna Winwood could tell.

Sir Clifford was especially unhappy to have to be hosting one of his wife's gatherings. Generally, he hated them. He hated them, that is, after he tired of playing "lord of the manor" for them. The fact that he was not actually an English lord left him little to fall back on for the rest of an evening once the initial "How do you dos" and "So delighted you could grace us" were over with. After the initial pleasantries, he reverted back to his all too

American, Pittsburgh steel tycoon personality and his affected gentility, which Lady Opal had worked so hard to engender in him, would evaporate with his second martini and his wife would be vexed for the duration of the evening.

Tonight it would prove to be especially difficult for his lordship because of the day's events on his estate. He could not understand why his wife insisted on going through with the damned party. After all, a dead girl had been found in the bog! But Lady Opal, eerily calm after she finally emerged from her bedroom suite, had insisted that the dinner continue as planned. Besides, what could she do? Send out Indian runners to all the guests and inform them of the cancellation? No, the event would proceed as normally as possible.

Upon entering the kitchen Miss Edna turned her attention to Maggie whom, she was again surprised, she found in the kitchen making tea and tending to the produce that would become that evening's salad. Miss Edna, rarely at a loss for words, could only stare in amazement as the formerly distraught cook now very calmly, with the same eerie calm observed in Lady Opal, tended to her galley duties. Miss Edna could not have been more stunned by this rapid recovery if Maggie were all tarted up and had announced plans to seduce the vicar. And if that were not enough, Claudia Minnington was with Maggie, stroking her arm and reassuring her! Claudia, who seemed to think that meals magically appeared and, as far as Edna knew, had not until now even known where the kitchen or pantry were, was actually being kind to the help! Miss Edna Winwood's twitching inner sense began sending off warnings like fire rockets.

The sky darkened with thick grey clouds as the late afternoon turned into evening. Maggie had worked steadily, if a bit dazedly, preparing the various courses. Although Claudia had been in attendance, but had since disappeared, Roland was still nowhere to be seen. However, he was certain to arrive in time for the dinner party. Roland simply could not resist being there; his good looks, charm and plans to become an Anglican priest all contrived to make him the center of attention for the rich old ladies that attended his mother's affairs. It fed his vanity like a drug, and he very much enjoyed the high. There would be no doubt that he would turn up.

Snippy and Maggie eventually brought the salmon which had been provided by Fr. Burns in from the icehouse where it had been stored upon its delivery. Still iced and firm, it appeared to be as fresh as the day it was caught. Maggie needed to let it come to room temperature so that she could fillet it and cook it quickly when it came time to prepare the main dish. It would be served with a simple dill sauce, a favorite of Lady Opal's, right after a clear broth. At room temperature the salmon would be easier to cut and would also cook quickly and evenly, a cooking tip Maggie had been fortunate to learn from the nuns at the orphanage. She often had wondered what Lady Opal would do if one of her dinners were delayed or, worse yet, improperly prepared. This thought had struck her so many times that it seemed almost like an old friend, but for some reason this time it threw her into a fit of hysterical laughter which unnerved Snippy, who had been unfortunate enough to witness it.

Although she was not a guest at any of these dinners, Miss Winwood was permitted to stay and eat in the pantry with the other servants if she had no other plans of her own or if his lordship's workload warranted an overnight stay in order to get an early start the next morning. For this dinner, Miss Edna had elected to stay because her curiosity was aroused and her inner sense was promising an interesting evening ahead. She felt certain that tonight would bring some light to poor Dora's death. That is why, when she'd heard Maggie laughing in the kitchen, she was nearby enough to rush in to see what was the matter.

She found Maggie in a heap on the floor behind the counter, mounded high with salmon fillets. Snipwhistle gave Miss Edna an exasperated look of total bewilderment and seemed to find himself completely immobilized with shock. Miss Edna hurried to Maggie, who had by this time begun to sob dramatically, and knelt down by her side and tried to help her to her feet. A few minutes of coaxing and gentle lifting and Miss Edna was finally able to get Maggie up on her feet.

The two women stood up and Maggie dried her eyes and straightened her apron. As Miss Edna steadied them both by means of the counter next to them, they were both surprised, and somewhat dismayed, to find Lady Opal in the kitchen, in her dressing gown, observing them with sharp eyes and an unreadable expression.

"Is something the matter?" Lady Opal inquired, coolly.

"I'm so sorry, Missus!" said Maggie, quite shaken. "I suppose the news just hit me again. I'll be fine now, thanks to Miss Edna."

"Would you like me to send for Claudia for you again? She, ah, had a tremendously calming effect on you earlier," suggested Lady Opal.

"No, Missus, that won't be necessary," replied Maggie, most emphatically. "Miss Edna and I are about to have a bit of tea and I am sure I'll be fine after that. The dinner is coming along brilliantly."

"Very well," said Lady Opal, after a pause. She regarded Miss Winwood with a very cool look and turned and left the kitchen, presumably to go back to her rooms in order to finish dressing.

"Damn and blast!" Miss Edna caught herself saying the rather masculine expression that had been a favorite of her father's just loud enough to be heard by both Maggie and Snipwhistle. "What was she on about? Why would she be so keen on having Claudia tend to you, my dear? That's unusual enough to make the evening papers!" Miss Edna tried to mask her intense concern with something that she hoped would pass as a witticism.

"I-I don't know," stuttered Maggie. "Let's just have that spot of tea and let me get on with my work." Her manner suggested that she did know, but Miss Edna decided to let it go....for the time being.

40.

How Maggie got that damn dinner together she would never know. For three hours she kept her head bent to her tasks and, with a little help from Snippy and none at all from Miss Claudia, she was right where she needed to be when the guests started arriving at half past 7 o'clock for drinks. Snipwhistle was the perfect picture of an English butler, showing no signs of emotion or the stress of the day in front of the guests as he answered the door and showed them into the drawing room. The same dignified reserve could not be observed in most of the guests.

Nearly everyone that Snippy let through the door was atwitter with gossip about the unhappy events of that morning at Dogmoor. Their excitement generated an electricity in the air and all of them were abuzz, even before the liquor was distributed. Even Verona Walton, the stage actress, seemed to be in the mood for some common gossip. Her presence alone would have been worthy of gossip back in the day. As a stage actress, Miss Walton would, naturally, be unacceptable social company at such a gathering until a rumor went around London that the King was a fan. It seemed that a royal nod could be useful in gaining access to social circles normally closed to certain types of personages. Verona Walton, a somewhat mannish woman, usually behaved quite stuffily at these gatherings as if the aristocracy, to which she now had unprecedented access, was beneath her. She behaved as though she had been knighted by His Majesty rather than simply applauded. Tonight, however, she was almost girlish.

No one was more filled with obvious glee than Elinor Drumville. Her outward appearance, its usual quiet demur, was betrayed by the positively alive watery blue eyes which danced in her head as she went about the room greeting the other guests. Owen Corwinton actually asked her if she had done something with her hair, she looked that different. And Elinor could not remember a time that she felt more alive as she glanced around the room to see if all the regular attendees had arrived. As of yet, they had not, at least the one in particular that Elinor was eager to see.

Snipwhistle had just offered a libation to the latest guest to arrive when Lady Opal and Sir Clifford entered the room. Lady Opal was elegant in a beige evening gown with delicate sapphire earrings and necklace. Sir Clifford was in his usual dark blue business suit and was looking even less enthused than usual at one of these affairs. As they entered the room to greet their guests everyone there practically swarmed them in order to be the first to express condolences and to try to glean a bit of news from them. Only Elinor settled comfortably instead into the chair she had chosen. She would wait to share her obsequies with her hostess until a more opportune time and, although she relished the thought of reminding her ladyship of their afternoon together the other day, Miss Drumville had a bigger prize in mind for that evening.

Trays of martinis and sidecars made their way around the room several times. Poor Snippy could scarcely keep up with the guests as they excitedly imbibed and gossiped. The art of cocktailing before dinner had been introduced to Dogmoor by Sir Clifford who, upon arriving in England so many years ago, could not comprehend why no one in his new country knew what a cocktail was. The Minningtons social circle caught on to the singularly American tradition straight away and all the Minnington dinner parties were preceded by drinks and nibbles. It was amazing how much more freely conversation flowed after the drinks were poured. The "cocktail hour" catapulted the parties at Manor Minnington into a reputation for their gaiety and charm. And it was, after all, free for the taking.

Lady Opal made her way around the room chit chatting with her guests, her arm uncharacteristically entwined with that of her husband. Normally the two separated and Lady Opal played the grand hostess of the manor and Sir Clifford talked business with anybody there that he thought might be interested. Tonight, however, Mrs. Minnington seemed reluctant to let Mr. Minnington go far from her side. She seemed, quite literally, to be leaning on him. Most of the guests understood why, or at least thought they did. After such an ordeal it would only be natural for a wife to want the support of her husband. A general swell of sympathy filled the room. This groundswell of goodwill toward them lasted right up until the Minningtons got to Miss Elinor Drumville.

Elinor had been sitting and holding court in a corner of the room as she always did; her eyes were bright and alive but her conversation was conservative and reserved. This was certainly not the Elinor that everyone knew and, well, knew. Usually under circumstances such as this Miss Drumville would be buzzing like a bee in clover trying to gather and spread as much information, or misinformation, as the case may be, as she could.

Tonight, however, Elinor seemed to be waiting for something, more like a lioness hiding in the savannah grass. She smiled her most indulgent smile at each person who came by her to wish her a good evening and inquire as to her health, but she spoke not a word about the unfortunate occasion of the morning. Her eyes seemed to be saying a lot, but no one was sure what they were saying nor did anyone linger long enough to find out.

This was the posture she maintained until Lord and Lady Minnington made their way to where she sat. Wide eyed with innocence, Elinor accepted the personal welcome and greetings from her hosts and returned the salutations. Everyone in the room, it seemed, had quieted down and was trying to see without being seen trying to see, what might transpire in Elinor's corner. They were not disappointed.

After the initial exchange of greetings Elinor's eyes returned to their shifty and, therefore, more familiar look, shiftier than most had ever seen, in fact. Her mouth curled up in what might be called a smile and she asked in a voice dripping with faux innocence, "Is it true that the body found here today was that of Dora Finch, the maid at the 'Tea Cozy'? And isn't she, or should I say wasn't she, a friend of your cook?" Something in the way she asked that question, the way her voice almost seemed to be cooing, suggested to everyone else in the drawing room that it was time to start paying more attention, whether they were caught at it or not. In doing so they saw Lady Opal go pale, so much so that her complexion clashed with her dress. Many decided that it was time for another cocktail as they anticipated the show that was surely about to begin.

Elinor smiled a very contented smile, for she knew she had struck home with Lady Opal. Suddenly, the doorbell rang and everyone's attention was shifted from the drama brewing in the parlor to see who the late arrival was. The familiar and jocular voice of Sir Oswald Bunbarrel filtered into the drawing room. It seemed to momentarily break the tension that had gathered in the room like moss, until Corwin Owenton jabbed Clive Wright in the ribs and pointed towards Elinor. If it were possible, her smile had taken on an even more smugly sinister look.

41.

"She hates that old sod, you know," said Clive to Corwin, quietly as he pretended to sip his sidecar.

"For heaven's sake, everybody in London knows that they can't stand each other," replied Corwin to Clive, pretending the same with his martini. Indeed, everybody in London, it seemed, did know about the feud between the two and they knew how it originated.

"'Hell hath no fury'" quoted Clive.

"Yes, but even for a woman scorned, old Elinor has gone over the top. She looks as though she's about to drink the old goat's blood!" remarked Corwin. "Just look at that expression, would you?"

Indeed, old Elinor's eyes, lively with excitement as they had been upon her arrival, were now cold and hard, set in two narrow slits. Their watery blue had become ice and, set as they were above a grin that would have sent shivers down a ghoul's spine, they portended a confrontation of monumental proportions. Everyone in the room did as Corwin and Clive. They froze over their drinks and waited to see what would transpire between the two old adversaries.

Sir Oswald sounded his jolly self as he entered the drawing room and allowed himself a drink from Snipwhistle, whom he thanked, as was his gracious custom. He greeted the Minningtons with a somewhat sympathetic expression of "damn rotten luck" and continued making his rounds among the guests in the room. Following his employer into the room was Jasper Dunwoody, Sir Oswald's extremely handsome personal secretary. Elinor took a sharp intake of breath and one did not have the impression that it was because she also found Jasper to be so good looking. Even the Minningtons *both* froze when he walked in, being as he was a servant and not an invited guest. The other guests, their eyes fixed on Elinor, did not even consider the breach of etiquette because everyone in attendance now knew what the theme of the night's drama would be.

"The old rascal brought *him* with him tonight. That's odd for one of these occasions, isn't it?" This time it was Verona Walton whispering to Corwin over her cocktail. Her attempt to smile coyly in Jasper's direction gave Corwin the distinct impression that she might have fancied him. Her overall mannish appearance, however, gave Corwin pause, but he checked himself of the unflattering remark that was forming in his head. Instead, he simply nodded in agreement with her observation.

Unavoidable as death and paying taxes to the crown, Sir Oswald Bunbarrel eventually made his way to Elinor's seat and gave her a curt bow.

"Good evening, Elinor. You're looking as lovely as I've ever seen you," he said, employing one of his favorite insults on his elderly nemesis.

Elinor did not flinch. "Yes, Sir Oswald. And I cannot tell you how absolutely delighted I am to see you here this evening," the tone of her response sounding at once sincere and, therefore, foreboding.

The air in the room was fairly crackling with the electricity of the moment. Each and every guest there had heard this exact same exchange between the two old enemies innumerable times. They were familiar old barbs from familiar old warriors. This evening, however, not a soul failed to notice that Elinor seemed to be expressing genuine delight at seeing Sir Oswald and each soul wondered what specific delight lay behind those cold, steely blue eyes which were riveted to the old gentleman. All other eyes were riveted on the two of them, as though they were two boxers about to commence a match or, more appropriately perhaps, two swordsmen about to thrust at one another.

Himself aware of something different in Elinor's demeanor, Sir Oswald attempted to deflect what appeared to be an impending blow by dismissing her altogether and turned to someone else in the party and continued to exchange pleasantries. Elinor watched him for a few minutes, as though she were waiting for the right moment to strike, the perfect timing to jerk the gaff to hook her fish. Snippy was beside himself trying to keep up with drink requests.

"Sir Oswald?" The voice was artificially sweet and held the hint of something deadly, like some exotic poison.

Sir Oswald stopped still in his place, knowing that something was coming. How many times had the two of them gone around with each other in public gatherings, so often in that very room? His contempt for her was real, as it usually was, when he turned to her and replied "Yes, *Miss* Drumville?" He knew that emphasizing her status as an old maid would rankle her. Everyone else in the room knew it, too.

History was made when Elinor seemed not to notice at all! Her eyes, still narrow, still cold, and still focused on Sir Oswald grew narrower and colder still as she leaned slightly forward in her chair, her hands resting on her cane. Snippy snuck a sip.

"How many of the Minningtons' affairs have you been to and tonight you finally bring one of your own with you?"

So that was it. She was going to bring something out in the open that nobody in polite society had before, even though it was hardly news to anyone. Queen Victoria had left that gift to her subjects, at least the upper classes. Private business is just that, private. Of course, in the judgment of many of the assembled guests, by bringing Jasper Dunwoody with him, Sir Oswald had left himself open to whatever may come. It seemed terribly out of character for him to flaunt his current secretary at a social event such as this. All of the guests, both of the hosts, one extraordinarily handsome young man, and one servant waited with bated breath to see what would happen next.

"Whatever do you mean, Elinor?" Sir Oswald sounded nonchalant.

"I mean, Sir Oswald, that I find it distasteful of you to flaunt your indiscretions in polite company," came the reply, chilled and even.

The old gentleman was unmoved, even if Jasper appeared flushed. Sir Oswald appeared to be more interested in the dish full of cashews before him. "I find it hard to believe, *Miss* Drumville, that you would imagine yourself as being able to recognize an indiscretion, never having had the pleasure of one of your own."

Clive, Corwin and two or three other gentlemen present all seemed to develop a slight cough at the very same time.

"Really now, Sir Oswald," Elinor's tone seemed to chide her old foe and erstwhile object of affection. "The subject of whether or not I have enjoyed such things is rather irrelevant since I have always believed that what belongs behind closed doors should stay behind them. What *is* hard for me to imagine is that you would bring your *young man* here to the manor house as though it were an East End pub." One could almost hear the quotation marks around "*young man*" as she said it. She remained quite unperturbed and her gaze, steady.

In a room that was most unnaturally quiet considering how many people were in it, Sir Oswald briefly regarded Elinor before deciding what to say next. Though he was aware that rumors had circulated about him for years, it was true that no one had ever brought up the question of his sexual orientation publicly before this. It did begin to appear that bringing Jasper with him had been a mistake, even though Jasper truly was only his personal secretary. There had never been anything else between them, contrary to whatever whoever might have thought. Sir Oswald had only brought him along because he had heard of the death of the Finch girl and knew that Jasper had a friend who had been somewhat close to her. Finally, he spoke.

"Mr. Dunwoody is my personal secretary and only my personal secretary," he said, beginning softly but slowly building to a crescendo. "And just because there happens to be a handsome young man in my life currently is no reason to unleash your insanely jealous fantasies since there is not now, nor has there ever been, one in yours, you contemptible bag of bile!"

Elinor choked back the anger rising within her. "Heaven only knows what you people are capable of, with so much to hide," she insinuated, hinting broadly and hoping that someone might find reason to be suspicious enough of these perverse and unnatural beasts to connect them, however tenuously, to the death of the young woman.

Sir Oswald's response was quick and did not leave much time for the dropped hint to be picked up. "Don't bring Heaven into this, you old witch, or I shall be forced to summon the local vicar to shrivel you up with a blessing!"

"In *my* Bible what you and your kind do is called an abomination!" spat Elinor, losing her composure at last.

"In any book, madam, you would be an abomination!" Sir Oswald, as it happened, delivered the final line of the melodrama.

Snipwhistle, who had discretely left the room, rang the curtain down, much to the relief of the audience, by announcing that dinner was ready to be served. Lord and Lady Dogmoor led the procession of guests into the dining room. Snippy collected glasses and with one last glare at Bunbarrel, and nary a glance at Jasper Dunwoody, Elinor, bringing up the rear flank, followed the others into dinner.

42.

Miss Edna Winwood sat in the kitchen with Maggie O'Shea doing her best to console her and simultaneously to question her about her friend without being insensitive or intrusive. The last couple of hours had provided Maggie with enough work in preparing for the dinner party to have kept her mind occupied, although she felt as though she were in a fog, at best. Now that the guests had arrived and were being seated, the greater portion of her work was finished. All that was left was for her to see to it that Fr. Burn's salmon was cooked and served in its proper time. This period of lessened activity allowed Miss Edna the opportunity to spend some time with the distraught young cook.

Unfortunately, the seemingly constant interruptions from Snip-whistle had hampered her efforts. Every time that she thought she might have reached the perfect moment to broach the subject of Dora Finch, the butler would rush in from his pantry and give a report on the happenings in the front of the house. It appeared that there was a battle of epic proportions being waged between Sir Oswald and his ancient adversary, Miss Elinor Drumville. And while Miss Edna could not admit to being unin-terested in those proceedings, especially with the addition of Mr. Jasper Dunwoody in the mix, her primary goal for the time being was to try to get information out of Maggie. A lesser person would have been torn between the two ends, but Miss Edna was much more disciplined than the lesser personages of the world. So, after each interruption, she would quietly tuck the informa-tion away, for future consideration, and single mindedly turn her attention once again to Maggie O'Shea.

This alone had been a vexing proposition since Maggie was both in shock and busy with the details of a Minnington dinner party. However, Miss Edna persisted and, through her combined efforts at comforting and soliciting information, she was able to coax some details out of the haggard Irish lass.

"Really, Miss Edna," said Maggie as she pulled the salmon out from under the broiler and began transferring it onto the serving platter. "I am truly grateful for the kindness you're showin' me and the interest you have in poor Dora, but I really don't know what more I can tell you."

"Yes, dear, I can only guess at how difficult this is for you," replied Miss Winwood soothingly. "She was, I understand, your closest friend since childhood days at an orphanage in Ireland?" Miss Edna did not know why, but that fact seemed important.

"Yes ma'am, that is true enough. We've been friends since we were barely out of nappies it seems. After we each left St. Saviour's and went our separate ways with our adoptive parents, it seemed a miracle that we should turn up together again, decide to move to England, and end up living so close to each other. 'Twas a blessin' indeed." A tear welled up in one of Maggie's green eyes and rolled down her freckled cheek.

Poor thing, thought Miss Edna. "She was so quiet here and at the 'Tea Cozy'. I wonder, was she a happy girl?" Miss Edna hoped she did not sound too leading.

"Ah, sure'n she was a quiet and proper young lady but I would have to say that for the most part she was happy. We had many good times together. Of course, there were the natural sadnesses that we girls suffer through now and again," came the reply.

"Any recent sadness in her life that you would like to tell me about?" urged Miss Edna, ever so gently.

"Well," began Maggie, "Fr. Burns' visit did concern her at first. She wondered why he'd be coming all the way from Ireland to see us. But sure'n that turned out to be good news. I received a bit of an inheritance, as you know."

"Yes and how very nice that is for you!" Miss Edna hoped to encourage more conversation.

"Then there was a great disappointment with a young man she was interested in." Maggie seemed embarrassed to go on.

Although she already knew, Miss Edna gently prodded Maggie for more. "What disappointment, dear?"

Maggie paused a moment, considering her answer. "Let's just say, ma'am, that Dora wasn't the type he was interested in."

"I see," Miss Winwood said thoughtfully. "Did she have an argument with him over it, do you suppose?" She was fishing. A lover's spat, especially under the circumstances presented by Mr. Randiffle's true persuasion, could possibly produce murder, was her primary suspicion.

"Oh no, ma'am! Most emphatically no!" responded Maggie. "Dora may have been one of the poorer class, but she was much too fine a person for that. No, ma'am. She was very upset by it, of course, what girl wouldn't be? But she never confronted the young man a'tall a'tall."

"No, of course not," Miss Edna agreed consolingly. "She was a fine young woman, wasn't she?" The question was rhetorical and Maggie understood it so.

They sat quietly for a few minutes while Maggie poured the dill sauce over the salmon and set it in the window to the butler's pantry, where Snippy picked it up and took it out to be served. As the butler attended to the masters of the house and their guests, Maggie and Miss Edna prepared to eat their portion of the meal. Maggie had reserved a few portions of salmon for themselves, the ones that did not quite look up to snuff for her ladyship's table. "Sure'n there's nothing wrong with them," reasoned Maggie, so she had cooked them up for the staff to enjoy. She kept Snipwhistle's in a warming oven, hoping that he would be able to get to it before it over cooked too much.

Just as the two women were prepared to start their dinners, in popped, to their complete surprise, Elinor Drumville. Her cunning eyes roved about the kitchen and when she was satisfied as to its occupancy she smiled her infamous smile and entered the room.

"My dear Cook," she purred. "I just had to stop in and tell you how superb everything is so far. I cannot wait to get back to the main course. I am certain it will be wonderful."

Miss Edna looked crossly perplexed. "Why aren't you in there right now enjoying it then?" she asked.

"Age, my pet, has many disadvantages." Miss Edna hated being called "pet". Elinor continued. "I simply had to use the powder room. I suppose the excitement of the evening got to my system. Either that or the unsavory company foisted upon us by that old goat, Bunbarrel." Here she looked expectantly at Maggie, as though she thought there might be some sort of sympathetic reply to that remark from the pretty Irish girl, friend of the deceased.

Looks like old Elinor is fishing in my pond, mused Miss Winwood to herself. With a quick look at Maggie, she came to the rescue. "We are simple servants, Miss Drumville, and have been privy to neither the excitement nor the guest list," Miss Edna lied. "But I do know that Maggie has prepared a spectacular salmon dish with dill sauce that is simply ravishing to look at. I cannot begin to imagine how it will taste, until, of course, I taste it. Yours will be getting cold."

Elinor regarded Miss Edna with the cold stare of what was left of her dignity and, giving a slight nod to the two of them, returned to the dining room.

"The old biddy," said Maggie. "Thanks for fending her off me, Miss Edna."

"Oh, believe me, it was my pleasure." This time Miss Edna was completely and singularly sincere.

The two of them smiled at their small triumph and started in on what was, indeed, a delicious dinner. The asparagus was perfectly crisp, the potatoes silkily smooth (Mr. Minnington loved his mashed potatoes) and the salmon, even these lesser specimens from Fr. Burns' ice chest, were scrumptious.

The conversation turned light, mostly remarking on the good food and the good fortune that Maggie had found in the visit from the Irish priest. Who would have thought that she would have come into money from her adoptive family? What was she planning? She was not sure. And so on and so on.

Miss Edna was thoroughly enjoying the dinner and the company when, suddenly, she bit down on something very hard in her salmon. The surprised look on her face caused Maggie concern; she thought maybe something was wrong with that piece after all.

Waving away the cook's concern, Miss Edna, as delicately as possible, removed the offending object into her napkin.

The two women bent over and peered at the mysterious object. "Is it a fish bone?" asked Maggie fearfully.

"No, I don't think so," replied Edna. Cleaning it off the best she could with her napkin, she realized that it was, of all things, a small gold loop with a diamond on it. A woman's earring.

"How did that get in a piece of salmon?" asked Miss Edna of Maggie O'Shea. "Are the leprechauns feeding the fish gold and diamonds in County Cork?"

Maggie's mouth hung open and her face was pale as pale could be. "What is it child?" Miss Edna inquired urgently.

"That earring, ma'am! It's Dora's! She was wearing that pair when she was here just the other day. It was her favorite pair. They were the only things she got of any value from her adoptive family, the rotters."

The two women looked at each other in wonderment and then back at the earring in Miss Edna's napkin. Her twitching inner sense was getting stronger with sensations of foreboding.

Part V

43.

The sun shone brightly once again on Sunday morning. The November air responded to the sun's rays by warming itself up a bit. Those citizens who were religious and had aroused themselves for church remarked to each other that it seemed like a spring morning rather than one so close to winter. Even the birds appeared to enjoy the sun and their singing added to the seemingly spring-like feeling. It was looking to be a simply lovely day.

Miss Edna Winwood was not a religious person and had not aroused herself early in order to attend church. It was not that she had anything against religion. She enjoyed going to church, in fact. However, she only enjoyed going to church when nobody else was there. She preferred the quiet, peaceful calm of an empty church to the noisy distractions of a Sunday service.

Miss Edna was also not noticing the weather. The bright and beautiful morning had gone practically unnoticed by her. By the time she had finished her morning toilet and put the kettle on for tea, the morning had warmed significantly because, by then, it was after ten o'clock.

It was not like Miss Edna to sleep so late, even on a Sunday. But she had been up late the night before at Manor Minnington. The police had had to be summoned, naturally, upon the discovery of the earring. By the time the Chief Inspector arrived at Dogmoor with his assistant detective in tow and had questioned the entire party—which Miss Edna had not seen the need for; she was, after all, the one with earring in her salmon—and had satisfied himself that nobody knew anything helpful, it was well after midnight. Detective Frambley had been given the duty of securing the earring as evidence and, after one last reassurance from Maggie that she was absolutely certain that she had seen Dora wearing that earring on the last day she had seen her, they left the stunned society circle to wind itself down and take its leave of Manor Minnington. Nobody had even been in the mood for dessert.

As she waited for her kettle to boil, Miss Edna ruminated on the events of the previous evening. For some reason she found herself irked at the remarks made by Elinor Drumville. Miss Edna, who considered herself a very well mannered lady, had always believed in minding her own business and that whatever Sir Oswald or anybody else did in private was his own affair. But it was more than Elinor's aspersions that were worrying Miss Edna this morning. It was her intrusion into the kitchen during dinner. "That old cow thinks she knows something," thought Miss Edna, with an admittedly unladylike reference to Miss Drumville.

Far and away the most interesting event of the evening had been a comment made by Detective Frambley which had apparently been unwelcome by Chief Inspector Sheridon. Upon examining the earring and the salmon from which it came, the two policemen had consulted each other and had remarked that "one had been missing" from the dead girl, a fact that Miss Edna had herself pointed out on the morning the body was discovered. As they had examined the salmon itself, the detective made an observation about how the shape of the bruise would fit the shape of the fish. The Chief Inspector, realizing that the remark had been overheard by Maggie, Edna and Sir Clifford—who had accompanied the policemen throughout the investigation in his house—shot Detective Frambley a withering glance that said "Shut up, you idiot."

This exchange had brought an end to the questioning. Nothing further had been asked, nothing further had been proffered.

Chief Inspector Thornton Sheridon and Detective Frambley left and the guests departed soon after. Maggie was so upset that Sir Clifford sent her to her room and allowed that the kitchen and dining room could wait until the next day. He also offered Miss Edna the use of her room, considering the lateness of the hour, but she had decided that she wanted to return to her own flat. In an unusually compassionate gesture, Sir Clifford had offered her his own car, rather than try to call a taxi into Surrey at midnight. Miss Edna, who could not drive, declined her employer's gracious offer but did accept the offer of a ride into London with Corwin Owenton. Frankly, she would have rather hired a taxi. She knew that Mr. Owenton would want to rehash the events of the entire evening on the way. It had been, after all, one of the Minningtons more colorful gatherings. But she managed to fend off the incessant chatter of her Good Samaritan by pretending to be a much too distressed female to engage in conversation. What she had wanted was time to think.

She stifled a bit of a yawn as she poured the water over the tea bag in the little Brown Betty she used to brew her tea. When she had finally gotten to bed she had not slept much at all, only in snatches, for her mind was wrapped around the mystery of that earring in the fish. As her tea was steeping she yawned again and realized how unaccustomed she was to such late hours. She much preferred to go to bed early in order to be up early and refreshed and ready for the day ahead of her. Facing the prospect of a day wasted with weariness, she suddenly got the idea that she should go to the "Tea Cozy" for a bite to eat. For some reason, as soon as she thought of it, she felt a surge of energy. She drank her tea as she dressed and made herself presentable and, by eleven o'clock, was on her way.

The public house was fairly quiet when she arrived. The several customers there were mostly elderly and single, although there was one young couple enjoying their Sunday morning at a table by the window. Miss Edna surveyed the dining room and chose a table that would put her in easy proximity of the hostess' station so that she might keep up some conversation in the event that business were to pick up and keep her too busy to linger for conversation. Petal Chalmers, looking less effusive than she

normally did, took on a positively maudlin look when she recognized Miss Edna as she settled herself into her table. She had, in
the past couple of days after Dora last was at the "Tea Cozy",
come to find out that Miss Edna was a lady of importance and
that she had an important connection to the Minningtons. She
hurried over to where she was seated, happy to see that the table
she had chosen, while it was not the best table in the house, it
was in near to her hostess stand.

As she placed her order for tea and scones, Miss Edna had
the sense that Miss Chalmers was eager to discuss these recent,
sorry events. Not in the sense of a sinner who is eager to confess
his sins, nor even in the sense of a busybody who thrives on gossip, but in the sense of someone who is desperate to inject herself into the thrill of the tragedy. Miss Edna could not help herself
thinking that. She did chide herself for her cynical view of human
emotions; after all, Petal Chalmers had befriended young Dora
and undoubtedly had feelings for her as an employee. However, Miss Edna could not divest herself of the notion that Petal
was more intrigued than grieved. The impression that she gave
overall was one not unlike the melodramatic performances of
actresses in the silent pictures that Miss Edna remembered fondly
from her youth.

The unfortunate truth was that Miss Edna was not far wrong
when it came to this assessment of Petal Chalmers. She was,
indeed, a woman of dramatic emotional swings. As proprietress
of the "Tea Cozy" she could be, for her customers, the gushingly
happy hostess one moment and, minutes later for Dublin Joe,
a sharp tongued harpy or wounded queen, depending on the
circumstances. Over the years, old Joe Shannon had become so
accustomed to the range of his lady love's emotional gambits
that he hardly noticed them any longer. The ordinary customer
was not usually subject to the darker side of Petal's moods, but,
then, Miss Edna Winwood was by no means an ordinary customer.

Edna Winwood let her mind wander away from her hostess after she had placed her order for tea and scones and was
momentarily left alone. "She'll be back soon enough," mused
Miss Edna, knowing that she could not have rid herself of Petal's
desire to talk about the murder of Dora Finch even if she had

wanted to and was equally aware that she had not wanted to. This was, after all, the precise reason why she had wanted to come to the "Tea Cozy" in the first place.

As she awaited Petal's return, two issues seemed to preoccupy her thoughts. The first was the earring in the salmon. How in the world could a dead girl's earring get into a piece of fish? One could understand if it had been the cook's earring. Accidents like that, though unpleasant for the one dining to consider, do happen. But it was difficult to imagine the accident that would drop Dora Finch's earring into a salmon. It had been sent from Ireland having been caught fresh in the morning, iced to just below the point of being frozen, expressed to Manor Minnington in an heroically expeditious effort, and been placed immediately in the estate's ice house. This had been to guarantee its freshness and had enabled Maggie to make use of the gastronomic windfall for the dinner party that had been planned for the following Saturday. Swimming happily off the coast of Ireland before dawn, dead and nearly frozen in an ice house in Britain by late that afternoon: it seemed a Herculean effort, at the least.

Miss Edna was amazed at the coincidence of that happenstance alone. Fr. Burns had indeed gone to a great deal of trouble to ship a trunk full of fish to Surrey. Could he have had *that* much affection for the two girls? Or had something else motivated him to make such a dramatic gesture? This seemed, to Miss Edna's growing suspicions, more like an attempt to make up for something for which someone might feel terribly guilty, some dreadful faux paux, perhaps. She wondered what it might have been. Might it have had something to do with Lady Opal and the strange reaction he had when he learned of Dora having visited there? It was intriguing, but what possible connection could Opal Minnington, English aristocrat, have with an old Irish Roman Catholic priest from County Cork?

The other issue that occupied her thoughts was the offhanded reference to the bruising on the corpse that she had heard Detective Frambley make to the Chief Inspector and which was followed immediately by a rebuking glance from Sheridon. The fact that the detective seemed very embarrassed at his slip up only added to her feeling that the remark was of some significance. Something about the bruising was obviously relevant to the fact that Dora's earring was found in a piece of salmon. There was only one obvious conclusion to be reached, thought Miss Edna. "Could the police think that a piece of fish is the murder weapon?" The thought was too bizarre even to consider, but what else could it be? The pieces fit, but it was insane. There was nothing about it that made sense outside of a low comedy sketch. Miss Edna was perplexed by the whole thing because, of course, there was nothing funny about the death of a young woman.

Her thoughts were interrupted by the delivery of her order. Normally, Miss Edna would have discouraged conversation with the lingering hostess while she tried to eat, but today she happily encouraged Petal Chalmers to remain tableside to share her "grief". This was easy enough to do since Petal showed no hurry to leave her guest alone after placing the tea and scones on the table. She stood there with her tray, made a soft sobbing sound, and gave a forlorn look in Miss Edna's direction.

Realizing that she would not have to be too crafty to get Petal to talk, Miss Edna simply asked "How are you, dear?" Her assessment had been correct. Petal Chalmers did everything but sit down with her and began to pour out her troubles to her distinguished customer.

"Oh, Miss Winwood," began Petal, "I cannot *begin* to tell you how awful I feel about all this!" (Miss Winwood suppressed the urge to smirk for it was fairly obvious that she *could* begin.) "It's all I can do to get my work done. Joe and I have been struggling for two days with our grief over Dora's death."

Miss Edna stole a quick glance in the direction of the bar and did not notice anything particularly grief-stricken about Dublin Joe Shannon. "Then again, he is Irish," she thought. "They are used to this type of thing." She wondered why she had given vent to such a bigoted thought. Perhaps some of her employer's bad habits were rubbing off on her.

"I rue the day that young Mr. Minnington came in here, if you'll pardon me for saying so," continued Petal. At the mention of her employer's only son Miss Edna was drawn back to the hostess' conversation. She had been right about Petal Chalmers; she was going to be very eager to tell all she knew.

"I do not mind you saying so," said Miss Edna in her most soothing tone. "Just exactly what happened when he was here?" She had heard or, more properly, overheard, the story a couple of days ago, but she wanted to hear Petal's version. She was worried that the young heir might somehow be involved in all this but, for the life of her, she could not understand why he would want Dora Finch dead.

The invitation to speak was all that Petal needed to launch into a very long and detailed, somewhat melodramatic at times, account of how Roland Minnington had "sat at that table right over there and spilled the beans" about the terrible secret hidden from Dora by her young man.

Unfortunately for Miss Edna, the mention of Erskine's dirty little secret had launched Petal off onto a diatribe about homosexuality and how she "just couldn't understand *those* people"—a sentiment that was totally irrelevant to Miss Edna's purpose at the moment. She tried to think of a way to bring the conversation back to her intended topic but, uncanny as it may seem, the entrance bell rang just then. Miss Edna, who was happy for the distraction, could scarcely believe her eyes when she saw who walked in the door. She must have had quite an expression of surprise on her face because even Petal noticed it and paused long enough to see what might be the occasion of such a wide eyed look from the normally cool and collected lady at her table. She turned in the direction of Miss Edna's stare and was herself dumbfounded to see none other than Erskine Randiffle standing just inside the door.

Before either woman could overcome her surprise Erskine came directly to Miss Edna's table and asked if he might speak to her in private. There was such a pleading urgency in his voice that Petal, without needing to be asked, gave them both a nod of her head and unwillingly retreated into the kitchen. Miss Edna motioned with her own head for Mr. Randiffle to be seated. With a look of relief on his handsome face that was almost heartbreaking, Erskine hung up his coat, which he had carried in, not really needing it on such a nice day, and sat down.

"Shall we order you some tea, young man?" Miss Edna was solicitous because she was hoping for some information, as well as being moved, of course, by his apparent exasperation.

"No, thank you," replied Erskine. "I wanted to talk to you if you would be kind enough to listen to what I have to say. I do not know who else I could speak to about this and am not entirely sure why I would want to speak to you about it. But I saw you in here the other day and have the feeling that you overheard the unpleasant encounter between the hostess and me. Plus, you are Lord Minnington's personal secretary and I am gambling on the hope that I might be able to trust you. I feel an uncomfortable need to explain things to someone who will listen with an unbiased ear."

In addition to being elated over just such a happy coincidence as this, Miss Edna also took note of the young man's use of "Lord Minnington". She did not often hear it stated so formally, her employer preferring the use of his first name. However, she did not let herself be distracted by that amusement. She most definitely wanted to hear what he had to say about Dora and whatever he might divulge about his involvement with her in her last hours.

"Of course you can trust me, Mr. Randiffle. Do calm down and have some tea." Miss Edna motioned to Petal, who had taken a position at the kitchen door to try to spy discreetly on what was transpiring, to bring more tea.

"You know my name?" Erskine was surprised and perplexed at the same time. He did not see it as a good omen that Lord Dogmoor's secretary should know who he was. It especially concerned him since the body of an acquaintance of his had been found on his lordship's estate.

Recognizing the anxiety in him, Miss Edna considered the best way to proceed with her inquiry in order to produce the best results. She decided to just be herself and take her customarily direct approach. "Please, calm yourself," she said with an air of casual authority. "I do know your name and who you are. I am afraid to tell you that certain aspects of your private life are no longer private, thanks to circumstances and wagging tongues." At that precise moment, Petal delivered the extra cup and a bigger pot of tea. This time Miss Edna did not suppress her urge smile, considering the irony of the moment.

When the two of them were alone at the table once again, she looked young Erskine directly in the eyes and asked, "What is it that you wished to see me about?"

Her direct approach seemed to have been the right choice, for in no time Erskine Randiffle was confessing to Miss Edna those "certain aspects" of his private life. By the time she had finished consuming a scone and a cup of tea he had recounted the events of the previous evening's party, as he had been told them by Jasper, and admitted that he could not have had anything to do with Dora's death because he had spent the entire of Thursday night at Jasper's flat. "As soon as I left here I whistled for a taxi and went to find Jasper. I needed his advice. I was afraid for my position at the firm. As it turns out, I spent the night with him", he blushed. "In fact," he went on, "I was at Jasper's flat again all last night. We needed each other," he blushed again as he said it.

Her interior sense told Miss Edna that she was hearing the truth from the young man. Although she had not really considered Erskine Randiffle as a serious suspect in her musings about the crime—he had not really even entered her mind until this moment—she could see why he would be a prime candidate with the police. The need to hide his secret from the world and from his employer, the disappointment undoubtedly felt by Dora, the possibility that she could make trouble for him to spite him (although that seemed unlikely from a girl like Dora)—all these things could be counted against the young man.

Her inner sense may have assured her that he was sincere but it also kept up a nagging twitch that there was more to gain from this conversation. She decided to broach the subject of Roland Minnington and why he might have done what he did in regard to Dora and her affection for Erskine. She did this with some trepidation for if his lordship ever found out that she had been asking these types of questions about his son in such an unsavory set of circumstances she might find herself looking for a new employer. Still, her natural curiosity pushed her out further on the proverbial limb.

"Tell me, Mr. Randiffle, what possible reason could Roland Minnington have for exposing your secret to Dora Finch?"

Erskine's face turned crimson with anger at the mention of Roland Minnington's name. He took a sip of his tea, as if to collect his thoughts, and finally simply stated, "It was business."

Though she was not expecting any particular answer to her question, this was certainly the least likely one she might have. "What do you mean, 'business'?" Miss Edna could barely conceal her surprise.

Erskine opened his mouth to reply and then, suddenly, seemed to have thought better of it. "Miss Winwood," he said instead, "would you care to wait here while I go fetch Mr. Dunwoody? I think this is something that you should hear from him. It would also be an opportunity for him to confirm my whereabouts on the night Dora died. He lives only a bit from here. I could be back within half an hour. Would you please consider waiting?" His tone was imploring.

Miss Edna, who in her own heart knew that nothing short of war or pestilence could cause her to budge at that moment, nodded in quiet acquiescence to Erskine's request.

"Oh, *thank you!*" he said effusively and hurriedly departed from the pub.

Petal Chalmers was already on her way back to Miss Edna's table even as she watched Erskine's back go out the door. This time, however, she would not find her customer in the mood to chat. This fact would not be clear to Petal immediately because her own curiosity about what the two of them had conversed about was nearly maddening. With a manner full of hope for more, Petal approached Miss Edna and asked, "Can I get you anything else?"

Edna Winwood sat for a brief moment; her expression hard to read at first. Then she turned calmly to the hostess and replied, "Yes, I am hungrier than I realized and would like to have a full English breakfast, if that is at all convenient."

"Why, yes, ma'am, of course," came the reply. Petal had not expected that!

"Oh, and since I will be here for a while longer than I expected, and since it will take you some time in the kitchen to prepare my breakfast, might it be at all possible for you to pop down to the newsstand straight away and get me the 'Sunday Times'? I always read the 'Times' on Sunday while I breakfast. I realize that this is a terrible imposition on your good nature and hospitality, but it doesn't seem to be terribly busy in here right now, does it my dear?"

A completely surprised Petal Chalmers, mouth agape, simply nodded to her customer and, taking a quick look around the pub to make sure that no one needed anything for the next few minutes and after telling Joe where she was going and why, she put on her coat and made the short trip to the newsstand.

It had been a long time since Miss Edna had had a full English breakfast and, after the scones, she was not sure how she would be able to deal with one. However, it was the first and most logical thing she could think of to keep Petal busy in the kitchen so she could have some time alone to think. The idea of the "Times" had just appeared to her, as if on cue. She did like reading it on Sundays and was elated when the hostess agreed to go get one for her. That was a surprise bonus and would afford her a few minutes more time alone before Erskine returned with Jasper.

Tracing the handle of her teacup with her right index finger, Miss Edna ran through her mind all of the events and circumstances of the last several days. She recalled Lady Opal's strange reaction to hearing about Fr. Burns and the somewhat extravagant gift of salmon. Why? Then there was Claudia and her mother. How surprisingly and uncharacteristically caring Claudia had become over the weekend, practically doting on her mother in what was apparently a distressful time for Lady Opal. Once again, Miss Edna found Opal Minnington in the middle of a strange situation. Could the legitimate heir to Dogmoor have had something to do with the death of that young girl? Miss Edna could hardly believe such a thing but, she realized, stranger things have happened in the history of her beloved Britain. The question was one of motive. Why would Lady Opal want Dora Finch dead?

This thread of thought brought her to Roland Minnington and she asked herself that same question about him again. What possible connection could Roland have had with Dora Finch?

Would he, and why would he, want her dead? What did young Mr. Randiffle mean when he said Roland's involvement was all about "business"? And speaking of young Mr. Randiffle, how did all this homosexuality play into it? Could there be a conspiracy of secrecy among those people that would have resulted in the death of a young woman who felt scorned and betrayed by one of them?

Then, the most perplexing of all, there was the earring in her dinner last evening. Somehow, Miss Edna was certain, that the earring was crucially connected to the remark she overheard the detective make to the Chief Inspector. The policeman had obviously suggested that there might have been a connection between the bruise and the salmon. That could possibly explain the earring in the fish, odd as that may seem. Who in their right mind would use a fish to try to murder somebody? It all seemed so incredible. The facts seem to fit, but they simply did not make sense.

Petal Chalmers returned with the "Times" and placed it on the table. Miss Edna seemed hardly even to notice, she was so deep in thought. Petal excused herself to the kitchen in order to prepare her guest's breakfast order. Alone once more at her table, Miss Edna returned to her thoughts. She could almost feel that there was something in the midst of all those facts and circumstances that would provide the answer to who killed Dora Finch. The problem was, she could not as yet pull that answer out of the mist of confusion that clouded her inner vision.

There she sat, ignoring her "Times", waiting for her breakfast, and ruminating on all these things.

44.

It was half past twelve when breakfast was served to Miss Winwood at the "Tea Cozy". The toast and eggs and sausages and baked beans were all arranged in generous portions on the plate, all topped off with a grilled tomato. "Thank goodness there's no black pudding on it," thought Miss Edna as she looked at her plate with some embarrassment. She had never cared for black pudding and was embarrassed to be seen setting into such a huge breakfast at such a late hour on a Sunday. It caused her to feel somewhat slothful. "Full English Breakfasts" were advertised as available all day long in many public houses and cafes, but she had never had reason to order one so near lunchtime before. She wondered to herself how many breakfasts were served for lunch in Great Britain.

This distracted revelry was interrupted by the arrival of Erskine and his friend, Jasper Dunwoody. It had only taken Erskine less than three quarters of an hour to retrieve his alibi witness. They came directly to Miss Edna's table, hats in hand, and bid her a good afternoon. With a quick and, again, slightly embarrassed glance down at the plate of breakfast food in front of her, she offered each of them to be seated.

As they sat down, even Miss Winwood could not help but be impressed by the splendidly handsome appearance of Mr. Jasper Dunwoody. She did not consider herself to be a woman of silly femininity when it came to men, and rightly so, because she was not, but she could not help admiring this truly handsome young man. His impeccable manners and fine attire only added to the appeal that he had for her and others, she supposed. She almost felt sad that he would be involved at all in this sordid affair that was unfolding. However, she pressed on.

"How can I help you, gentlemen?" Miss Edna had decided to let them start the conversation and see where it went.

It was Jasper Dunwoody who spoke first for the two of them. "Miss Winwood, we appreciate that you would allow us to interrupt your Sunday breakfast (Miss Edna felt the slightest blush rise in her cheeks) and we do not wish to take up too much of your time. It is, however, imperative that you know that Erskine has had nothing to do with poor Dora's death. Erskine was with me all afternoon—and all night—on Thursday."

This time it was the two young gentlemen who blushed. Miss Edna felt sorry for them both. It must be terribly difficult to have to admit these things about themselves to others, she thought. However, sympathetic as she might be, she still was searching for information. Her inner sense told her that neither one of these two were involved with Dora's murder, but they might know more than they even realize about what happened. So, resolutely, she continued the conversation.

"I am sure you both understand that the only thing this admission does is establish a motive for Mr. Randiffle here. The authorities may see this as a perfect reason for wishing Dora out of the way. Unless his employer is as understanding as your own, Mr. Dunwoody" (Miss Edna prided herself on being politic), "his position may very well be in jeopardy if his private life were to become publicly known."

Mr. Dunwoody spoke again. "Surely we would not come out into the open with these personal matters otherwise. Wouldn't the police understand that? It is already likely that Erskine will lose his position, simply because of the implication of his involvement with the murdered girl."

"Yes, it is possible that the police will consider that," Miss Edna saw Jasper's point. "But unless you can provide other witnesses who were with the two of you between the time Miss Finch was last seen in the kitchen of Manor Minnington and when her body found, then your alibi is only corroborated by the two of you. It does not look good." It dawned on her too late what the implications might be of having someone else as witness to where the two of them were and once again she was embarrassed. One could not really blame her for that misstep. She was not accustomed to same sex attractions and what all their ramifications might be.

As though he read her thoughts, Jasper Dunwoody spoke to rescue her from her embarrassment. "Thursday evening we were with a large group of people at one of our favorite drinking establishments. Many of our friends saw us together there until late in the evening. Friday morning we each had to go to work. Surely the coroner can narrow down the time of death?"

Miss Edna smiled. Smart, too, she thought to herself.

This time it was Erskine who spoke, to Jasper. "Tell her about young Minnington." Jasper had Miss Edna's complete attention. She was somehow sure she was about to hear something useful so she gave Jasper an encouraging look of expectation.

"Well," Jasper seemed hesitant. He did not like the idea of speaking of the aristocratic class in the manner he was about to. He was, after all, associated with it by virtue of Sir Oswald and, on top of that, Edna Winwood was Roland Minnington's father's personal secretary.

"Speak up, young man," prompted Miss Edna. "If you have something to say about young Roland, then say it."

"Well," he started again, "if you are looking for someone who is hiding unsavory activities, you might want to look into Roland and what he's been up to in London lately and what he is apparently up to in Dublin."

Miss Edna was intrigued. "Continue, please," she said calmly, putting the lie to her own escalating sense of thrill at what was sure to be an interesting revelation.

"I know you were at Manor Minnington last evening and undoubtedly heard the hoopla raised by Elinor Drumville against my employer, Sir Oswald. Those two old cats have been fighting since the Flood. But some of the things to which Miss Drumville referred could have only come from one source."

"And you are suggesting that Roland Minnington is that source?" questioned Miss Edna.

"I do not know how the two are connected, but Roland is the only possible explanation for her insinuations."

Miss Edna raised her eyebrows. "I am afraid your employer's son is involved in some very unpleasant business, Miss Winwood," continued Jasper. "The genesis of Saturday evening's pugilisms was the fact that I had turned down an offer that came to me from Roland by way of a common acquaintance we have."

Now Miss Edna was *very* intrigued. Without prompting, Jasper went on.

"A young man named Trevor who, by the way, is well known to the local constabulary, had acted as a sort of a liaison between Roland Minnington and myself, requesting that I join Roland's... um....stable."

"Stable?" Miss Edna was completely in the dark with that one.

Blushing again now at what he was about to say, Jasper continued. "Yes, ma'am, that's the only word I can think of to use. You see, Miss Winwood, Roland Minnington is not the pious seminarian he would have everyone believe. His real ambition lies in prostitution, not the priesthood."

Miss Edna stared blankly, obviously not comprehending the handsome young man's meaning.

Sensing this, Jasper said, "Speaking quite plainly, Miss Winwood, Mr. Roland Minnington is a homosexual himself and is planning a business empire of homosexual male prostitutes. He sent Trevor, who is a prostitute and that is why he is so well known to the local police, to ask me to consider being one of his 'high end' boys, as I believe it was put to me. I told Trevor, in no uncertain terms, that I was not interested and that if he ever approached me again with a question like that I'd thrash him. I suppose that it was this second rebuff that set Roland on his course to try to ruin me."

"S-second rebuff?" Miss Edna could not help herself stammering. She was completely stunned. She did not even realize how out of character she was at the moment, she was so completely taken by surprise.

"Yes, ma'am," continued Jasper. "He had approached me himself one time for a more, shall we say, personal invitation, but I told him no." Here he turned to Erskine. "He's attractive enough, I suppose, but he is a Minnington and I would not consider a dalliance with local nobility. Besides, I had already met and fallen for this young fellow here beside me." The two of them smiled at each other. "So you see," he turned back to Miss Edna, "Roland Minnington had plenty of reason to come into this very public house to discredit me by trying to get at Erskine through Dora. Playing priest, he told Dora all about Erskine and me. He is a twisted one, he is. I surmise that old Elinor either overheard it or was told it by someone else who had." Here he shot a glance in Petal's direction.

Miss Edna sat quietly, still stunned. Her inner sense had not prepared her for quite this much information.

"Go on. Tell her the rest of it." Once again it was the otherwise silent Mr. Randiffle who spoke. Since he was on quite a roll, Jasper did not hesitate this time.

"Also, the other Minnington youngster is not without dirty hands," said Jasper.

"Claudia? What's Claudia got to do with all of this?" asked Miss Winwood, fearing more talk of prostitution or homosexuality, or both.

"Claudia Minnington is known among certain circles for her use of narcotics," Jasper continued. "She is often seen here in London at well known drug habitués and is rather gratuitous in her use of laudanum and poppy tea, it seems, and is generous toward those who supply her with it."

Miss Edna had never been terribly conversant on the subject of narcotics. Laudanum had been a popular drug in its day, a mixture of opium and alcohol, she knew, but she thought that it had been used by the lower classes and that its time had passed. The other, poppy tea, she had never really heard much of, outside of Oscar Wilde's "Picture of Dorian Gray". She had not read that in a long time. She was vague on the subject of that particular concoction, but her memory gave the distinct impression that it was not good.

The three of them sat quietly together for a few minutes. Miss Edna had much to digest and the two young gentlemen realized it. They were a tad uncomfortable, naturally enough. They had no idea how the personal secretary to the current Lord Dogmoor would react to the news that his heir was procuring and that his daughter was a drug addict. Independently, they each began to wonder if they had done the correct thing.

For her part, Edna Winwood simply was left without words. Her mind was reeling with the information just presented her. Although she was loath to believe that the two Minnington children could be involved in these atrocious activities, she was inclined to believe the testimony of the two young men. Her inner sense was satisfied that they were telling the truth. She found this very disquieting, however, because, as she sat there thinking, she was only just beginning to realize the implications. She suddenly found herself and was the one who broke the silence.

"Gentlemen," she said as she noticed for the first time the worried look on their faces, "I believe you. The ramifications are most unpleasant to consider, but I believe you."

Their relief was palpable. "Thank you!" they said in unison.

After a moment, Erskine looked perplexed. "So you believe that I did not murder poor Dora?" He wanted to be reassured of exactly what it was that Miss Edna believed.

"Yes, young man, I believe that you had nothing to do with Miss Finch's death. I am not sure what I think happened in that regard. But I believe that the both of you are 'in the clear', I believe the police expression is," Miss Edna said reassuringly.

Jasper and Erskine looked at each other with relieved smiles. Miss Edna could tell by the movement of their arms that they had reached for each other's hands under the table. Jasper Dunwoody, as gallant as he was handsome, insisted on paying for her breakfast as it surely had grown cold as they sat and talked. She looked down at her plate for the first time since the young men had arrived and it impressed her as being thoroughly unappetizing. She accepted Jasper's kind offer and signaled to the hostess.

Mssrs. Dunwoody and Randiffle were standing, expressing their gratitude once again and saying goodbye to Miss Edna as Petal Chalmers came to the table to check on her guest and, she hoped, to find out what had been going on. Her hopes were dashed because all three of the table's occupants were obviously going to be leaving. She received payment for Miss Winwood's meal from the tall, handsome blond man and Miss Winwood herself stood up to leave, thanking her for the meal and apologizing for not eating it. Petal watched as Miss Winwood picked up her "Times", retrieved her coat from its nearby hook, and departed with the two young men. She turned her disappointed attention to her Joe who, upon seeing her looking in his direction, tried in vain to find something to do.

45.

The day was still quite bright and even warmer than it had been when Miss Edna had first left her flat. Standing outside the "Tea Cozy" in the sunlight, she pocketed her gloves as they did not seem necessary. It was such a nice day, in fact, that she decided a walk would be in order. Miss Edna always felt she could sort things out better if she could take a walk and she certainly needed all the aid a walk might offer her right now. So, she adjusted her scarf loosely around her neck, reassured herself that her hat was securely upon her head, and she turned toward the direction of St. James's Park, one of her favorite places to walk.

St. James' Park was near enough to be a healthy stretch of the leg on a nice day. Miss Edna had frequented it quite often over the years. Walking there had helped her figure out many issues that arose from her business dealings with Sir Clifford. From helping him to construct the perfect contract to how to present himself to the Lord Mayor more recently, she had found solace at St. James. Seldom had she a personal problem that required a stroll through the park. Her own life was in near perfect order.

This was one problem involving her employer that might have implications for her personal life, however. The accusations that had just been leveled against his two children were certain to be ill received. As a father, he had the right to know what mischief his children were getting into but he was surely not going to like it. Miss Edna could not think of anything less pleasant in life than having to tell Sir Clifford what she had just heard. But she knew that she had to tell him. What else could she do?

As she walked purposefully along she pondered these things. Suddenly, she stopped and did an about face. Where she realized that she needed to be going was in the other direction. With a renewed determination showing on her face, she made her way toward the Victoria Embankment for a walk along the River Thames. It was not, however, a view of the river that she thought would make a difference, nor Whitehall Park. Miss Edna had become suddenly aware of what else she could do. She could talk to Chief Inspector Thornton Sheridon at Scotland Yard.

The walk along the Thames was brisk and quick. Miss Edna had a determination in her step the likes of which she had not had in some time. Many others were out enjoying the unusually warm weather, but she seemed not to notice them at all. In fact, one might suppose that she no longer noticed how nice the day was or if it was even day at all. She had only one thing on her mind and that was that she was resolved to tell what she knew to the proper authorities.

It was barely half past two in the afternoon when she arrived at Scotland Yard. Entering the building, she realized that she had no idea where to find the Chief Inspector but to her rescue came a uniformed young man who asked if he might help her. She told the young policeman that she needed to speak to Chief Inspector Sheridon about a matter of great importance. Then, almost as an afterthought, she added, "Please tell him that it is Sir Clifford Minnington's personal secretary asking for him".

"Yes, ma'am, I'll tell him," replied the policeman. "You are a lucky one; he's not usually in on a Sunday." The policeman had evidently not yet heard about the events at Manor Minnington and it had not even occurred to Miss Edna that it was Sunday and that the Chief Inspector might not be at work. She reckoned that the events at Manor Minnington were precisely what had brought the Chief Inspector into the Yard on this Sunday and not, as the young man supposed, her good luck.

It only took Chief Inspector Sheridon a few minutes to arrive at the lobby and greet Miss Edna. She was impressed already with the efficiency of Scotland Yard. It was, after all, a large building and here was the Chief Inspector already.

"Yes, thank goodness for the telephone," replied the Chief Inspector when she returned his greeting and remarked on his promptness. "I was not expecting to see you again quite so soon, Miss Winwood, after last night at the manor house."

"I was not expecting to see you so soon, either, Chief Inspector. But some information has come to me that I think you might be interested in hearing in regard to the unfortunate circumstances at Dogmoor." Miss Edna believed in getting right to the point, especially with the men of Scotland Yard, not that she had that much experience with them.

"Right this way then, Miss Winwood," the Chief Inspector smiled as he indicated the way she should go. He wondered what this quintessential English spinster would have to contribute to the investigation, but he had learned that surprising things come from surprising sources. Once they were safely ensconced in his office, Miss Edna launched into the reason for her visit.

"I realize you are busy, Chief Inspector, so I'll get right to the point," she began. "I do not know whom, if anyone, you have in mind as the perpetrator of the crime against young Dora Finch, but I think I can steer you away from one obvious suspect on whom you would be wasting your time."

Chief Inspector Sheridon Thornton raised his eyebrows in surprise but did not say anything. He merely nodded and waited to see what Sir Clifford's personal secretary had to say. Miss Edna spent the next several minutes detailing, as discreet in her speech as she could possibly be, the personal issues involving the young man that had been seeing Dora frequently at the "Tea Cozy". For his part, the Chief Inspector listened intently, appreciating how difficult it must be for a lady such as Miss Winwood to speak of these delicate and personal, and certainly unusual, matters regarding Mr. Randiffle and his friend, Mr. Dunwoody.

As she came to the end of her narration, Chief Inspector Sheridon, jotting down a few notes in his pad, thanked her for her trouble and assured her that he would verify with the individuals involved the facts as she had just relayed them. Having the feeling that she was about to be dismissed, Miss Edna continued, "That's not quite all, Chief Inspector".

Once again his eyebrows rose in surprise and he said, "Oh? What else do you have for me, Miss Winwood?" At his invitation to continue, Miss Edna recounted for him the allegations made against Roland and Claudia Minnington by Jasper Dunwoody. She did so with considerably more difficulty than her previous statement and Thornton realized that she was taking a tremendous personal risk in coming to Scotland Yard to repeat these allegations to him. He listened with great interest as she told him about the drugs and prostitution in which the young aristocrats were alleged to be involved. His note taking was a bit more copious this time, especially noting the name "Trevor" in order to make inquiries with the local constabulary about him. "I guess I'll be making another trip to Manor Minnington today," he said more to himself, but unfortunately just loud enough for Miss Edna to hear.

Finally having divulged all the information she had to share with the Chief Inspector, Miss Edna took a deep breath and waited for him to finish with his notes to see what he had to say to her. She felt certain that she had no more to tell him yet she also felt certain that there was something more. Her inner sense was tingling within her and, though she did not relish the thought of being near Sir Clifford when he heard these allegations against his children, she also felt there was something more to be learned at Manor Minnington. She had a growing yen to participate in solving the mystery of Dora Finch's murder.

As she expected, the Chief Inspector thanked her again for her information and acted as if he were ready to show her how to find her way back to the entrance of the building. As he stood up from behind his desk, she suddenly found herself asking him a question.

"Chief Inspector," she began, "I could not help but overhear the remark your detective made at the manor house last night about the bruising on the side of Miss Finch's head. Do you suppose that that might have anything to do with the earring I found in my salmon?" Miss Edna was beginning to form her own opinion about what might have happened.

The Chief Inspector paused but a moment and continued to rise from his chair. He was already angry with Detective Frambley over this indiscretion of the night before and now he was angrier still. "This is precisely what I was afraid would happen," he thought. He did not relish the idea of amateur sleuthing.

"Don't worry yourself about that, Miss Winwood," he said, rather patronizingly she felt. "We'll be running down all the leads we have. Do you need a ride to your flat? I can arrange a policeman to take you home."

"No, thank you, Chief Inspector," replied Miss Edna. "I do not live too far from here." Then she had a flash of inspiration. "But, I would appreciate a ride out to Surrey if you are going to be going out to Manor Minnington this afternoon," she smiled at him, innocently. "There are some papers I need to work on this evening for Sir Clifford and in last night's excitement I am afraid I forgot to bring them with me." She did not relish the thought of lying, especially to the police, but she wanted very much to be there when the Chief Inspector questioned the residents of Dogmoor. "Do you think you might oblige me and save me the cab fare?"

What could he do? The Chief Inspector knew he was trapped. On top of everything else, he did not want to accuse Sir Clifford Minnington's secretary of lying, but he had the distinct impression that that was exactly what she was doing. With a reluctance he hoped he was hiding from her, he agreed to give her a lift to her employer's home. Within minutes, they were, along with Detective Frambley and two uniformed policemen, traveling the road to Surrey together—a merry little group.

46.

The ride to Dogmoor was quiet, no one speaking much to any-one. Especially quiet was Detective Frambley. He knew from the look on the Chief Inspector's face that he was still in trouble for what had happened the night before and he correctly surmised, by the presence of Miss Winwood, that the Chief Inspector was not going to forgive him for that slip up any time soon. For her part, Miss Edna looked out the window watching the countryside go by, allowing herself to conjure in her mind one or two possi-ble scenarios that might have resulted in murder. As she contem-plated the crime, she also thought briefly of her involvement in solving it. She wondered if the moors would look as lovely after this afternoon was over.

The butler, Snipwhistle, dutifully answered the door when they rang and showed the group into the drawing room. Miss Edna remained in the company of the police and went along with them into the drawing room rather than to Sir Clifford's office. She deftly pretended not to notice the quizzical look she received from the Chief Inspector who did not really wonder why she remained with them instead of going about the business she had told him she had there. He shot another disgruntled look at Detective Frambley, who was not as deft as Miss Edna in pre-tending not to notice.

Presently, Snipwhistle returned with Sir Clifford and was about to leave them to their business when Chief Inspector Sheridon spoke up. "Please, Sir Clifford, have your butler remain here a moment. We are going to need him shortly."

Sir Clifford, who under the best of conditions was not an easy man, fumed at the Chief Inspector. "What do you mean you '*are going to need him shortly*'? What does he have to do with the police? Don't tell me you suspect my butler of murder?" That last question was asked with considerable sarcasm.

The Chief Inspector continued, unperturbed. "We shall need him, your lordship, to summon the rest of the family. We are here to ask some hard questions in the course of investigating the murder to which you have referred."

"Hard questions," Sir Clifford's sarcastic tone continued. "What '*hard questions*' do you have for my family?"

Here the Chief Inspector turned to the rather startled butler. (Miss Winwood felt very sorry for old Snippy.) Addressing the servant, Thornton Sheridon said, "Would you please gather the rest of the family? At least those who are present in the house, of course." It had occurred to the inspector that perhaps, on a lovely Sunday afternoon, not all of them would be at home.

Snippy looked at his obviously irritated employer and replied to the Chief Inspector, "At once, sir. I believe everyone is home, although I am not entirely certain. The young people come and go quite a bit." With a slight bow, he left the drawing room on the policeman's errand.

Nobody said anything for a few minutes, until Sir Clifford noticed that his secretary was there in the room with the policemen. "What's the matter, Miss Winwood? Why are you here? Rounded up by the cops as a suspect, too?" Sir Clifford's sarcasm was getting out of hand.

"No, your lordship," replied Miss Edna quite directly. "I am not a suspect. At least, I do not believe I am."

"She is not a suspect," injected the Chief Inspector. "She's simply here as a witness." He had decided to give up on the hope that he was going to be shed of her anytime soon and gave the only reasonable excuse for her being in the room with them during the questioning. Since he did not realize that she had arrived with the police, Sir Clifford grudgingly accepted the answer.

As the lady of the house, Lady Minnington was summoned to the drawing room first, before her children. Miss Edna noticed that she did not look quite herself again today. It would have been understandable, since a dead body had been found on her estate, but she had been behaving strangely since before Dora's death. She had been in a nervous state since Fr. Burns' visit. She made a mental note to herself to discuss this with the Chief Inspector, should the need arise.

Soon after Lady Opal arrived, her son came strolling quite casually into the room. He looked around at the assembled family and police and, as though he dealt with Scotland Yard everyday, relaxed himself in a chair, crossing his legs, a wry smile on his face. He did not seem the least bit curious as to why he and they were all in one room together on a Sunday afternoon. Miss Edna looked over at the Chief Inspector but his face gave no indication as to how, if at all, this impressed him.

A few minutes later and Snippy returned with the news that Miss Claudia could not be located at this precise moment. If she were out of the house, he would inform her immediately upon her return that she was needed by her father in the drawing room. The Chief Inspector thanked the butler and dismissed him.

Everyone in the room, except for Roland, had an air of anticipation. Sir Clifford even laid aside his sarcasm and waited to hear what the Inspector had to say. Miss Edna could feel the anxiety level in the room rising and Lady Opal took a seat near the window. It was to the young seminary student that the Chief Inspector first spoke.

"Sir, you can confirm for me that you are Roland Minnington?" he began.

"No, I'm the Archbishop of Canterbury," Roland had apparently inherited his father's gift for sarcasm. "Of course, I am Roland Minnington. Who else would I be?" He did not seem exactly belligerent toward the man from Scotland Yard, but certainly arrogant.

With a practiced poise that came from years of police experience, the Chief Inspector continued as though he had been given a simple, and appropriate, answer. "Mr. Minnington, I should like to know where you were on this past Thursday evening." He posed it as a statement, not a question. This would assert his authority in a gentle manner. He hoped that he would not have to assert it in any other manner.

"Thursday evening? I was where I am every evening when I am at hospital, attending vespers at St. Bartholomew's," he replied. Miss Edna thought it a pious alibi and could not help but to hold out some hope for her employer's son.

"And after vespers?" the Chief Inspector continued. Unlike Miss Edna, he apparently had not been struck by the young man's piety. Again, this would be thanks to years of police experience and an unhappy familiarity with the darker side of human nature.

Without hesitation, Roland Minnington recounted his further whereabouts. "After vespers I took a stroll and got a pint at a pub before deciding on whether or not to meet friends or to simply return home for dinner." Almost as an afterthought he added, sneering, "I do have a car."

Unimpressed, the Chief Inspector carried on. "And what did you decide to do?"

"I met friends," Roland was now distractedly playing with the fringe on curtain, something Lady Opal hated to see him do, usually.

"What friends were those, sir?"

"Oh, just friends," smiled Roland. "Nobody terribly important and nobody you'd know."

The young man's arrogance had just opened a door for the Chief Inspector and he was quick to walk through it. "Is that so? How about a young fellow by name of Trevor? Is he one of the friends you met that night?"

Finally, his look was not quite as smug and he stopped playing with the fringe on the curtain. Roland Minnington, however, quickly regained his composure and replied, "I'm not sure I know that name, Chief Inspector. It's not ringing any bells."

"That's too bad, for your alibi, I mean," said Chief Inspector Thornton, "because we have had a chat with a young man of that name who seems to think that he knows you. In fact, he has told us things that indicate he knows you, ah, rather well, shall we say?" Sheridon was going to try to break this young man's story by making up one of his own. He had, of course, not yet conversed with anyone named Trevor but, employing an old police tactic, pretended that he had just to see where it would get him with young Minnington.

It had its desired affect. Roland turned crimson and one could not determine whether it was from embarrassment or rage—or both. It turned out to be rage. His mind raced, wondering just what that fop might have said to the men of the Yard and just what comeuppance would be his when he, Roland, got hold of him. But Roland did not see himself beaten by the policeman just yet.

"I have no idea what or who you are talking about," he denied flatly. "I am not at all acquainted with anyone by that name."

"It's little use to deny it, young man," the Chief Inspector continued in his own little lie. "We have him at the Yard right now. It would not take much to ring them up and have them bring him here for further questioning."

Somehow the thought of having the male prostitute brought to his parents' home unnerved Roland, at last. What would Trevor do when he arrived? He would obviously be able to identify him and who knows what the police already knew from that vile mouth of his. Roland sat quite still for a moment or two considering. All eyes were on him as he began to show signs of nervousness now—tapping his fingers against the arm of the chair, shifting in his seat—and the room was thick with anticipation as everyone wondered what might happen next. Even Lady Opal had found enough wherewithal to be able to show curiosity about her elder child in her somewhat glazed over eyes.

As if he had just awakened to what was happening in his drawing room, Sir Clifford finally spoke, this time to his son. "Well, Roland. Who is this Trevor person?" His voice sounded unusually calm and yet everyone in the room familiar with him tensed. "Roland?"

Roland fidgeted with a button on his cashmere cardigan. He could feel the jaws of the trap closing in on him. As his situation became more obviously helpless, his rage returned and he turned toward his father.

"Trevor is a young man I know, father," he said. "In fact, I know him very well, very well indeed." There was an edge in Roland's voice that no one in the family had ever heard before. To the police, trained in so many of the more unpleasant aspects of man, and to Miss Edna, who was simply observant and clever, it appeared that young Roland had a great deal of pent up anger that was about to be vented. And Sir Clifford, it appeared, was to be the recipient.

Sir Clifford restrained his own anger and simply asked his son to continue. "What do you mean, Roland?"

"What I mean, father," he spat, "is that Trevor Willis is a business associate of mine."

Here the Chief Inspector decided to regain control of the questioning. "What kind of business associate, Mr. Minnington?" he asked calmly.

Roland took a breath to steady himself but not necessarily to calm himself down. When he spoke, the edge in his voice was still there and it seemed to still be directed toward his father. "Oh, it is a business of a very personal nature, Chief Inspector, as I am sure you already know if you have spoken with Trevor. He solicited me one night near Blackfriar's Bridge and the rest, as they say, is history." The rise in Roland's voice seemed to indicate that he was losing his composure, almost to the point of becoming manic.

The Chief Inspector pressed on. "He solicited you for sex, Mr. Minnington?" The policeman wanted to be certain of the facts.

"Yes!" shouted Roland. "He solicited me for sex! And I happily paid him for the experience. I had been looking for someone such as Trevor and believed myself to have had quite a stroke of luck when we met."

"Were you that, ah, lonely?" Detective Frambley interjected.

"Lonely? No, you twit!" Roland fairly laughed at the detective. "It was not because I was lonely. I had plans for a business venture of my own that I wanted to take back to Dublin with me when I returned to school." Here Roland was speaking to his father again, his voice sharp with anger once more. "Trevor was just the man I needed to get things started. He knew the right people and how to work the streets. I was going to provide cover and organization."

"So you were planning to establish a male prostitution ring in Ireland?" asked the Chief Inspector.

"I believe they call that 'pimping', Chief Inspector," Detective Frambley added in an official tone.

"Thank you, Detective," Chief Inspector Sheridon's reply was stated in such a manner that Detective Frambley knew not to speak again unless spoken to. Sheridon turned himself again to young Minnington. He wanted to draw as many incriminating statements as he could and then challenge his alibi. With this purpose in mind, he continued, "The Irish do not impress me as a people who would be much interested in that type of solicitation. What makes you think your venture would be at all successful there?"

"Ha!" replied Roland. "Dublin is not the backwater town that many of us here in Britain believe it to be, Chief Inspector. There is a good deal of commerce and a certain cosmopolitan air there. Not at all like London, of course, but lots of potential," and here he sneered, "even among the good Catholic men in town who don't seem to mind stepping out on their wives and lady friends on the odd occasion for, shall we say, a taste of a different slice of life?" He was being deliberately crude in order to irk his father.

Sir Clifford's composure was crumbling. His nostrils were beginning to flare as he breathed. Miss Edna was certain that an eruption was imminent. She was not entirely incorrect.

"Get out," he said to Roland in a murderous tone. "Get out of this house before I throw you out and do not ever come back." Roland stood looking at his father with a look on his face that promised hysterics at any moment. His eyes widened with rage and his mouth twitched as though it were looking for something to say but could not find it. The tension in the drawing room was immense. Suddenly, he turned and made as though he were going to storm out of the room.

"Just a minute, young fellow," Detective Frambley caught him by his arm and he reeled around. "I don't think the Chief Inspector is finished with you quite yet."

"Correct, Detective," said Sheridon. "We are not quite done here with you, young man. Be so kind as to retake your seat. There are certain matters we need to clear up before we let you go. There is still the matter of where you were Thursday after vespers. We will need to verify these facts with Mr. Willis." The Chief Inspector had an excellent memory for names, and a good thing. He had not known Trevor's last name until Roland's confession.

"Sir Clifford, is there a telephone that we might use?" asked Sheridon.

Sir Clifford did not seem to hear the Chief Inspector's question. He was looking at his son, plainly disgusted with what he saw. It was Miss Edna who spoke.

"The closest telephone is in Sir Clifford's office," she proffered. Knowingly volunteering the use of Sir Clifford's personal space without first consulting him was something that she would have never done under ordinary circumstances. It was a considerable breach in protocol. Somehow, however, Miss Edna did not think that her position with his lordship could be in any more jeopardy than it already was.

Chief Inspector Sheridon gave a nod to Detective Frambley, who understood that what he was supposed to do was to call the locals and have them round up Trevor Willis. The detective turned to Miss Edna for directions to Sir Clifford's office. "Turn left from the entry hall and it's the first door on the left," she told him in reply.

One of the uniformed policemen who had accompanied the Chief Inspector took charge of Roland Minnington—who had sunk, seemingly exhausted, back into his chair—and stood by him to be sure that he remained calmly seated. The other officer remained by the drawing room door. A quiet tension remained in the room. No one seemed to know what to expect next. It was almost a relief when Claudia Minnington was ushered into the room by the butler.

47.

The sense of relief was short lived. Claudia came into the room calmly enough and smiled at everyone present. Hers was not a smile of condescension, as been her brother's, but more dreamy, as though she were not completely aware of the reality of the situation around her. Hesitating for a moment in the doorway, she walked over to be near her mother, whose eyes seemed to plead with her. To come sit by her? Miss Edna wondered.

The Chief Inspector began as he had with her brother. "Are you Miss Claudia Minnington?"

Before she could respond, her mother interrupted. "Claudia, dear, could you go and get mummy some of your medicine before he starts. My nerves are feeling overwrought." Claudia smiled her dreamy smile at her mother, or at least in her general direction. Before Claudia responded to the request, however, if she were going to at all from the looks of things, the Chief Inspector spoke.

"What medicine is that, Lady Opal?" he asked.

"It's some sort of nerve tonic, Chief Inspector," replied Lady Opal somewhat crossly. "These events have had their toll on my nerves, as even you, a hardened policeman, must understand." Now it was Lady Opal's voice that was taking on an edge. Hers, however, seemed more from an excess of anxiety rather than anger.

"Nerve tonic?" the Chief Inspector gently urged. "Tell me about this 'nerve tonic' and when did you first try taking it."

Poor Lady Opal, thought Miss Edna. She had no idea where this was going because she was completely in the dark about what her daughter had been giving her.

Becoming flustered but, with her breeding behind her, trying not to show it, Lady Opal responded, "I am not certain what it is, Chief Inspector. My daughter gets it from an herbalist in the city, isn't that right, dear?" Claudia continued to smile dreamily. "She first gave it to me this weekend," a brief pause, "to help me over the tragic events that seem to have occurred here at my home."

Noting the pause in her answer, but ignoring it for the moment, the Chief Inspector inquired, "May we see some of this herbal remedy? Is there any in the house at present?" Chief Inspector Sheridon recognized the effect of laudanum use in Lady Opal and had already begun to theorize that that was why Claudia seemed to be a bit out of it. He wanted a sample to have examined at the laboratory at Scotland Yard to be certain, however.

Lady Opal's eyes brightened with hope. "Yes, I am sure there is, Chief Inspector," and, turning to Claudia, "Darling, go upstairs and get mummy some of your medicine. Then we can show it to this nice policeman as well." The mention of the word "policeman" seemed to have an effect on Claudia. She looked away from her mother and down at the floor, slowly shaking her head, her long brown hair falling forward and obscuring her face.

The Chief Inspector turned to Sir Clifford, "Your lordship, may we have your permission to look for this so called herbal remedy?" He wanted to be certain that, whatever they might find, he had covered all the bases under the government's rules of evidence, especially when dealing with the aristocracy.

Sir Clifford, for his part, seemed quite confused. He was still fuming inwardly about his son's recently revealed predilections and had no idea why there would be a fuss over some concoction of herbs that calmed his wife down so. "Aren't these people known for brewing this type of thing?" he wondered to himself, confusing the ancient Celtic Druids and the influence they might have had in Great Britain, and when. He also had no idea what his daughter had been giving his wife, so he granted his permission to the police for their search.

The uniformed policeman by the door was given the nod by the Chief Inspector and he proceeded up the stairs to Claudia's room, having been given directions to it by Sir Clifford himself. The rest awaited his return in silence. Claudia remained focused on the floor, if "focused" could be legitimately used; Roland sat with a blank and unreadable expression on his face; and Lady Opal, it was clear, was becoming increasingly agitated as she waited for the young police officer to return with her daughter's elixir, upon which she had learned to depend in the last few days. For his part, Sir Clifford pretended to be interested in seeing what was out of the window; he was so upset and confounded by what had come to light about his son. For her part, Miss Edna began forming another opinion about the crime.

Curious as she was about the murder and who committed it, she did find room in her mind and heart to feel sorry for her employer. It was hard to imagine Sir Clifford, the self-assured, often arrogant, American businessman to be humbled in this way. When his son had been accused of procuring prostitution, she had expected him to become enraged. When Roland admitted to it, she had expected a veritable eruption. To see him looking out the window, bewildered as he seemed, was not like the confident man who would have been standing before the Lord Mayor just days before, deftly brokering a business deal that would have an enormous impact on both London and his personal wealth. She wondered how he would come out of this turbulent day. She wondered if he could possibly forgive Roland. She wondered what he would do when he found out about Claudia!

She also wondered about the crime itself, and this occupied her mind much more so than her concerns for Sir Clifford. Roland certainly seemed a likely suspect. His bitter anger toward his father was evident. One could only guess what had caused such rage to build up inside a son against his father. Could he have killed Dora as an act of revenge, to embarrass his father in a most gruesome manner? Could he be that heartless to have used an innocent victim in sacrifice to his desperate desire to bring down his father? And then there was Claudia. Drugs do strange things to people, Miss Edna had observed. Under their influence at this very moment, Claudia and Lady Opal were behaving quite queer. Could some drug induced rampage have driven Claudia to a random act of murder? Or was it random? Might there have been some unknown grudge against Dora and the drugs had given Claudia the courage to act on her own anger? What might have made her that angry, angry enough to kill?   Finally, there was Lady Opal. Her behavior had been strange since Fr. Burns' visit. Nervous and jumpy at first then loopy and languid, apparently under the influence of her daughter's "medicine". What connection could she have had to the old Irish cleric? Whatever that connection might be, Miss Edna could not even hazard a guess but it would have to have been pretty powerful to give this lady of peerage a motive to murder a simple public house maid. As Miss Edna considered these things and looked at the people assembled in the room with her she felt certain that, barring some fiend roaming the moors, Dora Finch's murderer was in this drawing room.

Presently the uniformed policeman returned. In his hand he held a small silver flask. He handed it over to Chief Inspector Sheridon who removed the top and gave a tentative sniff of his nose to its contents. He recognized it immediately as laudanum. Replacing the top, he handed it back to the policeman to be held as evidence and turned his attention to Claudia.

"Miss Minnington, you know what we found in your room, don't you?" It was more a statement than a question. The Chief Inspector waited for a reply from the young aristocrat and finally repeated, "Miss Minnington?"

It was Lady Opal who spoke. "Of course she knows what it is," her voice was agitated. "It's the medicine she's been sharing with me. May I have some now, please?"

"I'm sorry, ma'am, but we cannot allow you any more. This is not medicine. At least not in these days." Chief Inspector Sheridon knew of laudanum's more laudable past, when it was, in fact, dispensed as a medicine. But those days were past, for it's addictive qualities had become all too sadly well known.

"Why can't she have any?" Sir Clifford had turned his attention from the window back to the assemblage in his drawing room.

"Because, sir, it is not medicine. It is a drug called laudanum, a mixture of opium and alcohol. Very commonly abused by the lower classes before the turn of the century, but not found often these days although, obviously, it is still out there."

The Chief Inspector's reply was yet another jolt to Sir Clifford. While he had begun to think that his daughter was finally behaving responsibly toward her education he now realized that all those trips into the city had been for drugs and not to study at Bedford's library! His daughter's often unruly behavior, which he had attributed simply to youth, had been the result instead of a dependence on drugs. In his own mind, he did not know if he were accepting a reality or questioning one. He turned to Claudia.

Miss Edna watched in painful anticipation. She was certain that the bombastic American would throw his daughter out of the house as he had his son. But to her surprise he did not address Claudia right away. Rather, he turned to his wife. Miss Edna involuntarily held her breath and wondered what was coming. After a moment, Sir Clifford finally spoke.

"And you, my dear. Why were you so keen on taking this garbage?" His voice was calm, but its tone was demanding.

Lady Opal wore a look of panic on her face. Naturally enough, she had been shocked to find out that her daughter had been administering a narcotic to her and yet, at the same time, she wanted more. Her nerves were so terribly frazzled already because of the murder and the police present in her home and now her husband was demanding some sort of an explanation from her. She was finding this pressure to be nearly unbearable.

She spoke the first words that came to her mind. "I don't know, Clifford."

Very unfortunate choice of answer, thought Miss Edna, for now she could see some of the old Sir Clifford returning. His face reddened with anger when he heard her answer. However, his voice remained rather calm, considering the circumstances.

"You don't know," he repeated. Miss Edna could tell he was struggling to maintain a calm appearance. "What do you mean 'you don't know'? Are you in the habit of using addictive substances so much that you do not know why you started using this one?" Miss Edna could not help feeling an odd sense of relief when she heard her employer's sarcasm return. The men from Scotland Yard watched to see what was going to unfold.

"No I am not in the habit of using drugs!" Lady Opal hostilely replied to her husband. "I don't know why Claudia gave me that poison. I never would have thought that my own daughter would give me such a thing!" Her words made sense but the look on her face told Miss Edna, and the Chief Inspector as well, that she was beginning to become unhinged.

At this point it was Claudia who surprised everyone in the room by finally looking up from the floor upon which she had previously been meditating. As though she had just awakened from sleep she lifted her head. Her eyes were clear and were fixed on her mother. There was a tinge of anger in her voice when she spoke.

"You remember, mummy. I gave you some when you became so upset after that priest's visit last week. Don't you remember?" Her tone was snide as well as angry.

"Priest," Sir Clifford interjected. "What priest? Was the vicar here?"

"No, daddy, not the vicar," replied Claudia, her voice dripping with feigned innocence but her glare still directed at her mother. "It was a Roman priest from Ireland. The friend of Maggie's from her orphan days. The one who sent us the salmon." Claudia's smile impressed the police and Miss Edna as looking quite predatory.

Chief Inspector Sheridon and his officers kept watching in silence. Detective Frambley had returned to the room, giving Sheridon a nod, indicating that his mission had been accomplished. The Chief Inspector, even though he maintained his official police detachment, could not help, despite all his years on the force, being caught up in the dramatic twists and turns unfolding for this family of nobles.

Sir Clifford, in the excitement, had apparently forgotten about the Irish priest and his gift of salmon. He had openly wondered why his family should have benefited from such a generous offering but had not really given it much thought. Now he was intrigued anew and more than ready to give it the attention it apparently deserved. He once again addressed his wife.

"Opal," he began, "why did a visit from an Irish Catholic priest upset you? Thinking of converting, are you?"

Lady Opal's mental and emotional state seemed to be declining rapidly. She fidgeted so nervously with her necklace that she threatened to break it and send pearls flying about the room. She did not even look at her husband when she replied, "No, I am not thinking of converting. That's ridiculous. I do not know what you are talking about. What priest?"

Claudia found her voice again. "Mother, how can you say that? You remember what priest it was. He was here to give Maggie the news of an inheritance, if you can call such a paltry sum an inheritance. He was from her orphanage. The one she and Dora Finch were at as children." Claudia's remembrance of the day, though it was offered in a way that was meant to seem helpful and informative, sounded menacing. Her next question proved that to be true. As though she were unsheathing a dagger, Claudia asked her mother, "Why don't you tell daddy about the box of letters and papers in your room?"

That seemed to be the proverbial straw on the camel's back because Lady Opal broke down completely in what appeared to be an extreme attack of anxiety. She put her head in her hands and cried hysterically. Rather than rush to her side, her husband stood and looked down at her. All others present, outside the family, felt keenly embarrassed, even the police. But they knew that, sooner or later, they would have to press on for more information. Presently, Sir Clifford spoke, addressing his wife.

"Yes, dear, tell me about the box of letters and papers in your room," he demanded firmly but not harshly.

The combination of events, her desire for more laudanum and the pressure from the police presence and now her husband's questions about her private papers had Lady Opal feeling cornered, like a fox at a hunt. She felt terribly exhausted by the whole ordeal and was desperate for it to end. Shooting a hateful look to her daughter, she addressed her husband.

"Yes, Clifford, there is a box of letters and papers in my room. It concerns things that happened before we were married, before I even met you. I had almost forgotten they were even there."

"But the priest, what was his name, reminded you of them," Sir Clifford asked.

"Fr. Burns. His name is Fr. Burns. Yes, he reminded me of them," Lady Opal sobbed.

"Why?" demanded Sir Clifford.

"Because he was the priest at the orphanage where Maggie and Dora were children, the place where they met," she replied.

"So, what does that have to do with you?" Sir Clifford was asking the questions which were on everyone's minds.

Odd, is it not, observed Miss Edna, how desperation can occasion resolve and give breath to new vigor in a person, because at this point Lady Opal seemed to regain her composure. She sat up straight in her chair and folded her hands in her lap. Her eyes were puffy and red from crying, but she was much calmer than she had previously been throughout it all. She looked at her husband and, without emotion, continued her explanation.

"Because, dear, I had met Fr. Burns at that orphanage more than 20 years ago. I had met him at that orphanage because I was there to have a baby and give it up for adoption. Dora Finch was my daughter by a lover I had had as a young girl."

She had stated it quite as a matter of fact and seemed quite relieved at having done so. Every pair of eyes, however, including those belonging to her children, was focused on Sir Clifford in expectation. Miss Edna, not at all a timid soul, felt herself shrink back from what surely would be an eruption of volcanic proportions.

Everyone in the room except Lady Opal watched and waited for Sir Clifford's reaction. Lady Opal alone seemed unconcerned. She remained seated in her chair, her hands folded in her lap. She had dried her tears and seemed almost happy to have it out in the open, that her secret was secret no more. Her burden, which she had carried for so many years, seemed finally to be lifted from her. Miss Edna reflected that perhaps the Roman Church was correct, that confession *is* good for the soul. Tension in the room mounted as they awaited Sir Clifford's response, but there was none forthcoming. He seemed, quite the contrary, eerily calm. He continued to look down on his wife seated before him with an emotionless face. No one seemed to know quite what to do.

It was a relief to everyone that Snipwhistle came into the room to inquire about tea. "Yes, Snippy," said Sir Clifford, usurping his wife's domestic role. "Serve the tea."

48.

The cook and the butler had been waiting in the kitchen as the police investigation continued. Each time Snipwhistle returned after his forays through the house to round up family members, he and Maggie would wonder aloud to each other what it might mean. Both of them thought, but both were afraid to say aloud, that perhaps the police thought it might actually be one of the Minningtons who was responsible for Dora's murder. But this was unthinkable! Maggie, when her Irish was up, had often thought of them as odd, but she would have thought that about any Brit when her Irish was up. She could not, in her worst moments, think of any of them as murderers.

When Snipwhistle came back to tell her that Mr. Minnington had ordered tea, Maggie felt a sense of relief at least in as much as she could perform a normal duty, although it was very much out of the ordinary to have so many for tea in on a Sunday afternoon. Sir Clifford tolerated the Missus' weekend dinner parties but had always insisted on quiet Sundays. When Maggie first started with them she thought him to be a religious man who wanted to obey the Third Commandment. It was not too long before she realized that all he wanted was quiet time in the house to prepare his business papers and presentations for the upcoming week. So it was unusual that she would have to feed a room full of people at tea time on a Sunday, even if they were only the police.

Fortunately, Maggie had something handy that she could use. In the excitement of the previous night she had found herself quite unable to fall asleep. She hated tossing and turning in bed to no point so she had gotten herself up and pulled the leftover salmon out of the refrigerator. Out of this she whipped up a delicious mousse. Last night she had wondered how and when she would get to use it. "Salmon won't last forever," she had reflected. It was almost a lucky stroke that Sir Clifford had just ordered tea, really.

As she prepared the salmon mousse sandwiches on small squares of trimmed white bread Snipwhistle put together the tea service. She handed the tray to him and whispered, "Well, Snippy, I hope there are no surprises in *this* salmon!" Snippy gave her a sympathetic look and then wheeled the cart into the drawing room.

The butler entered a room full of quiet people. Apparently no one had spoken another word since Sir Clifford had ordered tea. The atmosphere was heavy with discomfort and expectation as everyone in the room knew that soon there had to be something very unpleasant coming from his lordship. The teacart was placed in a convenient spot in the room and finally his lordship spoke. "Opal, serve the tea, won't you?"

He had said it in such a normal tone that Lady Opal simply got up and played her part as hostess of the manor. She had fleetingly considered telling her husband to serve it himself, since he had ordered it, but thought better of it. Her hands trembled slightly as she offered the customary late afternoon victuals to the men from Scotland Yard and to Miss Edna, then to her children.   Finally, she took a cup to Sir Clifford and he placed his on the fireplace mantle against which he had taken a position. Everyone had taken the tea because, whether they wanted it or not, they were unsure of what might have happened had they refused it.

Snipwhistle made to serve the sandwiches himself, as was his custom, but Sir Clifford halted him, speaking again. "That will be all, Snippy. Just place that tray on the table and we can help ourselves. Thank you." Slightly unnerved by his master's civil tone, Snippy set the tray down and exited the room and went back to the kitchen.

Lady Opal returned to her chair with her own cup of tea, having decided against a sandwich, and seated herself properly once again. Her anxiety was turning into anger and she directed her anger toward her husband who seemed to be in complete control of this horrible situation. All her dirty laundry had been aired in front of a servant and strangers, not to mention her children, and he was controlling the events unfolding in the room by coolly not saying anything other than telling her to serve the tea. Finally, she could take it no longer and, catching the attention once again of everyone in the room who had begun to grow uncomfortable as to what to do next, she said to her husband, "Clifford, do you mean to keep us all on tinder hooks or are you going to tell us what is going on inside that fevered brain of yours?"

All others present watched Sir Clifford. If Lady Opal's remarks had been intended to spark one of his customary outbursts—which is exactly what she had intended—it missed its mark completely. Rather than respond in anger, Sir Clifford remained calm, so calm it seemed cold—and, truth be told, somewhat frightening. He did not answer her question.

"Clifford, I demand that you speak to me! I am your wife!" Lady Opal was clearly affected by his aloof attitude and she appeared to have a mix of anger and fear in her voice and demeanor now. There was no one in the room witnessing these events that did not think that she wished she could have more laudanum at that moment.

"What is it you would like me to say, my dear?" responded Sir Clifford. "You've said so much already." Again, a steely cold, calm voice emanated from his lordship.

"Well say something! I've just admitted to an affair that resulted in a baby that I gave up for adoption before we married! Can't you say something?" Lady Opal was again bordering on hysterics.

Sir Clifford sipped his tea and replaced the cup upon the mantle. "If you insist dear, I can say something. I thought you might like to wait until we were alone, but if you wish I can say it now. It is something important that you need to hear."

Lady Opal, not at all certain that she wanted to be alone with her husband in the near future, tried to muster a steely glance of her own and nodded to him to continue.

"Very well, dear, I'll say it now," began Sir Clifford. "Do you remember our wedding day?"

Expecting a tiresome lecture on the sanctity of marriage and broken vows, Lady Opal simply nodded in the affirmative.

"Of course you do. It's every woman's special day, isn't it, my dear?" Sir Clifford was beginning to sound a little sarcastic, and therefore more familiar, at least to Miss Edna. "But there was more to remember about our wedding day than dresses and flowers and cakes, was there not?"

"For heaven's sake, Clifford, make your point," Lady Opal responded quite irritably. "I know you have a point in there somewhere, so make it." She would be sorry she spoke those words.

"The point is, dear, that the day before the wedding you and I met with an attorney. Do you remember that? And in that meeting you signed a paper, an agreement. Is any of this coming back to you?"

Frankly, it appeared to everyone in the room that none of it was coming back to her. She had a very confused expression on her face as she tried to remember all the events that went up to her wedding day.

"I cannot recall," she simply said.

"Well, let me refresh your memory. The day before we entered wedded bliss, you and I met with a lawyer from my Pittsburgh firm and we signed an agreement. This agreement set down certain conditions on our marriage. You see, I am not now, nor was I then, the foolish, naïve American you and your family thought I was. Even though I was quite smitten with you, I knew that you were not marrying me out of love. Well, love for me anyway. You were in love with my money. You and your parents both. Since it seemed to me, even at the time, that this was really more a business arrangement, a merger if you will, than a marriage, I had my lawyer draw up an agreement to be signed by each of us before the wedding agreeing to certain conditions."

"C-conditions?" Lady Opal had grown pale.

Her husband continued. "Yes, conditions. Among them a morals clause. If at any time either party had or would engage in and try to hide from the other a gross lapse in moral conduct, then the marriage could be considered ended and the offending party would have no claim on the aggrieved party's assets. Or words very much to that effect. Remember it now, dear? It made perfect business sense to me at the time." He smiled an unpleasant smile as he finished.

Lady Opal stared back at her husband, her eyes opened wide in disbelief—or fear—those observing her could not be sure. When she spoke, she sounded incredulous. "Do you mean that you intend to divorce me?"

Sir Clifford simply continued smiling his unpleasant smile. Miss Edna and the Chief Inspector looked at each other at the exact same moment and seemed to have the exact same thought. "Now *there* is a motive for murder!"

49.

Chief Inspector Sheridon, who, along with his companions and Miss Winwood, had had the dubious honor of witnessing this revelation, decided that it was time to take control of the room again. He had permitted the conversation to continue without interruption in order to ascertain if important information might be forthcoming. Now, however, seemed to be the proper time to reassert himself. After all, he was here to investigate allegations in connection with a murdered girl, not to become involved in an aristocratic melodrama. He set down his tea and stepped forward into the room and began to speak.

"I should think that we might want to take a bit of a break right about now," he said, the interruption completely changing the all too heavy tenor of the room. "The officers and I will take turns using the facilities, with your permission your lordship. I suggest that each of you tend to that, too, if you need to. I also must insist that no one try to leave the house."

To suggest to people of the Minningtons' social status that they ought to use the bathroom was crude to the point of being cheeky, but the Chief Inspector needed to completely rearrange the dynamics of the room. The conversation to which he had just been privy had provided very useful information but it was now time to use it for police work and allow the Minningtons to sort out their domestic issues in the privacy of their own time. A break for nature seemed the most convenient and natural contrivance both to regain control of the room and to loosen up other tongues that had heretofore been silent, meaning those belonging to Roland and Claudia. Taking turns provided a way of doing so by keeping them all in the house under the watchful eyes of the uniformed men.

In a move he would later regret, he turned to Miss Edna to say, "Madam, can you show me and my men where the facilities are here on the ground floor?"

Miss Edna was only too eager to help. As she had been watching and listening to the Minningtons and their woeful problems, she had also been thinking about the murder. It was as though she had two brains that could operate simultaneously, she was that clever. She took the opportunity to direct the police to the manor house's bathrooms and to have a private word with the Chief Inspector. And this is where he would end up regretting his move.

"Chief Inspector, might you spare a moment?" asked Miss Edna as she had adroitly directed Detective Frambley to the bathroom first. Sheridon resisted the urge to roll his eyes for he had the impression that some amateur sleuthing was afoot but, ever the courteous policeman, he replied to Miss Edna, "Of course, ma'am. What can I do for you?"

"Things look bad for the family," Miss Edna began.

"Yes, they do," replied the Chief Inspector.

"Have you formed any opinions?" continued Miss Edna.

"We've drawn no conclusions yet, ma'am, until the investigation itself comes to its conclusion," he answered her.

"A sensible position," concurred Miss Edna. "Might I offer my own opinion?" The urge to roll his eyes was getting harder to resist, but the Chief Inspector's courteous manner prevailed. Without waiting for his reply, Miss Edna continued, "I believe that, whereas Roland looks the perfect cad and seems to have the morals of a guttersnipe, he did not do it."

"Oh? And why is that?" the Chief Inspector feigned interest in her opinion.

Miss Edna had the feeling she was not being taken at all seriously, but she launched into her theory anyway. "Roland seems to have a great deal of rage toward his father, as I have no doubt that you witnessed for yourself just moments ago." Chief Inspector Sheridon gave her a slight nod. "His, um, business aspirations, if you will, appear to be motivated by a desire to lash out at his father and to embarrass him. Why he involved himself with Dora Finch is puzzling, but perhaps Mr. Dunwoody's explanation of revenge solves that. Whatever the reason, he had no reason to kill her. Unless he were completely mad he would not take the risk of exposure by coming under suspicion of murder. And, whatever else he may be, I do not believe Roland Minnington is mad."

The Chief Inspector could not help but be impressed with the lady's logic. He somewhat reluctantly allowed himself to further the conversation along. "That seems reasonable enough, but somewhat circumstantial. Motive would be easy enough to prove in his case, I think, mad or not. Opportunity has yet to be demonstrated, as of yet we are not certain of his whereabouts at the time of the murder." He carefully left out any discussion of means. He could tell from looking at her that she had not been as impressed with his logic as he had been by hers, so he said to her, "Apparently, there must be something more than that, Miss Winwood, I can tell by the look on your face. What else makes you think that was not Roland Minnington?" The Chief Inspector was beginning to be interested in what she had to say, in spite of himself. "Why not him?"

"Because in my opinion, untrained though I may be, a woman did it," said Miss Edna. The Chief Inspector's eyebrows rose and she had the feeling that she might actually have his attention, finally. "The crime was one of opportunity. The hastily hidden body in a shallow grave would indicate that, would it not? A murderer who was planning more thoroughly would have more than likely disposed of the body more efficiently." The Chief Inspector found himself nodding in agreement.

"Furthermore, the manner in which poor Dora was attacked would be indicative of a sort of spur of the moment decision. After all, who would plan to use a salmon to render someone unconscious?" Here she gave the Chief Inspector a knowing look, for she could tell by his eyebrows that she had made the correct assumption. She enjoyed her victory but a moment before continuing. "And why would someone bury an unconscious girl? An unconscious person might regain her senses and extricate herself from the ground. Surely the perpetrator assumed that Dora was killed by the blow and hastily covered the crime by digging a shallow grave in the bog. Roland would be unlikely to make that mistake. He's much too cunning and methodical. His detailed plans for his, um, business empire demonstrates that. However, a woman, particularly a woman under the influence of a narcotic substance, more than likely would make such a mistake."

Sheridon had to admit that the lady had a point and he grudgingly acknowledged as much. He was, however, going to reprimand Frambley again for his egregious slip of the tongue. As for Miss Winwood, he decided to ask her, "And which of our two remaining suspects do you think did it, then?"

He was surprised by her answer. "I don't know, Chief Inspector." He had begun to think that she had the thing solved already.

50.

After what he considered to be an appropriate amount of time, Chief Inspector Thornton Sheridon directed his men and Miss Edna back into the drawing room. As it had turned out, only Detective Frambley and one of the uniformed officers had actually had to avail themselves of the facilities, so not a great deal of time had elapsed. Sheridon was glad for that. The family had had just enough time to allow for the tension of the previous revelation to break but not enough time for any of them to regroup. As they returned to the drawing room, he saw that he had assessed the situation correctly.

Sir Clifford had returned to the window and was again pretending to find something interesting to look at, although by the appearance of his facial expression the Chief Inspector presumed him to be deep in thought. Young Roland Minnington was sitting in the same chair he had occupied before, looking at his mother as though he were amused by the whole episode. Claudia Minnington had taken a position on the floor in front of the fireplace and appeared to be watching the flames dance over the coals. Lady Opal was beginning to look more distressed and fidgety and kept looking hopefully toward her daughter. Sheridon surmised that she wanted another dose of laudanum. He decided that he'd resume his interrogations there. He motioned to the officer who had been holding the container of laudanum and took it from him.

"Lady Opal," he began, "are you alright?"

Opal Minnington started at the mention of her name. She looked at the Chief Inspector to answer him and spied the flask in his hand, which he had held in a way that would make that unavoidable. Her eyes fixed on the container of laudanum and she responded, "I am fine, thank you. I am just a bit frazzled by all the excitement. Might I have just one more sip of that mixture, whatever it is?"

"I am afraid not, ma'am", replied Sheridon. "We will see to it that one of the medical men attached to the Yard comes round this evening to help you with your nerves with something that is less likely to make you dependent upon it." The Chief Inspector had suddenly developed a sense of compassion for the woman before him. Hooked on a drug by her own daughter and the secrets of her life revealed to all the world. He could understand why she would want to alleviate all that anxiety with more drugs. Looking at the flask in his hand, he dismissed these sympathetic notions and turned his attention once again to Claudia.

"Miss Minnington, tell me where you get this," he inquired.

Claudia seemed to ignore him as she sat watching the fire. This led Sheridon to presume that she had just dosed herself with the laudanum before coming into the room. He was not sure how long its effects would last on her but did not relish the idea of remaining at Dogmoor until it wore off. As he was mulling this prospect over in his head, Claudia suddenly began rocking her head slowly back and forth and made a noise that seemed to be half hum and half giggle. The Chief Inspector repeated his question.

"Miss Minnington, please tell me about how you have come to be in possession of this substance." His tone was soft and yet demanding. His was a voice accustomed to being used authoritatively.

This time Claudia broke out into a laugh and her whole body rocked back and forth in front of the fireplace. Roland Minnington suddenly spoke. "Ask her again, Inspector," he said, a look of malicious glee in his eyes, "it looks as if you are getting through to her."

What manner of man is that, wondered the Chief Inspector silently to himself. He imagined that Roland more than likely knew the answer to his question, but he wanted Claudia to start talking and admit to it herself. As of yet he had not gotten much testimony from her about her own whereabouts. And after Miss Winwood's conversation in the foyer, he, also, was developing opinions as to the nature of the crime. Once again he turned to Claudia Minnington.

"Miss Minnington, are you quite alright? Perhaps you should take a bit more tea." He had decided to use a more subtle approach. Unfortunately, Claudia simply maintained her position on the floor and continued to have what was beginning to appear to be a laughing fit.

Sir Clifford, heretofore standing silently by the window, could tolerate no more. He went over to his daughter and angrily grabbed her by the arms and lifted her off the floor. Giving her a violent shake he demanded, "What in the devil is wrong with you, girl? Tell these men what they want to know!"

Detective Frambley and the Chief Inspector both stepped in to intervene. "We'll handle this, your lordship," said Frambley. "Why don't you sit yourself down over by the window," it was more a directive than a request.

Relinquishing his hold on his delinquent daughter, Sir Clifford did as the detective suggested and returned to the window and resumed his former stance. Chief Inspector Sheridon, who now held Claudia's left arm in his own hand, watched him as he stood looking out the window.

Claudia, for her part, did not seem to react to her father's violent outburst much at all, other than that her laughter had ended and she seemed to be completely out of touch with her surroundings. Sheridon turned to her and noticed that he now was holding her arm quite firmly and began to loosen his grip. As he did so he noticed that, in the fracas with her father, the sleeve of her loose woolen sweater had been shoved up her arm, leaving her forearm exposed. As he was about to let go of her, he suddenly noticed an odd mark on her forearm. With a snap of his head, he looked up and signaled for the officer who had previously been holding the laudanum to assist him. Together they gently walked Claudia over to a lamp to get a better look under the light. Looking up at the uniformed officer he said something that the rest of them could not hear—a fact that irritated Miss Edna a great deal—and the officer left the room. The Chief Inspector sat

Claudia down in a chair and straightened himself up, looking down at her and seemed to be deciding what to do next.

It soon became apparent that they were going to wait for the return of the officer so, as they waited, Miss Edna looked at her employer. Until just now she had tried to avoid doing so very much because she had felt so inappropriately conspicuous being there, even though she was the one who had finagled her way into the investigation. Seeing her employer and his family embarrassed by these revelations, however, had made her feel out of place. That feeling had been brief, relatively speaking, as her inner sense kept cloying at her, compelling her to continue her pursuit of an answer to the mystery confronting them. Still, she could not help but to feel pain for Sir Clifford. He may have many rough edges about him, but he certainly did not deserve to see his family fall apart before his eyes.

The return of the young officer ended Miss Edna's reflections and her attention once again was on the activities of the police interviews. The policeman walked quickly over to the Chief Inspector and handed him what appeared to be a white hand-kerchief. Inside the handkerchief there appeared to be some other object. Miss Edna resisted the urge to ask outright what it was. She was afraid she knew already.

After conferring briefly with the uniformed man and examining the contents of the handkerchief, Chief Inspector Sheridon returned to Claudia Minnington, who was still sitting quietly in her chair.

"Miss Minnington, do you know what I have here?" he asked.

Claudia looked as though she were going to ignore him again, but she eventually gave a shrug of her shoulders as an answer.

"This is a hypodermic needle, Miss Minnington," continued Sheridon. "The officer found it in your room just now. Tell me, please, how you came to be in possession of a hypodermic needle."

Claudia's head began to rock again and she appeared to be ready to laugh. "Claudia!" Her father's angry voice brought her back. She looked up at the Chief Inspector for the first time and, in a rather rebellious tone, replied, "What do you think it's for?"

"Yes, Chief Inspector," interjected Sir Clifford. "What are you saying? Why do you think that my daughter would have one of those things?"

"We can't be sure, sir, until we have it tested in the laboratory at the Yard," replied Sheridon, "but I suspect that it has been used to administer a dose of heroin."

Miss Edna closed her eyes. Her suspicions had been correct. She was now fairly certain who murdered young Dora Finch and why.

The Chief Inspector stole a look in Miss Edna's direction and made note of the look on her face. He was certain she knew what he was thinking but wondered how a lady of Miss Winwood's generation and breeding would know anything at all about the drug trade of London. He told himself that he would have to ask her that question the first time the opportunity presented itself. For the moment, he returned his attention to Claudia Minnington.

"Miss Minnington, have you used this needle to give yourself a dose of heroin?" he asked. "Do you use that as well as laudanum?"

The somewhat euphoric state that Claudia had been in seemed to be slowly dissipating as the afternoon's lengthy interrogations had continued. She was beginning to show signs of agitation. She picked at the sleeves of her sweater, threatening to unravel it, and she shifted uncomfortably in her chair. She looked at the Chief Inspector and replied, in a tone both passive and defiant, "What if I did?"

Sheridon's eyebrows told Miss Edna that he felt he was going to be getting somewhere finally. He continued addressing Claudia. "Well, for one thing, Miss Minnington, it is illegal to abuse pharmaceuticals and unless you can show me a doctor's prescription for the heroin then I am afraid you are in violation of the law. The same can be said for the laudanum, although it has been a long time since I have heard of it being prescribed as a medicinal." He looked at her with a smile that was meant to pacify her evidently increasing agitation. It did not appear to have its desired effect.

"So what?" she spat, clutching now at the arms of her chair.

"Presuming that a doctor has *not* prescribed them," he placidly continued, "there is the matter of *how* you came to possess these drugs. On the black market they cost some considerable bit of money, especially if you have developed a habit." He turned to Sir Clifford, "Is her allowance such that she can afford to purchase large quantities of drugs as well as the other things a young lady who goes to school might need on a weekly basis?"

Sir Clifford looked at the Chief Inspector, at once stunned, horrified, and angry. It was his anger that was most evident when he answered. "Absolutely not, Inspector! She gets what she needs for traveling back and forth to school and some supplies and the occasional dinner or lunch with her friends, but not enough to do all that *and* to be buying illegal drugs in alleyways!" Everyone else in the room wondered if his rancor were directed more towards his daughter or Chief Inspector Sheridon and the Chief Inspector wondered whether or not Sir Clifford had the slightest inkling as to how much illegal drugs purchased in alleyways cost.

He turned once again to Claudia. "Well, Miss Minnington? How did you pay for these drugs?"

Lady Opal surprised everyone by speaking. Her voice was flush with disbelief when she said, "My jewelry!"

"What about your jewelry, Lady Minnington?" asked the Sheridon, turning toward her.

Opal had wrapped her right hand around her left wrist and gently felt it. She wore no bracelet today, but acted as though she thought she had. She answered the policeman but spoke to Claudia. "Some pieces of jewelry have been missing in recent months. At the very first, I thought I had mislaid them somewhere, or perhaps had sent them out to be cleaned and forgotten to retrieve them. But there were more and more pieces missing—a ring here, a watch there. It was not until I went looking for the diamond bracelet that I had intended to wear to last night's dinner that I realized someone was stealing from me. I never dreamed it would have been anyone in this house, let alone my own daughter." Lady Opal's voice betrayed her deep disappointment.

Turning once again to Claudia the Chief Inspector asked, "Have you been financing your drug habit by committing larceny against your mother's jewelry box, young lady? It would be

better for you to answer truthfully now as it will go better for you later."

In order to help Claudia with the admission of her obvious guilt, Sheridon once again unfolded the white handkerchief and held it out to her. He said, "Do you recognize this?" In his hand he held a diamond bracelet. Lady Opal rose from her chair to get a better look. He could tell by the sorrowful expression on her face that it was, indeed, the missing bracelet of which she had just spoken.

Having resolved the issue of the missing bracelet, one crime had been solved, however this was not the crime that had brought the men from Scotland Yard to Surrey. There was still the matter of Dora's murder. Chief Inspector Sheridon decided to stir the pot by initiating arrest proceedings against Claudia to see what might happen.

"Miss Claudia Minnington, I am placing you under arrest for larceny and drug abuse. You may remain silent, but if anything that you might have told us comes out at trial and you have held it from us, it will go against you."

Lady Opal gasped, "No! You will not arrest my daughter! I will not prefer charges against her!"

"Are you sure, ma'am?" asked Sheridon. "This might be the wake up call that your daughter needs to reflect on where her life is going."

Lady Opal turned to her daughter. "Did you hear that? *He's* worried about where your life is going! Why aren't *you*? You are an heir to Dogmoor. Your father and I have worked hard to see that you and your brother would remain in the moneyed class for the rest of your lives and, hopefully one day, your children's lives. Why would you commit these foolish acts and throw away with both hands everything you stood to inherit?" Lady Opal's voice was approaching what one might consider being shrill.

Her questions, however, seemed to bring Claudia around and triggered a response. She looked angrily at her mother. "Inheritance? My inheritance?" she asked scornfully. "Tell me about my inheritance, Mummy. How long would I have to wait for it? How long before I would no longer be doled out my pitiful allowance by you and daddy?" Her voice was steadily rising. "And how much would be left at all after your bastard daughter got her share of it?"

With an uncontrollable instinct that was driven by anger and indignation, Lady Opal reached out and slapped her daughter across the face. "How *dare* you say that to me?" she asked, her tone low and harsh.

Just as he was considering if this might be an appropriate time for him to reinsert himself into the conversation, the Chief Inspector suddenly heard Claudia speaking again, saying "Yes, mummy's dirty little secret exposed for all the world to see. How much of Dogmoor would be left?" Claudia's voice was now steely and calm. She continued, "Roland and I have expensive tastes. Some of his boys have cost him quite a bit, haven't they Roland?" She smiled contemptuously at her brother. "That's how he got the idea to start pimping himself. And, yes," she spoke to the Chief Inspector but her eyes remained on her mother, her voice cold with hate, "the black market is expensive. A few of mother's baubles have kept me and my friends supplied with our favorite remedies for boredom. You asked me why I did not wait for my inheritance, Mother. I was protecting my inheritance from your little indiscretion. I wanted to be sure that there *would* be something for me to wait for. I *had* to do it."

"What are you saying?" asked her mother, afraid to hear the answer to her question.

With a deathly calm look on her bedraggled face and a completely emotionless voice, Claudia replied, "I killed Dora Finch."

Lady Opal recoiled in horror. Sir Clifford, on one of the very rare occasions in his life, could not speak. Even Roland's smug and arrogant expression was gone, replaced by slack jawed disbelief.

Turning to the men from the Yard, Claudia continued her explanation. "I had been in the pantry adjacent to the kitchen the day that Maggie had her visit from the priest. At first I was interested in trying to get my hands on some of her inheritance, but couldn't figure out a way to get any of it out of the little mick's hands. I was back there again looking for something to pinch when my mother and Miss Winwood had a little conversation. Mummy seemed very perturbed to know the little papist was going to be coming here. I kept my eye on her and noticed she was getting more and more upset by it. Something told me that there was more to this story. I decided to help calm dear mummy's nerves with a little dose of laudanum, telling her it was a potion of herbs I had found in London. I found her in her room amidst a pile of papers and photos spread out upon her bed. After she was high, I went through the pile myself and discovered that Roland and I had a half sister that no one, and I was betting even Daddy, knew about.

"On Thursday, when the silly cow was back crying in her tea to Maggie about some boy or another, I hid in the pantry again. I was not certain what I was going to do; all I knew was that I had to do something to get her out of the picture. Eventually she left and I followed her out into the dark. It was a stroke of luck that I thought of the salmon in the ice house. It had just been delivered. I ran in, grabbed a good, hefty one, and crept up behind her. With one good wallop to the side of her head she fell to the ground. After that, I simply buried her in the bog."

The family remained as before, as though frozen in tableau. Detective Frambley gave a low whistle, amazed as he was at how coolly the tale of murder had just been recounted. Chief Inspector Thornton Sheridon, when he came to himself, asked to use the telephone. As for Miss Edna, she simply observed the scene that had unfolded before her with complete sadness. Sometimes she hated being right.

51.

Sir Clifford and Lady Opal stood at the main entrance to Manor Minnington and watched as their daughter and son were led away by the police; Roland charged with procuring, Claudia with drug trafficking and murder. Chief Inspector Sheridon had rung up the local constable for assistance in transporting two prisoners and Dickey Olsen had arrived to perform that duty. Taken into custody, handcuffed and hunched over, Claudia shuffled to the waiting police vehicle. She stopped only once to turn back to look at her parents before being taken away. Her dark hair hung limply around her face and her face mimicked it—limp, expressionless, emotionless. One of the uniformed men assisted her into the automobile and the other did the same with Roland. They signaled Constable Olsen, who then started the engine, preparing to take them to Scotland Yard for further questioning and to have both arrests formally processed.

As the police vehicle's engine started up and was shifted into gear, Lady Opal felt a clutch in her throat. The emotional stress of the last several days was overtaking her. As she watched her son and daughter disappear down the lane, the very lane upon which Claudia had perpetrated such a terrible crime against poor, innocent Dora, Lady Opal began to cry. She turned her body towards her husband and wept on his strong, broad shoulder.

Sir Clifford put his arm around his wife and closed the door to Manor Minnington. His face was a curious mixture of emotions. At once, one could detect the pain he suffered because of his felonious children and the personal embarrassment the situation caused him. But, with all that, his eyes were steely and his brow set firm. His jaws twitched as he clenched his teeth together.

Miss Edna knew that something was about to be said that she should not and did not want to hear, so she and Chief Inspector Sheridon discretely excused themselves to Sir Clifford's office. For his part, Sheridon was eager to hear how this matronly secretary had come to the resolution of the crime.

"It's quite simple, Chief Inspector," replied Miss Edna when he inquired this of her. "After I ruled out any male involvement in the crime, I was left with two females; Lady Opal and Claudia. I could not believe for a minute that any mother, even one as vain and otherwise flawed as Lady Opal Minnington, could possibly kill her own child. It goes against nature. So, in my mind I had eliminated her as a suspect as well. That left Claudia. Once my suspicions regarding her drug abuse had been confirmed, I realized that she was the most likely candidate. I am so very happy that I read the 'Sunday Times'." She smiled at the Chief Inspector as she revealed her source of knowledge on such unsavory subjects as the illegal drug trade and its attendant violence. She continued, "There was also something she had said, something about how pitiful an inheritance Maggie O'Shea had received. That stuck out in my mind and I later realized that it supplied the perfect motive for murder. It seems that the love of money is, after all, the root of all evil, Chief Inspector."

"Very perceptive, ma'am", Sheridon congratulated her. He was beginning to have a fuller appreciation for Miss Edna Winwood and her powers of observation and deduction. In spite of himself, he added, "You might make a fine detective, at that."

Edna Winwood smiled in gratitude for the recognition.

Alone with his wife in the entrance hallway, Sir Clifford kept his arm around her shoulder and, taking her hand with his, led her to the sitting room. It was time for a chat with his wife. He knew she wasn't going to like it.

Still sobbing gently, Lady Opal allowed herself to be guided by her husband's strong arms into the sitting room and took a seat in one of the great leather chairs that flanked the fireplace. Sir Clifford sat across from her in the other. Snippy had already dutifully stoked the fire and the chill of the encroaching November evening was kept at bay from the room. Under other circumstances, the atmosphere in the room might have suggested a cozy interlude, the likes of which they had not shared in many years. Unfortunately, this was not one of those circumstances.

Lady Opal seemed to be coming around to her own senses once again and was beginning to realize that the strong arms of her husband had led her not to a place of solace, but to even more bad news. She had seen that look before in her husband's face and knew that it generally precipitated one of his characteristic outbursts. She braced herself for the tirade she felt certain was to follow, assuming that she would bear the brunt of the responsibility for the failings of her brood. "This would, after all, surely be bad for business", she thought to herself sourly.

Sir Clifford, however, did not launch into one of his familiar tirades. There was no shouting. He made no accusations. There were neither wild gesticulations nor his customary condemnations of all things British. On the contrary, Sir Clifford simply sat and stared at his wife. His aspect was still very stern, but one would not say he was glowering in rage at her. He simply sat and seemed to be waiting for the right moment to say something that was going to be very well thought out and very important for Lady Opal to hear and fully understand. This was quite unlike her husband and completely unexpected. Suddenly she found herself craving some more of her daughter's "medicine".

After several minutes of silence the room began to feel chilled despite the merry fire burning in the hearth. Lady Opal could stand it no longer and opened her mouth to speak.

"Clifford, I ..." she began, but was cut short by the expression on her husband's face which had clearly become a glare the moment she began to speak to him. Her mouth remained open, yet silent, as she watched him slowly rise from his chair across from her and turn to face the fire. Staring straight forward and standing as stiffly erect as a Beefeater guard at Buckingham Palace, he crossed his hands behind his back and began to speak, in a calm tone that was rather frightening for its lack of emotion and he directed his words to his wife.

He began. "Opal, you and I need to have a serious talk."

Opal held her breath. She had never been frightened by any-thing her husband might say. She had been annoyed and frus-trated before, yes, but never frightened. But right now his tone made her quite fearful and she wondered where this conversa-tion was going to go.

Sir Clifford continued, "Since our marriage so many years ago, I have been a happy husband and a proud father." His voice was calm and even, almost as if he were just musing to himself out loud. "Hell, I've even become a British lord living here in jolly old England. I have indulged you in your excesses—the clothes, the jewels, the parties—and have enjoyed watching you enjoy yourself. I have always felt that I was providing for you what you wanted, the proper life of a British noblewoman."

"Clifford, please, I ..." Opal began but was again silenced by a gesture from her husband's hand.

"Let me say what I have to say, Opal. This is not going to be easy." Sir Clifford paused a moment, reclasped his hands behind his back, and continued.

"Living in England has opened up for me a new business venture. My steel company will be able to expand quite nicely here, thanks to my meeting with the Lord Mayor the other day. I expect, my dear, that I shall become an even wealthier man in the very near future. I can only imagine the fun you would have had trying to figure out ways to spend it."

Sir Clifford paused again, smiling ruefully to himself at the thought.

Lady Opal, sitting on the edge of her chair, had been wait-ing to hear what, exactly, this talk was all about. She knew her husband had to be terribly upset after finding out about her rela-tionship to Dora. She had been wishing that he would throw his tantrum and be done with it. But what was it that he had just said that stood out in her mind? It surprised her when, quite suddenly, she realized what it was. She looked steadily at her husband and asked, "What do you mean, the 'fun I *would have had* trying to figure out how to spend it'? Whatever are you trying to tell me Clifford? That you are divorcing me?" In Lady Opal's voice there was a mixture of fear and indignation.

"No dear, I am not planning to divorce you," Sir Clifford calmly responded, still staring ahead at the giant marble mantelpiece. "To divorce you would cause too many problems."

"What do you mean 'problems'?" Lady Opal's voice was becoming less fearful and more indignant. "Are you saying that a divorce would be 'bad for business'? That's your usual excuse for damn near everything!"

Unmoved by the bitterness apparent in his wife's last remark, Sir Clifford continued. "Yes, dear, that is true. It would be bad for business. It is going to be a public relations nightmare as it is, dealing with a murdered girl, a felonious daughter, a homosexual pimp for a son, and a wife who cuckolded me, albeit before we were married. These are going to be bad enough to deal with, but in business, as long as I have not been personally responsible for what was done my people will be able to clean this mess up. We may take a bit of a hit, but it won't last long. But if I divorce you on top of all of it—well, that's a horse of a different color." (Lady Opal cringed despite herself. She always hated when he used that expression.) "You see, my pet, the simple fact is that if I divorce you then I become a divorced man. And even though there is ample reason to divorce you because of the circumstances of our marriage, it would look bad. It would look like I was abandoning you, leaving you alone to face your obligations as the mother of the beautiful fruits of our love. That would constitute a public relations fiasco, no mere nightmare. There would be no way of putting that in a positive light. So, that would be terribly bad for business, yes."

Lady Opal stood abruptly and was just about to launch into an angry rant against her husband and his infernal concern for his business affairs, but he silenced her by continuing.

"But it is not because of business that I am not divorcing you. The fact is, I could go back to America as a divorced man and continue in Pittsburgh as I had been before. But I don't want to go back to Pittsburgh. I want to stay here and proceed with my newest venture. But all of that is beside the point."

"Well for the love of God, what *is* the point?" Lady Opal was beginning to get quite agitated.

"The point is, my dove, that if we divorce all of these dirty little secrets will become fodder for public consumption. It would prove terribly embarrassing…"

"So, bad for business after all!" Lady Opal interrupted her husband. His demeanor was driving her mad!

"No dear. Business is not my concern here so much as the personal embarrassment we would each face in the event that this scandal gets too public and continues to grow."

Lady Opal was stunned. Did she hear her husband say that he was concerned for her name, her position, her dignity after what he now knew about her and her family and how, and why, they had arranged the marriage between herself and him? Something made her very wary of what Clifford was about to say next.

Sir Clifford must have sensed the hesitation in his wife and read it correctly. "Yes dear one, there would obviously be terribly embarrassing moments for us to face. But, to be perfectly honest, the real reason that I am not going to divorce you is that that would be too easy on you. I have other plans for you." Here Sir Clifford turned towards his wife, his face calm and even but with fire in his eyes. For a brief moment, Lady Opal was afraid for her own safety.

"W-w-what do you mean by that, Clifford?" she asked. "What is going on in that peculiar American brain of yours?" She meant it to sound insulting.

"Funny you should mention my 'American' brain, because America is where you are headed."

"America! After all I, we, have just been through do you intend to send me into exile back to Pittsburgh? I won't go! I am a citizen of Great Britain and I simply will not go!" Lady Opal stamped her foot in emphasis.

"America. Yes. Exile? You can call it that if that appeals your sense of wounded nobility. But Pittsburgh? No. No dear, Pittsburgh is not where you will be spending the next several years of your life." Sir Clifford almost sounded amused and Lady Opal would have thought he was going to laugh at his own joke if it weren't for the look in his eyes.

"Where then?" his wife was truly mystified now.

"Do you remember my grandmother, my mother's mother? You met her at our wedding."

Lady Opal had only the vaguest recollections of the members of her husband's family. During their time in Pittsburgh she had been forced to be in their company many times and had tried to tolerate their bourgeois behavior. She had tried even harder to forget all about them after she and her husband had returned to Great Britain. Sensing his wife's lack of clarity in these memories, Sir Clifford continued.

"Grandma Linden was at our wedding and gave us a silver bowl. It had been given to her and my grandfather at their wedding. I doubt you even know where it is, if it even made it across the pond when we moved here."

"So, your Grandmother Linden. What about her and what does she have to do with me?"

"That's who you're going to be living with. My Grandmother Linden in Scranton, Pennsylvania."

"*Scranton?*" Lady Opal shrieked. "Where on earth is Scranton?"

"Scranton is on the eastern end of Pennsylvania. It's not too far from New York City or Philadelphia. You'll be able to take a train to see a show on Broadway, occasionally." Sir Clifford's voice sounded soothing, too soothing. "Occasionally a shopping trip, if you behave yourself."

"Clifford! I demand that you explain to me what this is all about!"

Her husband continued, "It's quite simple, Opal. I am not divorcing you because then you would be free to do as you please. I want to be the one to decide what you are going to do after what you've brought down on me with your conniving ways. And I want you to live in Scranton with my Grandmother Linden. Oh, and did I mention that she needs around the clock care now? How much nicer it will be for a member of the family to be there to take care of her in her illness." Clifford Minnington smiled a sincerely insincere smile.

Lady Opal looked at her husband in utter disbelief. "You must be mad! Who do you think you are, the King? I will not be forced to leave here to take care of your sick grandmother in some godforsaken Yankee outpost called Scranton! You will not send me back to the States to punish me, Clifford Minnington. I repeat, I am a British citizen and *I-will-remain-here!*" Lady Opal punctuated her last phrase with staccato emphasis.

"Well, of course, you might wish to consider one other thing," cooed Sir Clifford in a very smug tone.

"*WHAT?*" spat Lady Opal.

"If you insist on remaining in England against my wishes, then I shall divorce you. And since it is clear now that our marriage was arranged the way it was, and that you were not truthful to me about your affair and your first child and that this is all publicly known now, then when I divorce you I shall owe you nothing."

Lady Opal held her breath. "What do you mean?" she demanded.

"I mean, that if we divorce you will be left as poor as you were when I found you. You will be entitled to nothing. That was what you agreed to right before the wedding. Remember, the paper I asked you about just this afternoon? That agreement entitles you to nothing and I will give you nothing. You can remain in your beloved England, but you will do so in poverty." Sir Clifford's voice began to rise. "After you sell your jewels and other possessions to get by for a while, what will you do then? You're not as young as you used to be. I doubt that some dumb shit American millionaire will be as taken in with you as I was those many years ago. Eventually you will be forced to sell this godforsaken firetrap of a mansion house that you love so much!" At this point he was nearly shouting, his previous cool composure having dispersed into the gathering gloom of the evening.

"You bastard!" Lady Opal lunged at her husband and struck him in the face with her open hand. The slap returned Sir Clifford to his previous, controlled disposition. Calmly, he turned back to the mantelpiece with his hands behind his back once more.

"Perhaps I am a bastard, Opal. But you are a bitch. Your choice is simply this. We remain married and you will leave England for as long as it pleases me. You will then retain a generous allowance from me as long as you are living in Scranton. Or, we divorce and the public scandal that results will ensure that I leave England for Pittsburgh to go on with my millionaire's life that you enjoy so much, and you remain here, penniless. The choice is yours."

They remained motionless in the sitting room, both of them standing and neither of them speaking. She stared at his back as he stared at the great marble mantelpiece. A long silence ensued. After what seemed like an eternity, Sir Clifford turned to his wife and gave her a cruel smile. He walked over to the door of the sitting room and opened it.

"Snippy!" his characteristic bellow had returned. "Pack her ladyship's things. She's going on a long trip."

From the office, Miss Winwood heard Sir Clifford calling for Snippy. "Well, he's finally had it out with her, I suspect," she thought to herself as she looked over the letter she had just finished typing. Reading it, she realized it was a new experience for her. She had never left an employment situation as a result of her own decision before. It had always been her employers that made that decision for her. Satisfied that the letter said exactly what she wanted it to say, she signed it, folded it, and placed it in an envelop with "Sir Clifford Minnington, Lord Dogmoor" written on its front. Rather than seal the envelop, she simply folded the flap inside it because it was her intention to hand her letter of resignation to Sir Clifford as she left Manor Minnington that evening.

The telephone call that Miss Edna Winwood had discretely made a short while ago had been to Sir Oswald Bunbarrel. Sir Oswald had offered her a position on his staff the night before at the dinner party. She had been gratified by the offer, but had turned him down. However, the recent tragic events at Dogmoor had helped Miss Winwood in her decision and the fact was that Sir Oswald had wanted to take her to Ireland with him. Even without the murder and subsequent mayhem, not to mention the tension this was going to bring about as far as working with Sir Clifford was concerned, she might have given serious consideration to that offer; only her sense of loyalty to her current employer would have made her choose otherwise. Miss Edna had been to Ireland only once, in her youth, and remembered it so fondly that, as of today, she was very receptive to living there in the employ of Sir Oswald.

It had taken her less time than usual to make her decision. She had telephoned Sir Oswald and accepted his offer and sat down immediately to compose her letter of resignation. One might be tempted to think harshly of Miss Winwood for deserting Sir Clifford in this, his hour of utmost need. After all, who knew more about his business dealings than she? Who would help him continue his preparations for a steel operation in London as he sorted out the mess of his personal life? Miss Edna regretted her decision for this reason, but was certain that Sir Clifford would be able to move on without her. He was, after all, a very determined gentleman.

For one thing, she suspected that Sir Clifford had been preparing for this contingency for some time. There had been much correspondence in the last two years between Lord Dogmoor and the States, particularly with one Estelle Linden. Though he never actually confided in his "Gal Friday", Sir Clifford was fairly transparent in what his plans were. The only thing Edna had not been able to determine beforehand was why. Why would he want to be shifting his wife to some small town in eastern Pennsylvania? That answer was provided this weekend. Sir Clifford had known, or at least suspected, all along that there was something that his wife had been hiding from him.

As she left, she closed the door to the office which had become so familiar to her these past several years. Having had second thoughts about handing Sir Clifford more bad news just now, she had decided simply to leave the letter on his desk, fully aware that he would be the only person to see it. She walked through the house to the kitchen to say goodbye to Maggie, who wept at the news of her departure. Having said her goodbyes to Maggie and then to Snipwhistle, Miss Edna Winwood departed through the doors of Manor Minnington for the last time.

As she rode back into London with Chief Inspector Sheridon and Detective Frambley, Miss Winwood could not help feeling a sense of relief. In the gathering dusk, she watched the cold, barren moors of Surrey roll past the window of the police automobile. She knew that she would miss her American employer, having become so accustomed to his manner, but also looked forward to her new position with Sir Oswald. "At least you can get a decent cup of tea in Ireland," she thought to herself.

However, she still had a nagging feeling in the back of her mind. There was something that still seemed not quite right about this whole affair. As they pulled out of the estate grounds, she wondered, for instance, how a man possessed of such astute business acumen, as was Sir Clifford, could be so completely clueless about what was going on under his own roof. How could a man with such an eye for every detail of the business world not be in the least suspicious of the clandestine activities of his two children, especially one involved with drugs? And with all the correspondence between Sir Clifford and Scranton, why would it be only now that he would choose to act on it?

These thoughts were leading Miss Edna to a place she quickly realized that she did not want to go. With a cold shudder, she suddenly understood as the pieces of the puzzle swimming around in her mind came together. She thought she knew the answer. Despite Claudia's confession, there was more to this story. The cold logic of her conclusion caused her to shiver involuntarily. She looked at the Chief Inspector, briefly debated telling him what her new suspicions were, and kept silent. It was too impossible to be believed and even she was beginning to doubt herself.

She hoped, as she continued to peer into the darkening skyline, that life in Ireland would be quieter than it had been in Surrey of late. Surely, it must be so. She gave a quiet sigh and closed her eyes, trying to burn into her memory the image of the familiar moors which she would never see again. She was grateful that her sleuthing adventure had come to an end, behind her now as were the moors she was passing. She allowed herself to look forward to less stressful days ahead, across the Irish Sea.

52.

From his wife's bedroom window, Sir Clifford watched with relief as the police vehicles disappeared into the distance. He knew that he would never see his personal secretary again, or at least that was his hope. He knew that she would have left a letter of resignation for him, having made up her mind to leave his employ, under the circumstances. He knew all this. He knew her very well. They had worked well together for the last several years. He was relieved because, in addition to being a brilliant secretary, she had just that day shown herself to have the makings of a brilliant detective, as well. That was something that Sir Clifford could not afford to have hanging about the manor house.

He turned from the window and looked at his wife. She lay sleeping on her bed, looking so much at peace that she seemed to deny the events of the day. Her sobs and protests had been silenced by the sleeping powder that Sir Clifford had mixed into a glass of water and had her drink.

He stood beside her bed and picked up a pillow. He observed it in his hands, its size and thickness. He contemplated once again how easy it would be to have her sleep forever with just a few minutes' effort. But he replaced it on her bed beside her and returned to the window.

So far it had all gone his way. So much so that he could not believe his luck. It had been pathetically easy to ply his daughter with the drugs she craved and make her susceptible to the suggestion that she had been the one to bludgeon Dora Finch and bury her in the bog. The revelation of Roland's homosexual prostitution empire had been an unexpected, yet most welcome, diversion that only added to the confusion of the day.

He turned again towards his wife. As she lay sleeping he almost could see Dora as she lay on the ground next to the hole he dug in which to bury her. The resemblance between the two was amazing.

Sir Clifford would never forget the day he first laid eyes on Dora Finch, a few years before. He had gone into the pantry looking for something and there she was, engaged in friendly conversation with his cook. He remembered that he had stopped dead in his tracks as if he had seen an apparition. It was as though he were looking at his wife when she was young, some twenty years before.

He had known immediately who she was and why she so resembled his wife in her youth. When Lady Opal had insisted on having a private safe in her bedroom he had acquiesced, but not without making certain that the workman who installed it had provided him with the combination. Opal never knew that. After he was sure that she had hidden away whatever it was she wanted the safe for, he had made it a point to see what it was. On a day when his wife had gone into London on a shopping spree, he had read with grim interest the papers and letters she was so desperate to keep from him.

As he watched her sleep he wondered why he hadn't simply murdered her instead of Dora. His wife was, after all, the guilty party. But, he knew, it was because he still loved her. He supposed that he had simply snapped. Love is a strange and mysterious force and can compel one to do strange and impulsive things. No one knew this better than Sir Clifford. He had not been able to bear it when she became unhinged after the visit by that meddling priest. Sir Clifford grinned as he thought of the gift of salmon and how it had been so handy for his use.

He once again turned to the window, just the barest hint of worry on his brow. "Will the old girl keep quiet?" He wondered.